# KINGDOM
# KEEPERS IV

### POWER PLAY

# RIDLEY PEARSON

# KINGDOM KEEPERS IV

## POWER PLAY

**Dısnep • HYPERION BOOKS**

*New York*

Copyright © 2011 Page One, Inc.

For information address Disney • Hyperion Books, 114 Fifth Avenue, New York, New York 10011-5690.

Printed in the United States of America

First Edition
10 9 8 7 6 5 4 3 2 1
V567-9638-5-11032

Reinforced binding
ISBN 978-1-4231-3857-0

visit www.disneyhyperionbooks.com
www.thekingdomkeepers.com
www.ridleypearson.com

*For my daughters, Storey and Paige,
and my wonderful readers—you make it magical.*

# KINGDOM
# KEEPERS IV

## POWER PLAY

# 1

"LET'S GET LOST," Finn said to the two girls.

DisneyQuest was a maze, a place where it was difficult to know where you were. An electronic funhouse filled with virtual rides, video games, and interactive attractions, the enormous building in Walt Disney World's Downtown Disney consisted of five floors subdivided into virtual worlds and activities, all interconnected in a way that seemed designed to disorient. Finn Whitman actually *was* currently lost—he couldn't quite figure out where he was or how to get out of there—but his suggestion to "get lost" stemmed from his spotting Greg "Lousy" Luowski at the other end of the gaming room, over near the Guitar Hero consoles. Luowski was the ninth-grade bully. Roughly the size of a kitchen appliance, the zit-faced, fingernail-chewing Luowski had it out for Finn, and Finn knew enough to stay clear of trouble. At least, *avoidable* trouble.

Over the past few years, trouble had defined him, had followed him as he and his four friends—now known as the Kingdom Keepers—had gained notoriety for their efforts to save Disney World from the

Overtakers, a group of fanatical Disney villain characters within the Parks bent on taking over and "stealing the magic." Guys like Luowski didn't appreciate sharing the spotlight with anyone, and at the moment Finn was roughly a million times more popular than Luowski.

"How about the simulators in CyberSpace Mountain?" Charlene said. Charlene was to beautiful what Mount Everest was to high. A cheerleader and phenomenal athlete, she was the poster child for the Kingdom Keepers. Her Facebook page had more friends than Ashton Kutcher's—well, not really, but close enough. Boys liked her. Girls liked her. Teachers liked her. Parents liked her. It was enough to make you hate her. But no one could. She was too ridiculously Charlene to ever have an ill thought aimed at her.

Finn considered the suggestion and glanced over to Amanda to get her read. Amanda was a different kind of pretty: mysterious, her looks often changing from slightly Asian to Polynesian or Caribbean. Amanda was not officially one of the five Kingdom Keepers, but she and her "sister," Jess, had unique qualities and unusual abilities that made them important to the team.

Amanda and Jess had once been part of a group of foster kids called the Fairlies—as in "fairly human." Kids who could bend spoons just by staring at them, or hear clearly at absurd distances, hold their breath underwater for ten minutes at a time, light fires by concentrating, dream the future, see the past. Kids labeled freaks and weirdos; kids once studied by the military but dismissed to a special home in Baltimore when scientists failed to duplicate or explain what was termed their "controlled phenomena."

Currently, Amanda and Jess lived in an Orlando foster home for wayward girls run by the iron-handed Mrs. Nash. Despite sharing not only the same address, but also the same bunk room, they now attended different high schools; Jess had qualified for an AP program and went to Edgewater High along with two of the Kingdom Keepers, Willa and Philby.

Amanda had come to DisneyQuest this evening because the event was a school-sanctioned function. She'd brought Jess as her one allowed guest. To Finn, it seemed like the entire ninth grade of Winter Park High was there.

Finn liked Amanda, which roughly translated to: he couldn't stop thinking about her, was often tongue-tied when trying to talk to her, and made a fool out of himself when trying to come off as cool. There was a friction that existed between Amanda and Charlene that he knew had something to do with him, but which he didn't like to think about. In general, he didn't like to think about girls all that much, but he couldn't seem to help himself.

"Okay," he said. "I guess." Finn didn't like roller coasters—actually was terrified of them—but wasn't about to admit it.

The other three Keepers were also in DisneyQuest somewhere, as was Jess. Even though only Finn and Amanda attended Winter Park, it had been months since the whole group had done anything fun together. Their last outing, to Disney's Hollywood Studios' Fantasmic!, had led to an encounter with the Overtakers that nearly got Finn killed. The idea tonight had been to meet here and stick together, but they'd separated by ride and interest—Philby and Willa had gone to the ground floor to battle pirate ships, while Maybeck and Jess had gone to the bumper cars. Charlene had taken off to the bathroom a few minutes earlier, and Finn had considered ditching her in favor of being alone with Amanda; but it had only been a passing thought and one he didn't fully understand. He liked Charlene. A lot. But not in the same incomprehensible way he liked Amanda.

Luowski spotted Finn and made a face like a football player who'd taken a knee in the wrong place. Finn didn't want to get drawn into that.

"Come on, let's go," he said, as Charlene returned.

The three took the stairs to the second floor, and Charlene led them to CyberSpace Mountain.

The ride was a virtual roller coaster that allowed visitors to pick preexisting twists and turns or to design their own. There were five levels of challenge, from easy to terrifying.

"I'll take mine lite," Finn said.

"Me, too," said Amanda. "I get sick on roller coasters."

"We should go together," Finn said, confessing, "because I'm basically a chicken."

"Oh, right," said Charlene. "You a chicken? I don't think so."

"Seriously! The Barnstormer is about as tough as I can take."

Both girls laughed. Then they exchanged looks that had they been Taser shots would have dropped each other to the ground.

Bill Nye the Science Guy tutored Charlene as she scrolled through selections to create a wildly scary roller coaster for herself. Maybe she was trying to make a point to Amanda, maybe she just loved roller coasters; but it had enough loops and jumps to make an astronaut puke.

She used her entrance ticket to store it. Then she quickly worked with Bill Nye to make another, very basic, ride. She saved it onto Finn's ticket.

"I love it as scary as it gets," she said looking directly at Amanda. "It's awesome."

They headed for the short line of people that waited for the next simulator. Charlene was bumped into by someone, so hard that had she not possessed the grace of a dancer, she would have fallen to the floor.

Greg Luowski.

She dropped the two tickets in the process. In a surprisingly polite gesture, Luowski asked if she was okay and collected the tickets and returned them to her. Finn caught this look in Luowski's eyes—the jerk liked Charlene; his bumping into her had been no accident.

"Lay off, Luowski," Finn said.

Amanda took Finn by the arm.

"Lay off what, Whitless? My bad for the knock-down. Can't I help her up?" He faced Charlene. "I really am sorry."

"No problem," she said. But Finn was still seething. "As in: we don't want any *problems*." She said this slowly, making sure Finn heard every word.

"I'll be around, Whitless. If you want me, you can find me."

"Try some deodorant, Luowski."

Charlene cupped her mouth, hiding her smile.

Luowski didn't just smell like a jock, he smelled like an entire team that had been working out in the summer heat for five hours. He smelled like a guy who hadn't showered since sixth grade.

"Or maybe I'll find you," he growled at Finn.

"I'm not worried," Finn said. "I'll smell you coming."

The line moved. Finn and the girls were shown up the stairs. The simulators were designed for a maximum of two people. Charlene lined up in front of door 1, Finn and Amanda, door 3.

"No holding hands, you two, if you get scared," Charlene called down to them.

Finn faked a grin; he was scared already.

A Cast Member wearing a name tag that said MEGAN accepted Finn's card from him and chose the only predesigned ride it contained. The door opened and Finn and Amanda were escorted into the simulator chamber. They climbed down into the padded seats of the red metal capsule. The seats faced a large flat-panel screen. Megan directed them to stow anything loose in their pockets. That was when Finn started to worry. She then pointed out the two red STOP emergency buttons, one for each rider.

Finn's stomach turned. He didn't like the idea of taking a ride that needed panic buttons. He pulled down the black padded chest brace as directed. Amanda did the same. Megan double-checked everything.

"You're good to go," she said. She hit a button and the simulator's lid closed slowly, locking in place. The only light came from the flat-panel display where the ride's parallel tracks stretched out in front of them.

"This was a stupid idea," he mumbled.

"You're telling me," Amanda said.

"But did you see the course Charlene created for herself? No way I would go on that thing in a million years."

"She wanted to impress you."

"That's ridiculous."

"Trust me. She picked the scariest stuff possible. It would terrify the guy who *designed* it. But she's going to come out of there and tell us she loved it."

He wanted to disagree, but thought she was probably right.

The lights dimmed. The ride began.

"If I scream," Finn said, "it's just to make it feel all the more real."

She laughed. But not for long. Her amusement was cut short as the roller coaster car began to move forward on the tracks in front of them. A light flashed in their eyes. Sound effects roared from unseen speakers and the car banked sharply left. Finn clutched the safety harness and shut his eyes.

"I hate this already," he said.

The capsule banked left, did a complete flip in that direction, and then lifted into a double loop, dumping them upside down twice in a row. Amanda's hair fell like a curtain. Finn squinted open his eyes: the track dropped straight down, about a thousand feet. They plummeted down, like on the Tower of Terror.

Finn screamed a word that would have gotten him grounded for a week if his mother had heard it. It just flew out of him.

"This . . . is . . . not . . . right!" Amanda cried.

They reached bottom, leaving Finn's stomach somewhere at his feet. He re-swallowed his dinner. The car shot up like a NASA rocket launch.

He screamed the same word again.

"She . . . tricked . . . us!" Amanda hollered. Then she screamed at a pitch so high it should have shattered the flat-panel display.

"Puke alert," Finn gagged out as they entered a triple loop.

"Please, no!" Amanda said. "Try shutting your eyes."

"Only makes it worse!" he choked out.

"Tell me this thing can't actually crash." She released another shriek at a volume that might have been heard in Miami.

"It can't actually crash," he said, though he wasn't

so sure. What if the simulator was put through stuff it wasn't designed to handle? he wondered. What if its bearings froze or its motor overheated? The thing was, even Charlene's ride, as crazy as she'd made it, hadn't seemed this bad. Had she tricked them, in order to sabotage Amanda?

That was the first time he realized that maybe Charlene wasn't the only one involved. A ride this violent carried the fingerprints of the Overtakers.

Finn remembered Megan telling them about the panic buttons. He reached down to punch the red emergency STOP button. Just as he did, the car lurched left, and he leaned so sharply in that direction that his hand missed the button.

"Did you see that?" he hollered. "I think it *knew* I was trying to stop it!"

"You're losing more than your cookies," Amanda said. "So this thing can think?"

The car dropped again. Rose and fell. Leaned ninety degrees left and stayed there. Jerked totally upside down and did three more upside-down loops.

Amanda struggled to reach her STOP button. But as she did, the track dropped away. She and Finn were thrown forward against their restraints. She punched down and hit the red plastic button.

"Got it!" she yelled.

The ride continued.

She hit it again.

They were flipped over seven times to their right, like rolling down a steep hill in an oil barrel.

"I swear I pushed it," she announced. "But nothing happened."

"Impressive," he managed to mutter to himself despite all the craziness, no longer thinking it was the work of the Overtakers, but *knowing* it. Wondering how they might have accomplished such a thing, and what, if anything, Charlene's role had been in it. She had designed the ride, after all. If it was the OTs, how had they organized any kind of attack given that their two leaders, Maleficent and Chernabog, were currently locked up somewhere in a Disney holding facility? The Kingdom Keepers' mentor and designer, Wayne Kresky, had believed that "With the head cut off the snake, the body cannot survive." But someone had clearly taken over leadership of the Overtakers. The ride going out of control could not be considered coincidence. The Keepers were under attack.

Finn reached down, able to press his STOP button. Nothing.

"It's . . . *them* . . . isn't it?" Amanda was no dummy. She'd figured it out on her own.

"Yeah," he said. "It's them. By now Megan knows"

—he gritted his teeth as the track lifted and fell so hard and so many times in a row that his neck hurt— "something is wrong. She's working to fix it."

"You're dreaming."

"Probably. But at this point, she's our only hope."

* * *

Outside the simulator bay, Megan was in fact hitting every switch and button possible. The system's mechanicals included a warning-light display used to alert Cast Members to potential simulator hardware failure: a single light that ran a solid green, amber, or red. It was currently *flashing* red—a warning level never seen before and one that attracted the concern and attention of three other Cast Members, including the ride manager.

"It's going to come off the gyros!" the manager shouted. "Like a wheel coming off a bike. The thing is going to basically explode if we don't stop it!" He, too, hit every known control trying to stop the ride. "What the heck?" he asked Megan, as if it were her fault.

"The power!" she said. "Call down and tell them to cut off the power."

* * *

"It's coming apart!" Finn yelled. On the screen, the parallel tracks rushed toward them at impossible speeds, reflecting the velocity of their virtual roller coaster car. Finn could barely look at it—another five loops coming up, then a series of left corkscrews and what appeared to be the edge of a cliff—another of the thousand-foot drops. It was no longer the pattern of the animated tracks that frightened him, but the sounds of grinding metal and the way the seats in the simulator were no longer level, but leaning heavily left. It was being made to do things it was not designed to do. Its parts were failing—the bushings, the bearings, servos, and gyros; it was like a car going down the side of a mountain with no steering and two of its wheels loose. It was going to crash.

"How could they know where we are?" Amanda cried out. "How is that possible?"

Finn didn't answer. He knew that when it came to the Overtakers, anything was possible.

"We have to stop it," he said, looking for options. He shoved his back against the seat and tried to slip out of the chest restraint. It was the same kind of restraint used on real roller coasters—a padded pipe that pulled down over your head. There was some slack in the way it fit. He got about halfway out before getting stuck.

"You're going to crush yourself!" she said.

The simulator spun sideways and rotated forward in full circles seven times. Finn felt his dinner coming up again. Each time he took his eyes off the screen he felt sick. He tried to focus on the screen the way his father had told him to focus on the horizon when seasick. The nausea passed. He was okay.

They fell hundreds of feet, facedown.

Finn squeezed back into his seat, unable to free himself.

"We . . . have . . . to . . . do . . . something!" he said.

"I'm up for suggestions," she answered. Oddly, Amanda sounded suddenly collected and unaffected by the flips and twirls and drops. She could actually string a sentence together.

Then it struck him: Amanda had a unique power.

"Push . . . it . . . open," Finn shouted over the roar of the simulator's disintegrating parts. Amanda flashed him a look, her dark hair hanging fully upside down, her cheeks vibrating like Jell-O. Her eyes strained to find the hatch door that Megan had closed electronically. Neither of them knew exactly what was up or down any longer.

"It's too strong! I heard it lock," she said.

So had he, but what choice did they have? "You . . . have . . . to . . . try!"

If the seal broke, maybe it would initiate an automatic shutdown.

"Could be dangerous!" she said. For me, Amanda

14

was thinking. How would they explain the damage to the simulator? Damage that would come from the inside? So far in her life her "gift"—as some called it—had only gotten her in trouble or made her the object of teasing. Subjugated at the age of eight to a foster home for freaks in Baltimore—the Fairlies—she'd been studied by scientists, doctors, and soldiers until she'd had no choice but to run away with Jess. She had no urgent desire to make a scene with her gift and bring all that down on herself again.

They jerked violently left, right, front, back, and left again. Finn's head felt as if it was going to come off his neck. *Dangerous?* he wanted to say. *Really?*

Amanda couldn't risk Finn's getting hurt. She released her bloodless grip on the chest restraint, reaching toward the screen with outstretched arms. Finn watched her close her eyes, bend her elbows, and flatten her hands, palms facing out like a traffic cop's. She pushed up over her head—all at once, and with every ounce of strength she possessed.

The metal bulged like it had been hit with a battering ram. Red paint flakes rained down. Sparks flew.

"Again!" he hollered.

"Too strong!" she complained.

"You're all we've got." The vibrations climbed toward a climax. The push had made the simulator lean even farther to the left; the grinding of metal was now louder than the sound effects.

He smelled electrical smoke. They were going to suffocate.

"EVERYTHING YOU'VE GOT!" he shouted.

The act of pushing drained Amanda. At low levels she could briefly levitate a person or object—cause them to float for a few seconds. Using up more of herself, she could shove a car a few feet in a parking space, or knock a group of people—or Overtakers—off their feet. Or bend a simulator hatch door. Finn needed her to give it her all.

"O . . . M . . . G!" she screamed.

On the screen, the track ahead of them rose, fell, and tilted to the right before . . . disappearing. It looked as if someone had simply erased the track—it broke off in space. Below the break was a rock canyon so deep that Finn couldn't see the bottom.

The simulator shuddered. The smell of an electrical short—like the air before a storm—continued to flood the cabin. Their screams were lost amid the groan and complaint of the failing mechanics.

The car reached the end of the track and flew off into space.

Amanda thrust her arms toward the overhead door, but this time like she was lifting an incredibly heavy set of gym weights. Going for an Olympic record.

"STEADY!" Finn shouted, as the car tilted down, now plummeting into the depths of the rock canyon.

The hatch door rumbled and bent, bulged and shuddered, the seal cracking open, first a fraction of an inch, then wider.

"MORE!!!!" Finn said, as the ground—a rock bottom, like a dry riverbed—rushed toward them at over three hundred miles per hour.

The cry of the metal hatch now overpowered any other sound. Amanda's face was scarlet and sweaty, her arm muscles bulging as her bones seemed to bend to breaking.

The sheet metal tore at the location of both pneumatic hook locks that secured the hatch.

Two inches . . . three . . .

The lid blew open.

The ride shut down. Smoke coiled from motors and servos.

A group of Cast Members rushed inside, aiming fire extinguishers that belched a yellow foam.

Finn and Amanda hung against the chest restraints as the simulator rotated forward ninety degrees, facing the ground. It made it hard to see what was going on. Some guy was shouting a bunch of orders.

Finn heard Megan say, "Are you okay? We're getting you out! Hang on, you're almost out."

The chest restraints released without notice. Finn and Amanda fell, crashing into the flat-panel display and cracking its safety glass. Finn helped Amanda up, and Megan offered them her hand. They climbed out.

"Wow," Finn said, "that's incredibly lifelike."

Amanda played along. "Must be expensive if they do that every time."

They exited from the smoke and chaos. Charlene stood there, her full attention on their joined hands. Finn hadn't even realized that he and Amanda were holding hands. He let go a little abruptly.

Charlene leaned in to examine the twisted wreckage. Smoke and steam and the gas from the fire extinguishers commingled. She fanned it away from her face.

"What happened in there?" she asked.

Amanda said, "I think next time I'll design my own ride."

"You don't think I had something to do with that . . . that . . ." Charlene stammered, ". . . with whatever happened in there, do you?"

"You mean just because you talked us into coming here in the first place and you designed our roller coaster? Now, why would I think that?" Amanda said.

"Finn?" Charlene pleaded.

"You gave us the card, Charlie," he said, using a nickname for her only he used. "You designed the ride." *And Maleficent's locked in a jail cell,* he felt like adding. Use of her nickname was an attempt at intimacy, to remind her that he still considered her a close friend, despite what had happened. But it backfired. Amanda heard him and clearly resented it.

"Really?" Amanda said to him. "You're going to sweet-talk her after she almost *killed us?*" She stormed off down the exit stairs.

"Amanda! Wait!" Finn called after her.

"I promise you," Charlene said, "I didn't do anything! I had nothing to do with this. It wasn't me!"

They'd been close friends for more than two years. Finn said, "Listen, do I want to think you sabotaged the simulator? Come on!" But she'd designed the ride, he reminded himself.

Finn couldn't let Amanda get away. He hurried out after her. Charlene followed at a run.

The building seemed more crowded. He recognized nearly everyone—even though there were four hundred kids in his grade.

"KK rules!" he called back to Charlene. His team had long since agreed that when in the Parks no one flew solo. The Overtakers took advantage of Keepers off on their own. In pairs or teams their chances for survival increased.

Finn shoved his way through the crowd, catching only fleeting glimpses of the back of Amanda's head. She was wasting no time trying to get out of there. She disappeared down the staircase—much too far ahead to hear him calling after her.

Charlene closed in from behind him.

He glanced over the rail, looking down, hoping to catch a glimpse of Amanda as she reached the bottom of the stairs.

His breath caught.

Not possible.

Snow White's Evil Queen stood amid a torrent of admirers, all begging for autographs. But the Evil Queen wasn't looking at her fans; she was locked onto Finn like a laser-guided missile.

He jumped back from the rail, out of the way of her gaze. A shudder of terror flooded him. If it was a legitimate Cast Member, fine. But if it was an Overtaker—if it was the *real* Evil Queen—then she could throw spells, conjure curses, mix potions to transfigure herself into an ugly old peddler offering a poisoned apple. In short, she was nothing to mess with.

*Amanda!*

He yanked his phone out of his pocket and sent a group text:

Possible OTs in DQ. Head 2 bus ASAP

Hopefully that would get the others moving. Presently, his job was to get Amanda and Charlene out of there.

The four other Keepers had smart phones just like his—gifts from Wayne and the Imagineers. Amanda and Jess didn't have phones. Even if they'd had the money to buy them—and they didn't—Mrs. Nash didn't allow her girls to have phones.

Charlene caught up to him and he launched himself down the crowded stairwell, fighting through the throng. As he neared the bottom of the stairs, Amanda came into view again.

The Queen turned to look at Finn. He averted his eyes, fearing a spell. She walked toward him, the bubble of her admirers moving with her. He stole one more glance in her direction only to realize she wasn't looking at him but over his head. He looked behind him . . .

. . . at Charlene.

From the step above, Charlene lowered her eyes to Finn and said, "What's *she* doing here?"

"You know who that is?" Finn asked, surprised.

"Of course I know who that is!"

"I've never seen her before. Not the real one."

"The real one? Is that the *real* one?"

"What do you think? You feel like giving her the pinch test?"

"AMANDA!" Charlene cried out loudly. She waved furiously, trying to get Amanda to turn around and join them. But Amanda was too caught up in the reason for her running off in the first place. Even more furious seeing Finn and Charlene on the steps together, she heaved through the crowd, ever closer to the Evil Queen.

"I texted the others," he tried telling Charlene. But then he saw what she was up to: she was taking a photo of the Queen.

Charlene mumbled, "What's she doing outside of the Parks?"

"Technically," he said, "we're on Disney property." He led her down the stairs, fighting his way toward Amanda. Charlene followed.

"Technically," she said, calling over his shoulder, "she belongs in the Magic Kingdom. The afternoon parade. Some autographing. Not inside DisneyQuest."

"Maybe it's part of our school event," Finn suggested. He wanted an easy explanation; he wanted to be told this was a Cast Member, maybe a college student in costume.

The Queen was slowed by her fans.

Amanda had disappeared, hopefully into an elevator or down another stairwell to the ground floor, where a variety of rides gave way to a long hallway and an exit that passed through the gift shop.

The Evil Queen seemed caught up in her popularity—a woman pulled in two directions, but favoring admiration over purpose. Finn and the Keepers had long since learned that the by-products of fame—the adoring crowds wanting autographs and souvenirs, the people invading your space away from the Parks—was a different, but very real challenge.

Charlene grabbed Finn's hand. He led her through the crowd, coming incredibly close to the Queen, but her fans formed a wall, and they passed by as quickly as they'd arrived. He let go of Charlene's hand and bounded down the less-crowded stairway.

He ran and caught up to Amanda, turning her by the shoulder.

"Wait up!" he said.

She spun around, her face streaked with the snail lines of fallen tears.

"Let go!" she said.

"I knew it was the OTs. They're here." His eyes refocused toward the entrance of the hallway that led outside. "There!" he said.

Cruella De Vil was looking right at them. Gaunt, pale, and wearing fur in Florida with her trademark cigarette holder in her right hand. She, too, was surrounded by a knot of fans wanting autographs. She raised her cigarette holder and pointed with her long, gloved finger.

"Look, kids," she said in her creamy voice, "it's the Kingdom Keepers."

The mass of fans turned toward Finn and Amanda, just as Charlene caught up to them. "She's right!" . . . "It's them!" . . . "Let's go!" Voices echoed off the ceiling and walls.

A mass of kids abandoned Cruella and rushed toward them.

Finn pulled Amanda to him protectively.

Amanda said, "Oh . . . no . . ." pointing back toward the stairway.

The Evil Queen.

The three of them were sandwiched.

Charlene's attention was on the low ceiling decorated with fishing nets and metal sculpture.

"I can handle this," she said. "Stay with me! I have an idea." She broke away from them just before the fans enveloped Finn and Amanda.

Finn had learned that the only thing worse than a hyper fan was an angry fan. No matter what, he didn't want to make any of the kids mad or they would harass and glue themselves to him, complaining and shouting and taking an attitude.

"Hey! How ya doing?" he said.

Amanda looked curiously at Finn, wondering what he was starting. But he knew what he was doing; he'd done it plenty of times before. Offered a pen, he started signing forearms, hands, the back of shirts. The crowd pressed in more tightly, everyone eager to get an autograph. This was what Charlene had immediately understood: their fans would protect them.

Given the distraction, Charlene had scrambled up the wall like a tree frog and was currently hanging upside down from the lights attached to the ceiling. As she moved, so did the human wall surrounding Finn and Amanda—the fans were leaping up and trying to touch her, applauding her, screaming her name. As long as Finn and Amanda stayed below her, the protective wall of fans that encircled them moved with her, keeping the Evil Queen and Cruella at a distance.

The two Overtakers—they *had* to be Overtakers— were also trying to push through to Finn and Amanda, but it was no use; they weren't going to beat out fifty wild fans.

Charlene continued on the ceiling toward the hallway. Finn and Amanda and their fans moved with her.

As the group reached the hallway, the room narrowed. Charlene dropped. Finn pushed rudely through that side of kids, dragging Amanda with him. A gloved hand caught his shoulder.

Taller than the young fans, the Evil Queen had reached above their heads and caught him.

She said, "You cannot stop us. We will do this with or without your help. If you run, you'd better keep running."

He ran.

Down the hall at a sprint, twenty of the screaming kids close behind. Through the turnstile, the gift shop, and into fresh air. Finn had rarely ever run so hard, and yet both girls were several paces ahead of him and increasing their leads.

When a good distance away, he dared to look back. Cruella and the Evil Queen had made no attempt to run after them.

*If you run, you'd better keep running. . . .*

Instead, Cruella was heading to a . . . pay phone.

She reached it and brought the receiver to her ear. It was the last Finn saw of her, but it struck him as so out of place, so odd, despite the fact that Cruella used telephones in her movies. Not pay phones. Not in Downtown Disney.

He arrived at the bus stop out of breath just as a bus was about to pull away. The driver braked for him and opened the door, and as he climbed on, he saw all six of his friends clustered in the back by the door.

Maybeck, a head taller than anyone his age, caught Finn's eye and nodded, clearly relieved to see he'd made it.

A telephone, Finn was thinking.

* * *

Philby contained his surprise when a pop-up window appeared on his lab computer. A bright-eyed sixteen-year-old with reddish hair and freckles, Philby was a geek in disguise. He looked perfectly normal, but his British upbringing and slight accent, along with having a brain like Einstein, set him apart from other kids.

Edgewater High's computer lab security software blocked pop-ups, prevented cookies, and limited Web access while simultaneously recording keystrokes. It was like working in the offices of the CIA or the NSA.

The lab had five long countertops with chairs, and eight laptop stations each. Currently, thirty-one students all faced forward where their instructor, Mr. Chambers, was stationed to the left of a large, interactive whiteboard mounted to the wall behind him. The whiteboard could carry anything from a mirror of one of the computers, to a PowerPoint presentation, or video. The instructor monitored software that showed a real-time thumbnail of each computer screen active in the lab. Mr. Chambers could click on any one of these at any time, seeing exactly what a particular student was doing. Chats were forbidden, as were aimlessly browsing the Web, downloads, or entertainment.

The pop-up on Philby's screen displayed an invitation to a video chat. Technically, because of the security software and firewall, a pop-up was impossible, which only made it all the more intriguing to him. Despite his computer expertise, Philby had never been able to hack the school's firewall—but not for want of trying.

Making matters worse, Philby and his fellow students had all signed ethics contracts, making it their responsibility to report any breaches or misuse of the system. By not raising his hand the moment the pop-up appeared on his screen, Philby had already violated that contract. It didn't escape him that Mr. Chambers could easily be watching his screen, could already know about the pop-up himself.

If caught in violation of the contract, Philby would be suspended from lab for a week, possibly expelled from the class for the semester. It called for diversionary tactics, nothing new to Philby and his friends, who had long since established a system to distract Mr. Chambers away from his monitoring software.

Philby caught the eye of Hugo Montcliff, a neighborhood friend with droopy eyes, greasy hair, and shirts that carried unidentifiable food stains. Hugo's father was a hard-drinking former policeman who couldn't hold a job. Hugo occasionally sneaked out at night because he couldn't take the screaming between his parents. Some nights he'd show up at Philby's house and sleep on the couch. Philby's mom had come to think of him as a kind of adopted son, and Philby considered him the closest thing he'd ever have to a brother. Philby signaled Hugo by tapping the desk twice and then pointing to his screen. Hugo nodded.

Philby then turned his attention to Mr. Chambers, knowing Hugo would open a drawing program when he was supposed to be creating a PowerPoint. As Mr. Chambers reached for his computer mouse, suggesting he'd spotted Hugo's divergence from the assignment and would therefore briefly only be monitoring Hugo's activities, Philby made his move.

Already wearing a headset for the sake of his own PowerPoint assignment, Philby accepted the invitation to the online video chat.

The pop-up window grew in size and a fuzzy video image appeared.

Philby brought his fist to his mouth to muffle his own gasp. Although difficult to see clearly, the white hair and cool blue eyes revealed the identity of the caller: Wayne.

The Keepers had neither seen nor heard from Wayne in several months—not since his hospitalization following the Fantasmic! adventure. He was believed to be in hiding, keeping himself out of the hands of the Overtakers, who would use any means necessary—including torture—to obtain the top-secret location of their captured leaders, Maleficent and Chernabog, or possibly to obtain other secret information that the creator of the Kingdom Keepers possessed.

"Are you secure?" The old man's voice was steady but troubled, even as heard over the static-ridden poor connection.

"Not exactly, but I'm okay for a couple minutes," Philby whispered.

Wayne knew more about the behind-the-scenes operations at the Parks than any other Disney Imagineer. He had helped to create a new hologram technology, had recruited Finn, Philby, and the others to model for what would become hologram guides in the Parks— Daylight Hologram Imaging, or DHI. The new holograms were an instant success. Families could be toured through the Parks by a talking teenage guide who was nothing but light, yet looked and sounded absolutely real. Park attendance jumped. Tourists traveled from around the world to see the new Disney phenomenon.

But Wayne and his Imagineering colleagues had advanced the DHI technology so the five students who'd modeled for them could also "cross over" into the Parks as holograms when they went to sleep at night. Once in the Parks, the DHIs could spy for the Imagineers or battle the Overtakers for control of the Parks.

A call from Wayne could not be taken lightly.

Philby had so many questions he wanted to ask: How had Wayne managed to breach the school's computer security? Why would he risk contacting Philby in this manner? When had Wayne gotten out of the hospital? Where was he now? Did his call have anything to do with Maleficent or Chernabog? But time was precious; he kept his mouth shut and listened.

"As you know, these are dangerous times," Wayne said. "Dangerous times require risk taking. My daughter, Wanda, whom you've met, has been my eyes and ears of late. She has been extremely busy carrying on my work—*our* work. But something has happened. She has been jailed by the police."

Philby wanted to cry out, but he held his tongue. *Wanda arrested?*

"I need Finn to offer bail for her release. This will require an adult, and we know Mrs. Whitman to be . . . supportive . . . of our cause. Wanda knows things that you five must know. Must act upon. Quickly."

*The Evil Queen*, Philby was thinking. *Cruella De Vil. It's happening again.*

"Tonight the five of you must be in Norway's Stave Church at eight PM. Not your DHIs, but your real selves. A picture is worth a thousand words."

"I have so many questions."

"Prepare for remote access to the server. You may need it," Wayne said. Philby knew this was a call to battle.

Since Maleficent and Chernabog were imprisoned by Disney, Wayne's concern suggested that the Overtakers had reorganized. But if Wayne was risking breaching the school's computer security, it implied something else as well.

"You believe they're monitoring our home computers," Philby said, guessing.

"You see why I contacted you? You understand the bigger picture. Finn is the natural leader, but you, Philby, are the navigator. Steer Finn in the right direction and he will lead you well."

The Overtakers were spying on them. It gave him the chills. He'd been IMing with Willa on a regular basis, writing stuff he didn't necessarily want anyone else seeing.

"Never underestimate their capabilities," Wayne

said. "We all have learned that lesson too many times."

"Where are you?" Philby blurted out. "Are you all right?" Wayne looked old and tired. He must be worried sick about Wanda, Philby thought.

"Unimportant. Do as I say. Do what I ask. Good luck. We're all counting on you."

The window went black, the connection lost.

"Mr. Philby?" It was Mr. Chambers from the front of the class. He was not in a charitable mood.

Philby slipped off the headset expecting suspension and possible detention.

"No videos. You know the assignment. Voice is okay. No video."

Philby realized that Mr. Chambers so trusted the school's firewall that he couldn't for a moment believe that anyone had managed to breach it. He must have assumed that the video on Philby's screen was something Philby had created.

"Sorry, Mr. Chambers."

Philby and Hugo met eyes, and Philby thanked him with a quick nod of his head. Hugo smiled and went back to work. He could see the curiosity on Hugo's face—he wanted to know what had required the diversion. Philby would have to invent a pretty convincing story: Hugo was not easily fooled.

Philby's heart raced. Wayne. Wanda. The Stave Church. The Overtakers were reorganized, still out there.

For the past several months he and his friends had not worried about such things. They'd actually had lives again.

But now, in a few short minutes, all of that had changed.

Again.

\* \* \*

Philby compartmentalized his ideas. His mind worked like a filing cabinet. He held ideas in drawers, opening one or two while closing others. He didn't think about it; it just happened. Once he had hung up from the chat with Wayne, he put all those ideas into a drawer and slid it shut, marking it as *urgent*. He'd been able to go about his classwork. But now, while other kids occupied the time between classes with hallway chitchat, Philby concentrated on the contents of that mental filing drawer. He made a list of what had to be done and in what order, with an emphasis on efficiency.

First, he would text Finn about Wanda. Next he would send a group text to all the Keepers about meeting at the Stave Church at eight PM. Then, once home, he would take his laptop over to Hugo's house to get off his home network, where the Overtakers might be monitoring him. He would access the DHI server remotely and lock it down, making sure there was no chance that the Keepers might cross over unexpectedly after going to sleep. Crossing over was not the danger; it was getting stuck as a DHI, failing to come back, what the Keepers called the Return.

Philby spotted Willa up the hallway. In that instant, he became just another ninth grader with a crush. She was standing at her locker, one hand on its metal door, the other at her side while staring into space. He suddenly tensed. His legs felt like lead.

He recalled the exact day this change in his attitude toward her had occurred. They'd been sitting at a table at the Marble Slab with the other Keepers when he'd been overcome with a feeling of curiosity. It was something he still didn't understand. But what it amounted to was: he wanted to be around her, to know more about her, to spend time with her. She was smart, funny, and thoughtful. Maybe not drop-dead pretty like Charlene, or the brooding kind of beauty like Amanda, but interesting-looking. Intriguing. More important to him was that they thought the same way. Often came to the same conclusions without any kind of communication. Like they were connected.

"Hi, there," he said, reaching her locker.

"You ever know you're looking right at something but can't see it?" At the moment, Willa was looking right at *him*.

"Yeah, I suppose."

"My sheet music is in here somewhere."

One thing on which they differed: she kept her locker a mess; his was neatly ordered. He studied her locker carefully, reached in and withdrew the sheet music. Her eyes filled with appreciation.

"You're awesome!" she said.

He wanted to hear her say it again.

"Wayne just video-chatted me in the lab," he told her.

"Yeah, right."

"I'm not kidding."

The locker door slammed into place and she locked it. Philby could sense both Willa's apprehension as well as her misgivings. He could *see* her think. She had an intensity that he totally got.

"But that's not possible," she said.

"I know. Isn't it cool?"

"It had to be some kind of trick. The school's firewall—"

"—was breached. Wayne breached it."

Spencer Randolph was staring at them from across the hall. A gifted athlete and popular tenth grader,

Spencer always seemed to be hanging around Willa.

"Don't look now," Philby said, trying to make it sound like he didn't care, "but Spence can't take his eyes off you."

"He always does that." Willa blushed. Philby didn't like seeing her blush over Spencer Randolph. She looked back at Philby. "Why would he do that?"

Philby felt confused: *Because you're smart? Because you're a Willa kind of pretty?* "He probably wants to go out with you," he said.

"Wayne, stupid!" she said. "Not Spence. I know all about Spence."

"You do?" How had he let that slip?

"Why would Wayne go to all that trouble just to get a message to you?"

"That's the thing," he whispered. "He said it had to be here at the school, that it couldn't be at my home, or Finn's, or any of ours because he thinks the OTs are monitoring our home computers."

"What!? But we . . . I mean, you and me . . ." Willa stammered.

"Yeah, I know. We have to stay off our computers. And no crossing over. Who knows what they're planning?"

"Just when I was starting to feel normal again."

"Yeah, I was thinking the exact same thing." He

added, "Normal, if you overlook that when we go to sleep we wake up in the Parks as our holograms."

"We've all been overlooking that for a couple of years now. I don't even think about it, you know? It's just . . . a part of me." Willa added, "We need to tell Amanda and Jess as well." The Keepers had applied the hologram technology to Amanda and Jess months earlier. Philby could remotely cross them over as DHIs as well. But this meant they were now at risk along with the other Keepers. It didn't seem exactly fair.

"Yeah. They'll need to know." Philby told her about the Stave Church at eight PM. He left out the part about Wanda for now. He wanted Finn to deal with that, as Wayne had asked. "I'm going to text the others, not IM. We have to assume that whatever we do online from home could be monitored."

"That's way creepy," Willa said.

"Yeah."

"But what about texting?"

"Probably safer than anything on the Internet. I don't see the OTs hacking Verizon."

"No. That's true."

The hallway bell rang, signaling another class for both of them.

Spencer had not gone away. The longer he stared, the more Philby felt like kissing Willa right there in the hall for everyone to see. Not that he would ever do it.

He shook his head and coughed out disgust at himself.

"What?" she asked.

"You wouldn't understand."

Philby wounded her by saying that. Hadn't meant to. He longed for a rewind button, another chance to say something different. But Willa was already on her way down the hall, her back to him. Spencer peeled himself off the wall and came up alongside of her, and Willa's step seemed a little lighter.

Philby stood there watching, sick to his stomach.

# 2

"**W**HAT ARE YOU DOING HERE?" Finn blurted out as he climbed atop his BMX bike. It wasn't just any bike, but a trick bike capable of doing stunts and jumps. Being on the bike gave him a height advantage over Charlene, which he appreciated.

"You don't have to sound so pleased," she said sarcastically.

"I didn't mean . . . It's just that Evans High—"

"Happens to be playing your school in soccer today," said Charlene.

"I didn't think soccer had cheerleaders."

"Am I dressed like a cheerleader?" In fact she wore tight jean shorts and an equally tight T-shirt. "Where are you headed?" Charlene asked.

"I'm going to see Wanda."

"I kind of figured that. Mind if I hitch a ride?"

The bike was small. Finn had ridden with Amanda before—on the seat behind him, while he stayed up on the pedals—but it felt a little weird to offer the same thing to Charlene.

"I don't bite," she said when he hesitated.

"No problem," Finn said, glancing around in the mass of kids, hoping Amanda wasn't among them.

Finn climbed off, helped Charlene on, and then straddled the bar. He rode away quickly. The message from Philby had injected a sense of panic in him. Wayne. Wanda. The police. He pedaled hard.

"We're meeting my mom. Only adults can bail someone out of jail," Finn said.

"And your mom agreed?"

"We'll see."

"You haven't asked her?"

"Not exactly." He changed subjects. "You got Philby's text about tonight?"

"Yes," Charlene said. "Do you know what it's about?"

"Only that Wayne told us we had to be there at eight."

"Why?"

"No idea."

"What do you think he wants?"

"It's got to be important," Finn answered.

"Do you know what he told Philby, exactly?"

"Why all the questions?" Finn asked. Charlene never asked so many questions; she was more of a "tell me what to do and I'll do it" person.

"I don't know. Curious, I guess. Am I asking a lot of questions?"

"Yes."

"Maybe I'm nervous," she said. "I talk a lot when I'm nervous." She put her hands on Finn's hips to steady herself on the seat.

Now he was nervous, too. He kept glancing back, worried that Amanda would see them despite the fact he was now several blocks from school.

"We're not supposed to use our computers at home," he said.

"Yeah, I got that," she said. "Hey, how come Wayne contacted Philby instead of you?"

Another question.

"I don't know. I don't have computer lab the way he does. I suppose that could be it." But it bothered him much more than he let on. Wayne referred to him as the leader; Wayne usually contacted him, not Philby. Was his leadership role of the Keepers in jeopardy? Had he done something wrong?

"What do you think it all means?" she asked. "Wayne contacting Philby. Wanda getting arrested. I thought with Maleficent and Chernabog locked up this stuff wasn't supposed to happen."

"It wasn't," he said.

"So?"

"So I guess things never go as planned."

* * *

Finn's mother was an actual rocket scientist. She'd eventually left NASA to raise Finn and his sister, the dual commitment proving to be too much, but she remained the smartest woman he'd ever met. And the fairest. Whereas his father got angry and upset about Finn's escapades as a Kingdom Keeper, his mother, a huge fan of everything Disney, supported Wayne's effort to keep the magic alive in the Parks. What was to Finn's father a silly ambition fraught with physical danger and risk was to his mother on the level of national importance. Because of this, he had recently opened up to her more, sharing the challenges the Keepers faced, sometimes even asking for her help. This was one of those times.

Mrs. Whitman, currently a brunette, was thin, happy-faced, and athletic. She hardly wore any makeup. Her shoes were what she called "practical" and her earrings "artistic."

"Bailing someone out requires money," she said from the other side of the kitchen counter. Finn and Charlene were both eating bowls of breakfast cereal.

"I know that. I'm sure Wayne will pay you back."

"And a bail bondsman. You put up a small amount and the bail bondsman promises the rest. It's complicated. If the person misses her appearance in court, then the bail bondsman loses his money, and in this case, *we* would have to repay him."

43

"She won't miss anything," Finn said. "Please, Mom."

"It would mean taking money out of our savings. Your father would never approve of such a thing."

"But if Wayne repays you, it's only gone for a day or two. Right?"

"*If* he repays me, yes. But you've no way to reach him. Correct?"

Finn hung his head shamefully. "Yeah."

"In two weeks the bank statements will arrive. By that time we have to have the money back in the account."

"Does that mean you're going to do it?" Finn didn't even try to contain his excitement.

"Not a word to your father," she said.

\* \* \*

The sign out front read: CITY OF ORLANDO, POLICE HEADQUARTERS. It was a normal-looking office high-rise. Finn, Charlene, and Mrs. Whitman checked in at a lobby reception desk and rode the elevator.

It was not the dismal, smelly, dimly lit space that Finn anticipated from television, but instead, more a combination of post office and doctor's office. There were some decent chairs to sit in, copies of newspapers and magazines. The overhead lighting was bright, the smell not nearly as bad as he'd expected.

A man in uniform sat behind a window of thick glass. He looked pleasant enough.

Finn's mother spoke to him for several minutes. She handed him stuff from the bail bondsman, filled out something on a clipboard. Showed her driver's license. It reminded Finn of her returning shoes at Nordstrom, or paying for an oil change.

"We can't get her out tonight," Mrs. Whitman reported to Charlene and her son. "Some problem with the courts. I can return tomorrow morning. Tuesday at the latest."

"She has to stay here?" Finn said. "That's terrible."

"She's going to make bail," his mother said. "It's just delayed a little. But we're allowed to see her."

Finn felt a huge weight lift. "YES!" he said, fist-pumping. "You are totally awesome!"

If Mrs. Whitman could have floated off the floor, she might have. "Come on. What are you waiting for?"

The three had gone through security to enter the building, but they were put through it again before entering the jail. The room they were shown to was plain. It looked like a very small version of their school lunchroom with six green plastic picnic tables bolted to the floor, overhead tube lighting, and lots of acoustic tile.

Wanda looked older than Finn remembered. She

wore an orange jumpsuit with ORLANDO CITY JAIL written across the front. Her hair was stringy. She'd been crying.

Finn, his mother, and Charlene sat on the bench facing her. A guard stood just outside the door.

"So, how are you?" Finn asked.

Wanda smirked, her twisted smile telling him more than he wanted to know. "Been better," she said.

"We've posted bail," Mrs. Whitman said. "Tomorrow sometime, I'm told."

"Thank you so much, but I wouldn't count on it. I've been told by the attorney they appointed that they may try for Homeland Security charges. That's probably why the delay."

"What did you *do*?" Charlene asked.

Wanda lowered her voice. "My father has me monitor bandwidth usage on the DHI server, the same way Philby sometimes does."

Finn nodded. If bandwidth usage surged, it meant extremely large data packs were moving in and out of the DHI servers. That, in turn, meant someone was crossing over or Returning. Wayne watched for unusual or unexpected bandwidth usage as a warning sign of possible Overtaker interference.

Wanda said, "There has been some unusual activity: data surges late, late at night. A spike at one point from the Animal Kingdom server. Others as well. We knew something was going on, we just didn't know what. So I hacked one of Disney's multi protocol routers. If the Internet is the information superhighway, I hacked a major intersection, a truck stop. That's probably why the Homeland Security charges. It's kind of like hacking Google or Microsoft."

"But you *work* for Disney," Finn said.

"That just makes matters worse. I look like a disgruntled employee."

"Oh, my," said Mrs. Whitman.

"I came away with more questions than answers. What seemed to be happening couldn't possibly be happening. I needed more data, more time to drill deeper. That was when I was arrested, in the middle of all that. It was only then I realized that I'd probably been set up. That I'd walked into a trap."

She looked each of them in the eye, making sure they understood the earnestness of what she was about to tell them. "Our friends," she said, meaning the Overtakers, who weren't their friends at all, "knew that if they made enough noise on the DHI servers it would attract our interest. Mine. Philby's. Someone's. They could then alert the authorities, who would follow the data mining back to its source and arrest whoever was messing around—in this case, me. That would then mean that I'd need to be bailed out, and who would bail me out?"

"Wayne," Finn answered. "Wait a second! Are you saying it was all a way to make Wayne show himself?"

"To draw him out," Wanda said, nodding. "That's my guess. A father's first instinct is to save his children. My dad nearly came here. If he had, he'd never have made it through the doors. They'd have had him out front. I'm sure of it."

"So he contacted Philby in order to not come here in person," Finn said.

"I made him promise not to come," Wanda said.

"Was the Internet stuff you turned up for real?" Charlene asked.

"We won't know without more tests," she answered, "more investigation."

"Do you know where your father is?" Charlene asked.

More questions, Finn thought. He said, "That's none of our business!"

"It is, if the police are going to torture her or something," Charlene said.

"Don't be ridiculous, Charlene," Mrs. Whitman said. "That kind of thing only happens in movies."

Wanda and Finn exchanged a questioning look.

"We've got to get you out of here," Mrs. Whitman said.

* * *

As the bus from the Transportation Center rolled into Epcot, Finn spotted a pair of crash-test dummies—CTDs—on Segways patrolling the parking lot and pointed them out to Jess. Moving her dark hair off her face to get a better view, Jess's features reflected off the bus window. She had a teardrop chin with full lips and wide-set eyes. She changed her hair color—which had turned horse-tail white after an encounter with Maleficent—several times a year. She pointed out the Segways to Amanda.

The overhead monorail line divided the enormous parking lots; the lane beneath it was used for the parking lot shuttles and as a pedestrian walkway leading to the Park's front gates.

A fun distraction for Park visitors, the CTDs-on-Segways were known to the Keepers as possible soldiers for the Overtakers. Some were nothing more than Cast Members in CTD suits, acting out a part. But others were robotic drones armed with high-tech detection and surveillance equipment outfitted with Bluetooth and Wi-Fi. Originally, these had been introduced to Epcot by Security—an effective and inexpensive way to patrol the Parks during regular hours and after closing. Their popularity had led to the Cast Member variety—CTDs that would talk and interact with the visitors. But somewhere along the line, the Overtakers had managed to electronically hijack control of at least a half dozen of the robotic variety. Seeing them now so close put Finn on guard.

"Well, if they're looking for you, they'll never spot you," Amanda said.

"Not with you looking like that, they won't," said Jess.

Finn wore an Orlando Magic jersey with a heavy chain around his neck, a Yankee cap sideways on his head, and mirrored sunglasses. His shorts went below his knees and he wore basketball shoes with Nike socks. There were probably a few hundred boys just like him in the Park at this very minute.

"You look sooooo stupid," Amanda said, prompting a laugh from her and Jess.

"Good," Finn said. It was true, he looked like an idiot, but that was the point. If he happened to be recognized in the Park as a Kingdom Keeper he'd be hounded for autographs; if he was hounded for autographs he'd win the attention of Security; if Security caught him or any of the Keepers in the Park without approval, his family could lose their Golden Mickey Pass—or worse—Operations Management could bring the hammer down. It was one thing to attend a school function in Downtown Disney, but something else entirely to be in Epcot without asking permission.

Operations Management did not want Park visitors seeing both the DHI hologram guides and the real-life models for the DHIs in the same Park at the same time. Finn and the four others were under contract not to visit any of the Parks without prior approval—approval they currently lacked.

"Plus, you're hanging out with two gorgeous girls," said Jess, striking a pose. "So we know who everyone will be looking at."

Jess was typically more modest than this. The comment from her drew a shrill laugh from Amanda. They seemed to be having more fun than he was.

"We need to keep our eyes on them," Finn warned. "Seriously."

"Okay. We get it," Amanda said.

He'd ruined the moment. He wanted to kick himself.

Entering Epcot, they passed beneath Spaceship Earth—which looked like an elevated giant golf ball—reaching the fountain plaza where a computer-controlled water show ran. It could mesmerize visitors for hours at a time. Pavilions rose on both sides: The Land, The Seas with Nemo & Friends, Test Track. Beyond the plaza was the fifteen-acre lake surrounded by the World Showcase pavilions, each representing a different country and duplicating its most famous architecture: the

Eiffel Tower in France; a Mayan temple in Mexico.

The autumn Food and Wine Festival was under way. Special booths offered food and drink. The mood was even more festive than usual. The place was packed. At a few minutes before eight PM, the sun set. The IllumiNations: Reflections of Earth show would take over the lake—and the entire Park—before long. There was a buzz in the air.

For Finn, the buzz felt more like fear. Seeing Wanda locked up had upset him. The idea that the Overtakers had tried to trick Wayne out into the open worried him. They were planning again. They were up to something. With Wayne in hiding and Wanda in jail, it fell onto him and the Keepers to figure out what was going on, and to stop whatever was planned. The only timetable was *right now*.

Finn, Amanda, and Jess arrived at Norway's Stave Church just behind Philby and Willa. The steeple on the dark brown wooden church rose forty feet in the air, while the interior space was quite small, a closeted, museumlike space.

The walls were dark wood, the ceiling, vaulted. The five displays depicted various scenes or famous people from Norway's colorful history. There were descriptive plaques alongside each.

The three girls drew together in the far corner and

immediately began talking the way girls do. Finn and Philby were left alone.

Philby reviewed everything he could recall about the video from Wayne; Finn detailed the visit with Wanda.

"A trick?" Philby asked.

"That's what she thinks."

"Makes sense."

"Yes, it does," Finn agreed.

"I wish she'd told you more about the data bursts."

"I knew you were going to say that," Finn said. "You are so predictable."

"It's what I do," Philby said, unapologetically.

"What could it mean?"

Philby shrugged. "All sorts of things. But it's kind of random that she'd hack a bank of Disney routers. That's like hacking the streetlights at an intersection. No wonder she's in trouble." He mulled it over. "What's interesting, I suppose, is why she'd bother in the first place. Those big routers . . . I suppose if you wanted to determine where the packets were headed . . . the firewall logs might be all you'd need."

Finn lost him for a minute while Philby was doing the math in his head.

"Listen, there's one other thing before she gets here," Finn said.

"Charlene," Philby said, naming the only girl not there yet.

"Yeah. I know this doesn't make any sense, but she designed our ride. She gave us the card."

"Do you know what you're saying?"

"Yes. Of course I do. And look, was it her alone? No. But that's even more disturbing. And today, she just materialized at school. Said she'd ridden over with the Evans soccer team. She's been asking all these crazy questions."

"This is Charlene we're talking about!"

"I know!" Finn said. "That's what got me! Since when does she ask a dozen questions in a row?"

"Since never."

"But she did today. She was like Sherlock Holmes or something."

"You can't accuse her. Not without evidence. It isn't fair. We just don't do that."

"I know," Finn said. "I get that. But I wanted you to know. Only you."

"So I should keep an eye on Charlene."

"That's all I'm saying, yeah." Finn added reluctantly, "Not that I like it."

"No. It's ugly."

"Speaking of ugly . . ." He told Philby about his seeing Cruella De Vil on the phone outside Disney Quest and how out of place it seemed.

"This is beginning to feel like a parallel universe," Philby said.

"Right?" Finn said.

Philby reached out and touched Finn's shoulder. "Just making sure we're not holograms," he said. Both boys laughed.

A father and son entered. The son was carrying a Kim Possible cell phone. The Kim Possible quest was an interactive mystery hunt where the participant joined a popular cartoon character's pursuit of bad guys. The phones gave clues and could lead you all over the Park.

The boy searched the church and apparently found the answer in a display description that his father helped him to read. The boy squealed and pushed a button on the device. The phone gave him his next location. The two left without having paid any attention to the five kids.

Maybeck arrived out of breath. He looked around the small area, making sure they were alone. He said hello, and then, "Did any of you see the CTDs out there? There was a pair trying to follow me. I lost them, but they were zoned in on me."

Appraising Maybeck, Finn said, "Not the best disguise I've seen." Maybeck liked the fan attention—loved it, was more accurate—and rarely changed his appearance. He wanted to be recognized. He wanted to be mobbed.

"I'm kind of hard to miss," he said.

"You reap what you sow," Willa told him.

"Where's Charlene?" Amanda asked, looking past him.

Philby and Finn exchanged a curious look.

Maybeck said, "She stopped to get us some food. I'm starving."

"It's eight o'clock," Philby said.

"So what? I can't be hungry at eight o'clock? I'm hungry all the time! I have a big appetite."

"I wouldn't mind something," Jess said. "That dinner tonight . . ." she said to Amanda.

"Mrs. Nash's tamale pie is basically microwaved dog food with boxed gravy and Doritos on top," agreed Amanda.

"Gross!" Willa said.

"You should be in the same room with it," said Amanda.

Maybeck said, "I don't think we should hang here too long. Not only are there cameras all over this Park—right, Philby?—but I wouldn't be surprised if those CTDs circle back and come looking for me. We'd actually be safer out there with the mob lining up for the fireworks."

"I love the fireworks," Amanda said.

Willa said, "So, why are we here, anyway? What's

going on? Do we even know why Wayne wanted us here?"

"Not yet, we don't," Finn answered. "What we know is that the OTs are active again." He told them about the jail visit with Wanda.

Philby tried to explain what Wanda might have been doing hacking the servers. "Disney has an elaborate set of firewalls in place. Think of it as one of those European fort walls around all of Disney World's data lines. One you can't climb. One with gates too strong to bust through—"

On cue, the door banged open. Charlene entered, struggling to balance a stack of small plastic plates, all holding food. Everyone hurried over to help her. Shortly thereafter, lips were smacking loudly.

"So," Finn said to Philby, "you were saying?"

"The point is, the firewalls log any 'events'—that is, attempts to breach them. There are subnet masks, ISP numbers, all sorts of data that can be traced and used to track down where the attack came from and who was behind it. If I'm Wanda, that's what I'm looking for: the person behind the data bursts."

"And if you're the OTs?" Charlene asked.

"If I'm the OTs and I'm attacking firewalls," Philby said, "then I'm either looking for a way in or a way out. A way in would give me access to other Disney data—"

"Like the location of where Disney might lock up certain other Overtakers," Maybeck proposed.

"Like that, yes. Or, you remember how we used the changes in temperature inside pavilions to try to track Maleficent? That kind of record would tell them everything they want to know."

"Energy use," Willa said.

Philby smiled. He loved the way her mind worked. "Absolutely. Disney has to keep Maleficent cold. They're not going to mistreat her, and she needs cold to survive. That would require more energy. That's a number, something easy enough to uncover. Those kind of records could be hacked."

"They're going to bust Maleficent and Chernabog out," Maybeck said, speculating. "It's a jailbreak."

Silence.

Philby began nodding. "Nicely done, Terry."

"Could it be?" Charlene asked.

"It makes total sense," Willa said. "They're trying to gather enough data to locate where Maleficent and Chernabog are being held. At the same time, they know that's going to attract our attention—Wayne, Philby, Wanda . . . someone. When that happens, they have a backup plan to lure Wayne out into the open and kidnap him. Maybe they want information from him, maybe they want to trade him for Maleficent and Chernabog, but it's all directed at the same goal."

"Freeing the boss," Maybeck said.

"And with Wayne in hiding and Wanda out of the way—" Willa said.

"It's up to us," said Finn, prompting another heavy silence.

The church door pushed open. A girl and her parents entered. They were also on the Kim Possible quest. The Keepers scattered, pretending to be interested in the various displays.

The mother and father looked on as the girl read a plaque, looking for the same clue the boy had earlier. Her father complimented her as she identified the king in question.

"Check the *A* box," he said.

"I *know*, Dad," the girl complained, a little snotty. "Are you going to let me do it, or not?"

He stepped back and the girl worked the phone. Then she stopped and looked across the room, her curious eyes finally settling on Finn.

She tentatively crossed toward him, her father keeping an eye on her.

"I've played this game, like, six times," she said, addressing Finn shyly, her parents now nearby. "But this is the coolest yet." She handed Finn the Kim Possible phone. He accepted it reluctantly. She hung her head slightly, embarrassed. "I recognized all but those two," she said, pointing to Amanda and Jess, "when we came in." Her parents looked around, not having a clue who the kids were. "I didn't want to bug you."

"I . . . we . . . all of us appreciate that," Finn said.

"Is this a friend of yours, dear?" the mother asked skeptically.

"Oh, Mom . . . come on! These are the Kingdom Keepers. You know . . . ? This is, like, the most awesome Kim Possible ever!"

Philby said, "We're not actually part of—OWW!" Finn had elbowed him.

The girl pointed to the phone in Finn's hand. "Read it!"

Finn read the message on the phone's small screen:

Hand your phone to the nearest Kingdom Keeper!
Press "OK" to continue.

Finn reread the message twice. Wayne's reach inside the Parks never failed to amaze him.

Maybeck came over and read the screen. "What if when you push OK it sends our location to our other *friends*?"

"I kinda need my phone back," the girl said.

Finn pushed *OK*. The screen changed.

Go to the KP cart in Norway. Tell them you're my
friend. —W
Press "OK" to continue.

Finn pressed *OK*.

Hand the phone back to the guest.
Press "OK" to continue.

Finn pushed *OK* and returned the girl's phone
to her. Before leaving she asked everyone to sign her
Epcot map. Bounding with excitement, she left with her
parents.

When they were alone again, Finn said, "We have
to trust it. This is why we're here."

"It could just as easily be a trap," Maybeck warned.
"Wayne gave us all phones," he reminded. "If he wanted
to contact us, wouldn't he just call us or text us? Am I
missing something? Why bother with the Kim Possible
thing?"

Charlene said, "We won't know until we try."

Willa said, "He is always paranoid about the OTs
eavesdropping. When he puts us on a quest, it's to tell
us something that no one else could figure out."

"I volunteer," Charlene said, raising her hand. "I'll
do it."

"Amanda and I could do it," Jess said. "We aren't Kingdom Keepers. We wouldn't raise any suspicions."

"She's right," Philby said.

"And if it's a trap," Finn said, "then they catch the wrong people and who knows what that means?"

Charlene said, "I thought you were the one trusting it?"

*Busted.*

"I said, 'I volunteer,' " Charlene reminded.

"I'll go with you," Finn said.

"But if they catch you . . . We can't let them catch *you*," Amanda said.

Some suppressed smirks. It was the Amanda-and-Finn show. For all to see. Including Charlene, who looked away.

"Finn's the only one of us that can all-clear with any consistency," said Charlene.

"I know," Amanda said. "I've seen him do it."

With Greg Luowski, Finn recalled. He'd suckered Luowski into taking a swing at him, while Finn was briefly transformed into his hologram. No one had explained the science behind how Finn was able to briefly transform himself into pure light—what he and the others called *all clear*; he supposed it made him part Fairlie like Jess and Amanda.

He supposed that *all clear* was a state where

mystical, metaphysical elements met the physical sciences. It worked two ways: Finn, as a mortal boy, could on occasion concentrate to where he suddenly turned into a hologram. It only lasted a short amount of time—his record was eighteen seconds—but in that state he could walk through walls or take a punch, because technically he didn't exist as anything but light. The second way was more difficult for parents and even Wayne to understand: a hologram was nothing but light. When projected or crossed over into the Parks as DHIs, the kids were technically nothing but light. But fear removed their state of purity. If, as a DHI, one of them became afraid, that hologram lost a percentage of data, depending on the level of fear. That resulted in a DHI that was part mortal, part teenager, part hologram, and therefore vulnerable to being wounded or captured. Finn had perfected a kind of visualization—a train coming at him from down a dark tunnel—that helped him achieve *all clear*, pushed him into that state of invulnerable light. It was a useful, even necessary tool, and one he'd been coaching the others to learn how to do.

"And while you two are out playing games, what are we supposed to do?" Maybeck asked, clearly complaining. "I'm not hanging here. I'm not big on churches."

"You'll divide into groups—split up between Norway and Mexico on either side of us," said Finn. "You watch for crash-test dummies. Text me if you see any. Charlene and I will do the Kim Possible quest and let you know what we find out. Amanda and Jess, stay with us to make us a bigger group. That way it's less likely we get spotted as Keepers."

Maybeck said, "You look so stupid, Whitman."

"So I've heard."

"At least he tried for some kind of disguise," Willa said.

Philby said, "It's a good plan. Let's get going."

Philby and Willa headed for China. After more discussion, Maybeck went by himself into Mexico.

An announcement filled the loud speakers: the fireworks were set to begin.

\* \* \*

A wooden cart sat tucked into a dark corner of the terraced path between Norway and Mexico, pushed against an island of trees and bushes. The Cast Member attending the unmarked cart wore a Kim Possible Adventure T-shirt. Finn, Charlene, and the sisters approached the overweight man, waiting for a small boy and his father to return their Kim Possible phone.

"W sent us," Finn told the Cast Member.

"Okay." The man had a gruff voice, unexpected of a Cast Member.

"We're here to do the adventure," Charlene said.

"I was told you would have two initials for me," he said to Finn. This had Wayne's DNA all over it.

"K.K."

"Can't be too careful," the guy said.

He rifled through some phones in the cart's drawer and handed one to Finn.

He launched into a memorized explanation of the game. Finn and the other three listened intently. Didn't miss a thing.

"Any questions?"

"I think we've got it," Finn said, checking with his friends.

"Off you go. Return it here, please. I'd tell you to enjoy yourselves, but I'm not sure that's appropriate."

The phone's screen told Finn to step away from the cart and to press *OK*.

The crowds for the fireworks clogged the pathway encircling the lake, forty people deep. The Park music charged the air with excitement.

Finn pressed *OK*.

The cartoon image on the screen of Kim Possible changed to a photograph of a tree. A written message read:

Go to this tree by the bakery café and press "OK."

"Where is it?" Finn said, spinning around.

"There!" Amanda and Charlene said at the exact same moment, both pointing.

"Okay. But let's not advertise," Finn said.

The girls lowered their arms.

Once at the tree behind the café, Finn pushed *OK.*

The tree began speaking. Or at least it seemed so real that Charlene jumped back. Finn felt shivers run up his arms as an old man's voice—a voice he knew to be Wayne's—spoke to them from a speaker in the shrubs designed to look like a rock.

"We all need a waiter now and then," said the voice. "Some can get a waiter's attention faster than others. This can have disappointing results."

As Finn slapped his pockets hoping to find a pen, he noticed Jess already scribbling on a piece of paper. Jess carried a pencil and paper whenever she was inside the Parks. She had previously had daytime "dreams" or visions of the future here while awake. She came prepared. Her uncanny ability to dream about future events had earned her a place as a Fairlie alongside "sister" Amanda. That power was corrupted and nearly harnessed by Maleficent, who'd put Jess under the effects of a horrible spell, which brought her together with

Finn and the Keepers when Amanda had sought their help to free Jess of the spell. Now, the Keepers benefited from her unique ability; on more than one occasion the Keepers had used a Jess diary page to "see" an event before it happened. They'd learned to pay strict attention to anything she sketched.

The phone's screen said to press *BACK* to hear the message a second time. Finn pressed the button. Jess continued writing.

"Got it," she said.

"What's that supposed to mean?" Charlene asked.

"We keep going. You know what he's like," Finn said.

The screen on the phone changed. An animated Kim Possible said, "Find a friend around front. Push *OK* and watch what he does."

Again, a photo appeared. It showed two garden gnomes and some shrubs. They located the identical setting just inside the Norway plaza, past the Stave Church.

Finn pressed *OK*.

The gnome spun around, his backside facing them. Finn pressed *OK* and the garden sculpture pivoted to face them again. He triggered the phone to repeat the effect.

"Whoa!" Charlene exclaimed. "Way cool."

"Please write it down," Finn said to Jess.

Charlene leaned against him from one side; Amanda the other. A Finn sandwich.

A cartoon of a dorky kid appeared on-screen. He said that Kim Possible had identified a signal post and that she needed their help in locating it. If the enemy saw that signal, they were told, bad things might happen.

"Is that supposed to be some kind of code?" Charlene asked.

"Don't know," Finn said. But he was thinking, So many questions from her.

The camera offered another photograph. The four of them returned to behind the bakery. Jess, with her keen artistic eye, found the scenery that matched. She positioned them all with their backs to the bakery patio and pointed to their right where the building ended at a knot of rocks and foliage.

"Go ahead," Charlene said. "Try it."

Finn pressed *OK*.

Nothing happened.

"Try again," she said.

"Up high," Amanda said. She knew better than to point and attract attention. One by one the other kids saw it: a red, triangular flag popping up from behind a wrought iron lamppost each time Finn pushed *BACK*. The flag reappeared and sank.

"Better write it down," he said, but Jess was already on it.

The Kim Possible character reappeared on the phone and told them how well they were doing and that they had one last clue to find.

Another picture.

Charlene spotted the location immediately: it was a rock face on the way back to the Kim Possible cart where they'd started.

The screen read: *Push "OK" to have your picture taken.*

"I don't know about having your picture taken," Amanda said.

"It's telling us to do it," Charlene pointed out. "We've done everything so far."

Finn said softly, "Maybe it's a way for Wayne to see that it's really us. That we're the ones on the adventure."

"That makes sense," Jess said. "It should probably be just you and Charlene in the picture."

"Agreed," Finn said. "You and Amanda keep an eye out, while Charlene and I do this." His personal phone vibrated in his pocket. He read the text. It was from Maybeck.

CTDs on Segways headed this way.

"Crash-test dummies," Finn said. "We need to hurry."
Finn texted back:

Diversion needed.

His phone buzzed back.

No prob

He and Charlene hurried out in front of the rocks and Finn pressed *OK*.

The cartoon character's thin voice told him to face the lake and press *OK* again when he was ready to have his picture taken.

He had no idea what might happen. A trap door? A net falling from the trees? With everyone's attention now focused on the lake, anything could happen to them and it would go unnoticed. If it was a trap, it had been cleverly planned. He and the others had walked right into it, eyes open.

His thumb hovered over the phone's *OK* button.

He pushed *OK*.

A bright light flashed quickly from within the bushes.

Finn believed this to be part of the trick—to blind them while someone attempted to capture them. He bumped his shoulder against Charlene and reached down and grabbed her hand.

But no one came charging toward them. Finn spotted Amanda looking back at them, and immediately released Charlene's hand.

Return the phone to get your photos.

Press "OK"

Finn pressed *OK* and was told what a great job he'd done for the Kim Possible team. How they couldn't have done it without him.

Jess and Amanda joined them.

Amanda said, "Did you see Maybeck? He was running through the crowd, a pair of crash-test dummies after him."

"Did they catch him?" Finn asked, anxiously.

She pointed. The CTDs stood well above the crowd on their Segways. But they were barely moving because of all the people. Maybeck had led them past Norway and had to be way ahead of them by now—a good job of creating a diversion.

Finn and the girls reached the Kim Possible cart.

The Cast Member greeted them. "Have a good quest?"

"I guess," said Finn, returning the phone.

"Here's your picture," the man said, pointing out the snapshot pinned to a corkboard.

As all three girls stepped up to see it, the Cast Member blocked Finn from joining them and slipped something into Finn's right hand. Slippery paper. Photos—Finn could tell by the texture. He stole a glance at the first of the photos but slid them into the only pocket in his absurd gym pants as the Cast Member shook his head, suggesting Finn wasn't to share these.

The image on the photo hit him hard: the Evil Queen somewhere in DisneyQuest. She was standing in front of four students: two girls, Greg Luowski, and a boy wearing a striped T-shirt, whose face couldn't be seen because of the Queen.

He'd only seen it for an instant, but there was no question in his mind of what he'd seen. The Queen was talking to the four kids and, more importantly, *they were listening.*

It hit him like a slap in the face. He had to show it to the others. He simply had to. But the Cast Member had warned him not to. Worse, he still didn't know what was on the second photo. He needed a minute by himself.

"I gotta go to the bathroom," he told the girls, as they turned from the posted photo.

"I don't get it," Charlene said. "So what if our picture was taken? What's it mean?"

"This is yours," the Cast Member said. "I hope you enjoyed your mission and will join us another time."

Charlene accepted the photo, though unhappily. "Can't you wait?" she asked Finn. "I don't think we should split up just now."

Sticking together was his rule. "Yeah, okay. I'll text the others. We'll meet at the ice cream place by the fountain. There are rest rooms near there."

"Why meet? Why not just go home?" Charlene asked.

"The mission is over, so we've been given all the pieces," Finn said. "We need to figure out what it means while it's still fresh in our heads."

"But those guys are out there buzzing around looking for us," she said.

Finn already had his phone out and was sending a group text.

"Ice cream," he said.

* * *

Maybeck was the last to reach the ice cream parlor. The other kids stood at the counter. The fireworks show continued, so they owned the place. Even so, they kept their voices low between greedy bites of mint chip, cookie dough, and royal fudge. If there was one thing the Keepers could agree on, it was eating vast amounts of ice cream.

Finn wasn't sure the others noticed Jess sketching on a napkin as the discussion began with Maybeck's heroic description of eluding the crash-test dummies.

"We need to figure out the Kim Possible mission," Charlene said, still edgy.

Finn looked at her differently now. He'd been to the bathroom, and he'd dragged Philby with him. There he'd taken out the two photos and, for the first time, taken a good look at both.

"That's Sally Ringwald," Finn said, naming a girl who went to Winter Park. "And that's—"

"Luowski," said Philby, who knew about the bully.

"Talking to the Evil Queen."

"I don't recognize the second girl—maybe Maybeck or Charlene knows her. What's the other photo?" Philby asked, for Finn had kept it tucked below the first.

"Who knows if we can trust these pictures?" Finn said.

"Are you going to show it to me or not?"

"I just think we have to keep open minds."

"Come on! You know me."

Finn peeled away the first photo revealing the second.

The photo was actually two images divided by a

black line. Both black-and-white, they appeared to be freeze-frame photographs taken from a Security video. On the left, it showed Charlene entering a rest room—time and date stamped as the night before while they'd been in DisneyQuest; to the right, was the Evil Queen entering the same doorway.

"Twenty seconds later," Philby said. "Charlene was still in there."

"We don't know that," Finn said.

"Of course she was! Who can pee and wash her hands in less than twenty seconds? She obviously met with the Evil Queen, just like these other kids." Philby looked back and forth between the various shots. "The question is not whether she saw the Queen; the question is why haven't we been told about it?"

"We can't jump to conclusions."

"Who's jumping?" Philby said. "Number one: she's been acting weird. Do you deny that?"

"No," Finn said, unhappily.

"Number two: she's been asking a ton of questions, just like a *spy* would."

"I know."

"Number three. She volunteered to do the Kim Possible thing with you. Now, I'm not saying she doesn't volunteer to do stuff with us, but when she does it's always—I mean *always*—something physical.

Something gymnastic or athletic. That's her talent. It's not to solve a mystery. That's Willa's turf."

"Yeah," Finn said.

"She was in the bathroom with the Evil Queen."

"Yeah," Finn agreed, reluctantly.

"Why?" Philby said.

"It was *after* that that she got weird."

"Yes, it was," Philby said. "You're right. So another way to look at this is that the Queen met with her, not the other way around."

"Meaning?"

"She cast a spell on Charlene."

"To spy on us."

"Maybe on the other four, too. Luowski and everyone."

"Maybe." Finn wasn't easily convinced that Greg Luowski could be a victim.

"So Charlene starts asking all these questions and acting weird."

"It makes sense," Finn said.

"So we've got to break the spell," Philby said. "Ten times out of ten, when it comes to breaking a spell put onto a girl, you break it by kissing her."

"Not me!" Finn said. "If I kiss Charlene . . . I am not doing that!"

"Amanda."

"Yes."

"Yeah, well I don't exactly want Willa to see me do it."

"You and Willa?"

"This is news to you?" said Philby.

Finn shrugged.

"That just confirms what Willa says: that boys don't get any of this stuff."

"What stuff?"

"You see?" Philby said. His eyes shifted left and right.

"Maybeck!" they both said at once.

Back in the ice cream parlor, Finn saw Philby pull Maybeck aside and whisper to him. Maybeck's face crunched like a crushed paper bag.

"First," Finn said to the girls, in part to keep them from noticing Philby's whispering, "was the waiter."

Jess read from her notes: "'We all need a waiter now and then. Some can get a waiter's attention faster than others. This can have disappointing results.'"

"Then the garden gnome," Finn said.

"The gnome turned around," Jess said, "then turned around again to face us."

At this point, Maybeck and Philby joined the group again. Maybeck flashed Finn a look impossible to interpret. Was he going to kiss Charlene or not? Finn couldn't tell.

"Then the flag," Amanda said.

"A red, triangular flag," Jess added.

"And then the photograph," Charlene said. "But what's any of it mean?"

The girls all looked to Philby.

"As to the first," Philby said. "There aren't any waiters at the Norway bakery. It's a cafeteria with outside seating."

"We didn't look inside," Charlene admitted. "Maybe we should have."

"Waiters deliver menus, food, and drinks," Professor Philby said, breaking the clue into smaller pieces. Philby was more like a college student than a freshman in high school. "What else? They take stuff away after we're through."

"The bakery sells all sorts of stuff," Maybeck said. "Meals, desserts, drinks."

"Just deserts," Willa said. A brainiac like Philby, Willa understood language the way he understood anything technical. "What if it's a play on words? Wayne does that kind of thing. 'Just deserts' is with one s. It means 'giving people what they deserve.' Maybe the clue has something to do with giving the Overtakers what they deserve."

"That's way too random, even for Wayne," said Maybeck.

Heads nodded in agreement.

"But a play on words isn't," Philby said, sticking up for Willa. "When I was washing my hands just now—you know those signs telling employees to wash their hands?—well, some wise guy had crossed out 'Cast Members,' and had written, 'Servers.' It's not 'waiter,' but 'server,' " Philby said. "We all need a server now and then. It's server, not waiter. 'We all need a server now and then. Some can get a server's attention faster than others.' It's a computer server."

"That works!" said Willa.

"Wayne knows I've messed with the DHI server before," Philby said.

Amanda said, "So the full translation would be: we all need a DHI server now and then."

"Yes," said Philby.

"You guys and who else?" Amanda asked.

"The OTs," Maybeck said. He looked cruelly at Charlene. Finn thought he was the only one to pick up on it.

Willa said, "And the gnome turning around like that?"

Jess read from her notes. "The exact mission was to 'find a friend around front.' "

"A friend spinning around?" Charlene asked.

"Not spinning," Philby said, "A friend . . . turning his back on you."

"Or hers," Willa said innocently. "A friend betraying you."

"Us," said Maybeck, still fixated on Charlene.

"A red flag," Amanda said. "The flag was red."

"A red flag means something you need to notice," Willa said. "Something you shouldn't miss."

"That everyone needs a server," Philby said, "and that a friend has turned his or her back on us."

"We've been betrayed?" Willa gasped.

Charlene said to Maybeck, "Quit staring at me. Why are you doing that?"

Finn caught himself holding his breath. Maybeck and his big mouth could ruin it all now. Finn caught a look from Philby—he was thinking the same thing: It's now or never.

Maybeck said, "I've just never seen you prettier."

Willa giggled. Amanda and Jess watched intently as Charlene blushed and said, "Seriously? Terry? What's with you?"

Maybeck took another step toward her while maintaining constant eye contact. This was Maybeck-the-mouth in action. The self-proclaimed chick magnet trying to prove himself.

"I don't know if it's the lighting," he said, "but you look like an . . . angel. Like a movie star. Like one of those girls on the front of a magazine—the 'it' girl, the girl everyone wants to be. The prettiest, smartest girl in the room . . ."

"Terry?" Charlene said again, her voice quavering.

He was a single step away from her now as he stopped.

"One memory," he said, "is all I ask." He reached up and cupped her head in his hand, his thumb stroking her ear. She tilted her head slightly toward his hand. Her eyes looked sad and happy at the same time.

Charlene, her voice strong once again, said, "I mean, come on!" She pushed Maybeck back with both hands. "You really think that stuff will work on me?"

The other girls erupted in nervous laughter. For a moment they'd seemed so close to a kiss. Amanda was blushing. Jess returned to her sketching, her head down, giggling.

Finn could see it was a face she was drawing—an upside down face—of a boy or a man. She hadn't put on the finishing touches yet. He couldn't be sure. But in the back of his mind a small voice asked: *Who?*

* * *

It was the Keepers' policy to leave their phones on at night. Parents rarely approved of that policy, and so each of the kids had come up with his or her way to get around the objections. Finn put his into vibrate mode and left it on his side table on a piece of aluminum foil, so that if it vibrated, the aluminum foil would rattle enough to wake him. He was a heavy sleeper. He didn't know what tricks the other Keepers had come up with, only that if called at night they answered.

He answered his on the fourth metallic buzz as the vibrations lifted the phone and carried it close to the end table's edge and a possible tumble to the floor.

"What?" He whispered into the phone, having already seen Philby's photo and name on its screen.

"Problems." Only Philby could sound like a male librarian at one AM.

Finn rubbed his eyes with his free hand, scrunched his pillow behind him, and sat up in bed. "This had better be good."

"I know you hate technical explanations, so I'm not sure where to start."

"Maybe start with the problems."

"I monitor bandwidth usage, as you know. The same thing Wanda did, but I don't go hacking Internet hubs. The DHI server. *Our* DHI server. All it takes is the ISP and—"

"You're right: forget as much of the technical stuff as possible."

Philby cleared his throat. "Let's put it this way:

because I have the port address to the DHI server now, I'm able to direct what Park we land in when we go to sleep. You and I can go to the Magic Kingdom, while Willa and Maybeck go to Animal Kingdom. The only catch is the Return. We have to be together for the Return."

"You woke me for a history lesson? *I know all this.*"

"Finn, I woke you because we had a spike in traffic volume about ten minutes ago. My laptop wakes on network usage. I have it alarmed. I got woken up by that traffic surge. It was a major hit. A DHI for sure."

"I thought you controlled that," Finn said. "I thought we only crossed over when you wanted us to. I don't get it."

"Exactly! I do! But if Wayne or another Imagineer wanted us over there, then that's what would happen."

"Wayne? You think it's Wayne?"

"I didn't know what to think. So I called you. It's Charlene, Finn. The graphic tag—the hologram's ID—is Charlene's."

For Finn it was almost as if her name was echoing over the telephone line. In fact, it was nothing but a little bit of static. "It would have to be her, right?" he said sarcastically. "The Evil Queen?"

"Wayne's Kim Possible thing warned us about the server. What if the OTs have control of our server?"

Finn didn't answer, his heart racing. Only Philby would understand if that was possible.

"I wanted to follow her in there. She's in Epcot. But I didn't want to pull a Maybeck and go alone and wander into a trap." Maybeck's DHI had once followed a girl around inside the Magic Kingdom only to go missing. He had never showed up for the Return, and the others had crossed back without him. This had left his hologram "stuck" in the Park, and a sleeping Terry Maybeck in a kind of coma in his bedroom. Until his hologram was Returned, the boy had not awakened. The kids now referred to this comatose state in several ways: the Sleeping Beauty Syndrome; SBS; or the Syndrome. Following Maybeck's mishap, they had instituted the buddy rule. Philby was simply playing by the rules.

"Can you help us get there?"

"Of course."

"I'll need to send the others a text in case something goes wrong. You and I cross over, find her, and Return."

"And if we don't Return, they'll need Wanda's or Wayne's help to come looking for us. Put that in the text."

"Okay," Finn said. "So I hang up and get back to sleep and I'll see you in Epcot?"

"True story."

Finn ended the call, sent the group text, and slipped

quietly out of bed. He had secretly oiled the hinges on both his closet and bathroom doors so they could be worked in the middle of the night without screeching. The dresser drawers were a little more tricky, so he took his time with them. Fresh socks. Fresh underwear. He dressed quietly and quickly—black jeans, black T-shirt with a pirate skull on the back. A brown hoodie. An old pair of running shoes he'd painted black. He pocketed his phone and wallet, which held a few dollars. Sometimes the phone worked when he crossed over, sometimes not. He crawled back into bed and did his best to settle down, knowing that Philby would have already programmed the DHI server to cross them over into Epcot.

He blamed Charlene's crossing over on the Evil Queen. It seemed more and more likely that she had put a spell on Charlene. Maybeck's failing to kiss her loomed large.

The more he thought about everything, the harder it was to get to sleep. He cleared his mind, picturing a dark tunnel with a faint pinprick of light far, far at the end—the same technique he used to go *all clear*. He watched the pinprick widen ever so slowly. Focused on that tiny speck of light in the sea of black as it grew larger. The train approaching.

And then, there was nothing.

* * *

Finn awoke near the fountain in Epcot's central plaza.
The fountains were shut off. In fact, the entire Park was
lit by maybe half the available streetlamps. The landing, or
arrival zone, for their DHIs was one of the biggest problems with the program. Philby could now control which
Park each of the kids landed in, who among them would
cross over, and, in a pinch, he could manually Return
them from his home computer. But the program transmit-
ted the DHI into a Park's central feature. In the Magic
Kingdom, it was the central hub in front of Cinderella
Castle. In Animal Kingdom, the island and the Tree of
Life. In Disney's Hollywood Studios, it was the elevated
area beneath Mickey's Sorcerer's Hat. Here in Epcot, it
was the fountain plaza just beyond Spaceship Earth. In
all cases, in all places, it meant their holograms landed in
open space. Finn's limbs tingled as he scrambled across the
plaza, reminding him that he was in his DHI state.

Epcot after closing was not the remarkable and
enchanting Park it was during its opening hours. It was
known to the Keepers as a haven for Overtakers. Crash-
test dummies on Segways. Gigabyte, a ginormous snake
that was part of Honey, I Shrunk the Audience, slithered in search of unwanted visitors. There were court
jesters in France capable of every kind of martial art.
There had been a time when Finn had been certain the

Magic Kingdom was the Overtakers' headquarters. But he was no longer so convinced.

"Over here," came a harsh whisper. Philby. Fifteen feet toward the lake from Finn. Sitting on the walkway with his back against the information booth that housed a pin exchange. "A pair of CTDs passed by here maybe five minutes ago."

Finn lay down flat and kept very still. The robotic crash-test dummies were nothing to mess with. "How do you want to do this?" he asked Philby.

"It's too big to just start searching around. It would take us days, not hours, to look everywhere."

"Then. . . ?"

"You know me: technology."

"Meaning?"

"The IllumiNations control booth on the roof of Mexico. I know for a fact that setup includes feeds for all of the Park's Security cameras. We climb to the top of the temple. As DHIs, we should be able to walk through the door. If I get freaked out and lose *all clear*, then you go through and unlock it for me. We use the Security monitors to find Charlene."

Fifteen minutes later, Philby was sitting in a chair working switches. The television monitor displayed four camera views at a time.

"Heck of a view," Finn said. Outside the window,

Finn had a clear view of the lake and the surrounding pavilions. He grabbed a pair of binoculars and began sweeping the area.

"True story." Philby allowed enough time to study the view from each Security camera, then he pushed a button and another four appeared. There were thirty-two camera views available.

Twice Philby spotted CTDs on the move, but no Charlene. Finn confirmed the CTDs through the binoculars. They began working out a system.

With the binoculars held to his eyes, Finn said, "What do you suppose they want with her?"

"A download," Philby answered. "Let's say she was put under a spell to spy on us, as we talked about. She asks questions; she looks over our shoulders. Then the Evil Queen and Cruella need a chance to download whatever she's found out."

"But she's not a zombie."

"Exactly. So who knows what state she was in when she crossed over? The CTDs could be looking for *her*. The Queen may need a stronger spell to get Charlene to talk. I'm just guessing at all this."

"It makes sense."

"Thank you."

"Movement!" Finn said loudly. "In front of Morocco. A pair of CTDs running . . ."

Through the binoculars he watched the dummies in full sprint. They were tall, powerful, and surprisingly light on their feet. A trash can rolled toward them. The first vaulted it. The second bent and knocked it out of the way like it was made of cardboard. Each dummy had the strength and speed of three men.

"Someone threw a trash can in their way!" Finn announced.

Philby worked the camera views. "It's her! It's Charlene!"

Finn had trouble finding her in the binoculars. He turned and watched on-screen as Charlene ran past Norway. Philby pointed out another camera view. Charlene, wearing a white nightgown, ducked behind Norway, then cut back through the bakery patio to— another camera view—the Norway courtyard. She hid as the CTDs ran past like something out of *The Terminator*. Then she turned to her left, scrambled up some rock, and disappeared into a dark cave.

"Maelstrom," Philby said.

Finn had failed to recognize the cave because there was no water coming from the ride's waterfall. "Smart! That's a great place to hide!"

"Let's go!" Philby said.

"I'll go," Finn said, volunteering. "You stay and watch for the CTDs."

"No," Philby said. "We stick together."

Finn wasn't going to waste time arguing.

A few minutes later, the boys were climbing Maelstrom's dry waterfall toward the ominous black cave entrance. The lip of the cave was moss-covered and slimy. There was water in the trough just beyond, so they kept to the left where a narrow ledge followed the water course. The deeper they penetrated into the ride, the darker it became. The boys used hand signals to communicate. Philby indicated for Finn to keep his eyes open.

Finn had no problem with that: his heart was about to burst in his chest.

As their eyes adjusted to the limited light, the Maelstrom world enveloped them: lush green bushes and trees, rocks, and stones. Strange things happened inside the rides and attractions in the Parks at night. The only rule was that there were no rules. Trust nothing, Finn reminded himself.

On Philby's signal, both boys stopped and crouched.

They saw a pair of yellow, glowing eyes, tightly set. *Trolls?*

Finn pushed past Philby and continued along the ledge. Philby followed him as they pressed deeper into the darkness, the only light coming from the faint glow of their DHIs. Not trolls, he realized, but polar bears.

Two giant white bears, one standing, one down on all fours.

"If those things come alive . . ." Finn said, his voice shaking.

"We're hamburger," Philby said, finishing the thought for him.

"Thanks for that image," Finn said.

"No charge."

Morbid humor had a way of sneaking into their conversations at the strangest times.

They moved past the polar bears. There was something large and squarish up ahead to their left. Finn knew where they were.

"The cottage," he said. "The start of the ride."

Finn's eyes had adjusted to where he could now see a life-size Norwegian standing in front of a cottage. Finn hurried over to a rock that was familiar to him from his last visit here as a DHI. He reached down and felt for the three handles he knew to be there.

"There's an ax missing!" Finn whispered.

Philby stepped forward. Leaning against the rock was an old-fashioned ax and a sword. There should have been two axes.

"It's her," Philby said. "That's why she came in here."

Finn took up the sword, knowing it well from

a previous visit. He handed the remaining ax to Philby.

"What would you have done?" said Charlene's voice.

They both looked up as she stepped out of the cottage, the ax gripped in her hand.

They hurried over to her. "It *is* you!" Finn said. They hugged.

"You're okay!" crowed Philby, also hugging her.

"Not really. Terrified's more like it." She addressed Philby. "Why did you send me here without telling me?"

"It wasn't me," Philby said. "It wasn't like that. We can explain—"

"We think," said Finn.

"But first we've got to Return. We've got to get you out of here."

"There are CTDs out there . . ." she warned.

"We saw," Finn said.

"We'll have to be careful," Philby said. "And if that fails . . ." He raised his ax.

A whizzing sound sizzled past Finn's ear. A chopstick lodged in the painted Styrofoam scenery behind them. The next one flew through his shoulder, his pure DHI state preventing it from wounding him.

"Incoming!" he said. He felt his own terror beginning to take hold—his fingers tingling—and understood the mortal danger it presented. "No fear!" he reminded.

"Easier said than done," Charlene cried out.

Yellow eyes glowed from across the stream. More arrows whizzed past.

"I can feel my hands," Philby said.

"Me, too!" Charlene said. "And my feet."

They weren't in a state of pure DHI, which made them vulnerable to attack.

Philby and Charlene ducked behind the small rocks.

Eight trolls—knee-high old men with beards, whiskers, and huge eyes—appeared across the water. They carried kitchen pot lids as shields, steak knives as swords, carpentry hammers, and the homemade bows and arrows. They jumped across the water and charged.

The kids stayed behind the rocks. The trolls split up.

Philby took an arrow in the arm and screamed as he pulled it out. "That thing hurts!" he cried.

A troll came at Finn, his steak knife glinting. Finn swung the sword and knocked the knife out of the troll's hand. Philby stood and pressed his back to Finn's so they could defend in two directions. Charlene, on her knees, battled ax against hammer.

One of the old men surprised Finn from the right,

stabbing him, but his sword passed right through Finn's hologram. The guy fell, off-balance. Philby kicked him across the water into the scenery.

"Soccer!" Philby shouted to Charlene.

She stood and kicked out at the trolls, sending them flying.

"Goal!" Philby cried, as one of the trolls flew though the door of the cottage.

"That's it!" Finn said. "We get them all into the cottage and trap them!"

Philby kicked one of the trolls, passing him to Charlene like a soccer ball. She expertly sent him through the cottage door. Finn battled with his sword. He heard Philby counting them down.

"Four . . . Five!"

Finn's blade clanked against the steak knife of a competent swordsman. Philby came to his aid, toe-kicking the troll toward the cottage, where Charlene finished him off by sending him inside.

"Six!"

"I sent one across the water," Finn said. "So that's seven."

The final troll dropped his hammer and threw up his arms in surrender. Philby grabbed his hands, threw him into the cottage, and Charlene shut the door. She used her ax handle to prop it shut.

The kids, out of breath, looked around for more trouble, but saw none.

"That was . . . weird," Philby said.

"You okay?" Charlene asked.

Philby approached her and kissed her on the lips before she knew what he was doing. The kiss went on longer than Finn would have expected.

Charlene and Philby pulled themselves apart breathlessly.

"What . . . was . . . that?" Charlene asked, not a twinge of complaint in her voice.

"How do you feel?" Finn asked.

"That's a stupid question," she said. "Besides, that's for Philby to ask, not you."

Philby looked tranquilized. "I . . . that was . . . it was . . ."

"He had to do it," Finn said.

"Excuse me?" Charlene said.

How would they know if she'd been put under a spell? Worse, how would they know if she'd come out of it?

"Do you remember going into the girls' room at DisneyQuest?" Finn asked.

"What kind of a question is that?"

"One that needs answering." He wished Philby would say something, but he remained stunned and unable to speak. He was staring at Charlene like he'd gotten religion.

"It's none of your business. Eww."

Philby finally managed to speak. "It *is* our business. Do you remember who followed you inside the girls' room?"

She looked frightened. Her hologram's blue outline faded. "What are you two talking about?" She blinked furiously, as if about to cry.

"Do you remember going into the bathroom at DisneyQuest?" Philby asked, repeating Finn's question.

"Yeah, I suppose."

"Do you remember anyone else in there with you?"

"Like who? Amanda? Willa? Who do you mean? We were all there that night."

"Anyone else?" Philby asked.

The trolls were pounding on the door to the cottage to get out. Finn could barely hear himself think.

"How could you possibly know about this?" Charlene asked.

"Know about what?" Finn said.

"About . . . When I was in there, I kind of lost track of time."

"What do you mean?" Philby asked.

"I mean I lost track of time. I spaced out or something. This girl was standing behind me asking if I was all right."

"Because?"

"Because, according to her, I was just standing there staring into the mirror. Not moving or anything. She said it was . . . 'awkward,' was her exact word. But how could you possibly know that?"

"And the girl," Philby said, "the one in the bathroom. Had you thought about her before just now? Before we started asking questions?"

Charlene shook her head. "What's going on?"

"We can explain later," Finn said.

"You'll explain now," she demanded.

"Later," Finn repeated.

"I'm not going anywhere until you tell me what's going on." She crossed her arms tightly.

Philby was not pleased. He said, "We think the Evil Queen may have enchanted you . . ."

"To spy on us—the Keepers," Finn said.

"That she crossed you over tonight—because I definitely did not," Philby added.

"That the CTDs are out there looking for you," Finn said.

"That we've got to get to the Return and get you out of here."

Stunned, Charlene took a moment to process everything. "You'll explain it all later."

"Yes," Finn said.

"I kissed you to break the spell," Philby explained. "It apparently worked. You remember stuff you didn't remember before."

"Why?" Charlene gasped. "Why me? What does she want?"

"If we're right about them trying to break Maleficent out of jail, then who knows what they want? Who knows what they think we have? But we can't get caught. We're not going to let her get you again."

"I want to go home," Charlene said.

"Makes three of us," said Finn.

"We can't take the axes with us," Philby said. "They won't Return with us. And to leave them lying around the plaza would just tell somebody that we'd been here. We don't need to leave clues like that."

"How about leaving seven trolls locked up in the cottage?"

"That's their problem," Philby said.

They leaned Philby's ax and Finn's sword against the rock as they'd found them. Then they hurried to the cave entrance and climbed down the dry waterfall. They stayed in shadow, using trash cans, kiosks, trees, and anything else available to hide behind. They passed

Mexico and followed a perimeter route that took them near Test Track. A hundred yards from the plaza fountain, Philby stopped.

"Slower now," Philby said, taking a moment to catch his breath. "Extra careful."

They circled around the fountain, finally reaching the pin-trading station. A small, circular, one-story building, it held a large display screen that, when operating, informed guests of wait times for the various attractions. There was only one Return, one black fob capable of wirelessly connecting to the server and canceling the DHI projection. Finn had once asked Wayne for more of the devices—one for each Park—but Wayne had steadfastly refused, explaining that the act of Returning was the most dangerous part of the program. If two Returns were engaged within a few seconds of each other, they would theoretically cancel each other out, and the Imagineers had no idea where that would leave the DHIs—nor the kids who lay asleep in bed. If trapped between the two "worlds," the results could be devastating. The system would tolerate only one fob, one Return.

The Keepers were currently hiding the all-important fob in Epcot, in an intersection of purple pipes that supported the roof of the pin-trading post on the plaza. The pipes came together about head height, connecting with a single support column that rose up from the plaza. Where the pipes joined was a hidden space just big enough for the Return.

Finn reached up, his fingers searching blindly, and came down with it—a black rubber remote like a car door opener.

"Ready?" he asked.

Charlene nodded and reached for Finn's hand. Philby took her other hand, connecting them all. For the Return to work effectively, they had to stand near each other. Physical contact—like holding hands—worked even better.

"We'll text in the morning," Philby said, "and figure all this stuff out. Like what to do next. Like if there's some way to stop them from crossing us over."

"Like, why they chose me," Charlene said.

Finn stretched on his tiptoes holding the Return over the junction of pipes. As they crossed back, the Return would fall from his fingers, lodging in its hiding place. They would need to know where to find it the next time they crossed over.

With the three of them all holding hands, Finn counted down, "Three . . . two . . ."

He pushed the button.

# 3

BEING BACK AT SCHOOL was a major letdown. A regular part of almost every day, it was still the forgettable part; his time as a Keeper dominated Finn's thoughts. The one bright spot in the school day was, of all things, lunch. Not that the food was edible. It was not. But lunchtime was Finn's chance to hang with Amanda.

He stopped in the boys' room to make sure he didn't have something stuck in his teeth, or a booger lodged up his nose.

When his eyes shifted focus in the mirror, he saw Greg Luowski standing behind him.

"Hey, Greg." Finn was mindful of the Security photograph showing the Evil Queen talking to Luowski and three other kids. He was a bundle of nerves, especially because Luowski didn't say anything.

There was something different about Luowski's sneer. Maybe it was seeing his ugly mug reversed by the mirror. Maybe it was his piggish eyes, or greasy skin. Or maybe it was just Luowski trying so hard to look menacing. It was working. If they'd given grades for imparting terror, Luowski would have gotten an A.

Finn cupped his hands beneath the faucet, filled his mouth with water, and swished it around in his teeth to get rid of any cereal that might be lingering from breakfast. He did this in part to pretend that Luowski's presence didn't concern him, in part because his hands were shaking and he didn't want Luowski to see the effect he could have over him. When Finn stood up and looked in the mirror, Luowski was gone. The door to the boys' room hissed shut and Finn let out a sigh of relief. But he also wondered why Luowski had passed up the opportunity to bully him. The silent treatment was not Lousy Luowski's style.

Finn looked around to see if a teacher had entered; looked for *some* explanation. As far as he could tell, he was alone. He tried to let it go, to forget about it, but Luowski had gotten under his skin. He felt slightly sick, edgy, jumpy. His skin was crawling.

Amanda was sitting off by herself in the lunch room, a hopeful look in her eyes, which brightened as she spotted him. Her tray held salad, a bowl of fruit, and a glass of water. The lettuce was mostly white, not green; the fruit, canned. Even the water looked gray through the scratched plastic cup. He arrived with a yellowish mass on his plate that had been labeled creamed chicken and rice. With enough salt, it could be swallowed.

"Have you seen Greg-the-Gross?" he asked.

"Yes, you may join me," she said, ignoring his question completely.

"Lousy Luowski," he said.

"I'd be happy to have you."

Finn sat across from her. He stabbed at the yellow mound. "It lives," he said, putting his fork beneath the mass and causing it to wiggle.

She laughed. "In the hall earlier," she said, finally answering him. "His usual oafish self."

She looked pretty today, like every other day.

"Did he look . . . *different*?"

"A few more zits?" she asked. "A few less brain cells?"

Some creamed chicken and rice caught in Finn's throat. He washed it down with warm milk.

She stabbed her fruit. The consistency of rubber, it resisted her fork, like she was trying to stab an eraser. "I'm not exactly a fan," she said. "I don't usually pay attention to him."

She had trouble chewing her fruit. She said, "But did *you* happen to notice Sally Ringwald's new contacts?"

"Might have missed that." He sat up taller and listened carefully: Sally Ringwald had been one of the kids with the Queen in DisneyQuest.

"Pigmented. You know? Green. You can't believe the difference. She's much prettier now. Kind of Irish-looking."

"One of my mom's friends wears the blue ones. It's really disturbing. It's like I'm not supposed to notice or something. I'm supposed to pretend her eyes always looked like that. As if!" He paused. "Don't ever do anything like that, okay? Don't go changing yourself like that."

She blushed and returned to stabbing her fruit. Or trying to.

"Where did that come from?" he said.

"I don't mind."

In a desperate effort to change subjects, he blurted out, "Philby and I crossed over into Epcot last night to rescue Charlene."

"Rescue?"

"To help her Return."

"Did she ask you to?"

"No. It's just that Philby . . . he hadn't arranged for her to cross over in the first place."

"So you're the DHI police now? Is that it?"

"Ouch."

"She can't cross over without Philby's permission? What about Wayne? Or maybe the Imagineers? What if they crossed her over?"

"It . . ." He didn't have a great answer for that. "As it turned out, it was a good thing we went in after her. We ended up battling some trolls. The CTDs were out everywhere—probably looking for her."

"*Probably*," she said, stinging him.

Should he tell her?

"You can tell me," she said.

How come girls could read his thoughts like that? He never had a clue what a girl was thinking.

"We think she was under a spell." He lowered his voice. "The Evil Queen."

"Seriously?"

He reached into his back pocket—he only changed his pants about every four days—and passed her the time-stamped photograph of Charlene and the Evil Queen entering the DisneyQuest washroom.

He said, "There were two photographs last night. The one of the Queen with Luowski and Sally Ringwald, and this one. Notice the times."

"You kept this one from us?" She sounded upset.

"We kept it from Charlene, yeah."

Finn ate some more of the yellowish mush, but bit down on gristle and pushed his tray aside. He said, "She has no memory of the Queen being in the girls' room with her."

Amanda's concern carved lines across her face.

"Maybe the plan," Finn said, "is to cross one of us over each night until we're all stuck in the Syndrome. That would get us out of the way."

"If that ever happened," she said, "Jess and I would cross over and come find you. The OTs can't possibly know that you made it so we can be DHIs."

He spotted Sally Ringwald across the cafeteria. She was too far away for him to see her green contacts, but it prompted him to reconsider his encounter with Luowski.

"What if they were green?" he said.

"What if what were green?"

"Luowski."

"What about him?"

"His eyes. Contact lenses," he said. "What if Luowski looked different to me because eyes were green?"

"That's ridiculous. Greg Luowski has boring eyes," she said. "Hazel. Red hair, hazel eyes."

Finn said, "But what if his boring hazel eyes are now green like Sally Ringwald's?"

"Greg Luowski wearing pigmented contacts? Not possible. A guy like him never thinks about how he looks."

"But *we* should think about it," Finn said, persisting. "The Evil Queen corners Sally, Luowski, and a couple of others at DisneyQuest. Then, a day later, they both show up at school wearing green contacts. It's like those Goth groups, right? Green, as in Maleficent. Get it?"

"You're sick."

"It's not me, it's them!"

"It's your idea."

"We've got to look for others. And you have to get close enough to Luowski to see if I'm right."

"Why me?" she said.

"Because if he sees me he goes all Neanderthal."

"He didn't when you were in the bathroom."

"Just do it. Please! He's right over there by the drinks."

"Okay. I'll walk by him on my way out."

"What are you doing after school?" he asked.

"Jess and I were grounded by Mrs. Nash. She found out about our little trip to Epcot. We're in serious trouble. It's her three-strike rule. She threatened to send us back to the Fairlies," she said.

"That's not going to happen."

"No offense, but I don't think you're going to have a lot of say in it."

The school buzzer sounded. Lunch was over.

"See you." She stood along with half the kids in the room. She walked toward Luowski and the exit. Finn watched her every step. As she passed Luowski's table, she said something to him.

Then, at the door, she turned around and found Finn. She pointed to her eyes and nodded.

Her lips mouthed, "Green."

For a second he thought he might puke. It had nothing to do with the creamed chicken and rice.

* * *

Philby felt the prickle of hairs raising on the back of his neck, and knew he was being watched. Worse, he only associated that same level of dread, of impending disaster, with the Overtakers. But in school? Normally, it wouldn't have made any sense, but the photo of students with the Evil Queen had changed all that for Philby. No one was to be trusted.

The hallways of Edgewater High were jammed with students. Some were hurrying to class, some were flirting, some facing their lockers. But someone was watching him.

He crossed past Mrs. McVey's classroom and stood with his back against a bulletin board filled with thumbtacked essays on the promise of electric cars. He hoped the new angle would make whoever was watching him reveal himself. But the only person he saw was Hugo Montcliff, his neighborhood friend.

"Checking out the girls, or what?"

"Or what," Philby answered. He looked hard for someone focused on him.

No one.

"We've got Algebra."

"Yeah, so?"

"You okay?" Hugo asked.

"You ever get that feeling someone's watching you?"

"Like a girl? Me? Not so much."

"Do you think of anything but girls, Hugo?"

"Xbox. The new Guerrilla Warfare two-point-three."

The sensation had passed. "I was trying to have a little private time here," he said, wounding Hugo. For the first time he took his eyes off the kids in the hallway and looked over at Hugo. He must have hurt him bad because Hugo didn't look like Hugo at all.

"Hey," Philby said. "I'm sorry."

"Enjoy your private time," Hugo said. He charged off.

"Hugo?!"

He was about to run after him when he caught a pair of eyes staring at him from across the hall. A girl with dark hair. She looked vaguely familiar, though he couldn't remember her name. The girl from the photo? She broke off the stare and moved on.

Philby joined the river of students, trying to catch up with her. The more he pushed, the less progress he made. He pulled to the side and tried working along the lockers. He made some headway. There! He reached out and grabbed her shoulder, turning her around.

The wrong girl.

"Sorry!" he said.

"Loser," the girl said, brushing his hand from her shoulder.

He dragged himself out of the way of the crush. Against school rules, he pulled out his phone and sent a group text:

we hav 2 talk. Crzy glaze. after skool

Philby believed in science. Empirical proof. He believed in forming a theory, developing evidence, reaching a conclusion. He lacked all of that. He had only a few hairs tickling the back of his neck and some girl who might have been staring at a hallway clock for all he knew.

And yet he had no doubt—none, whatsoever. There were Overtakers in his school. They were watching him.

It turned his world upside down. There's no place safe, he thought.

* * *

Finn left school with Dillard Cole, his closest non-Keeper friend and full-time neighborhood pal. Dillard was neither athletic nor particularly fit, but he had a good imagination, a huge appetite, and was probably the best gamer Finn knew. At one time—what seemed like many years ago to Finn but wasn't actually so very long ago—the two had spent endless weekends and evenings "working the thumbs," as Dillard called video gaming. Following Finn's modeling as a DHI and his recruitment into the Kingdom Keepers by Wayne, their friendship had fallen off. The reason for the fallout had been, in large part, the secrecy under which the Keepers operated. But now, with newspaper stories "alleging" that Finn was one of the five Kingdom Keepers, Dillard understood the complications of the past and was letting the friendship come around again.

Finn found himself preoccupied with the idea of Luowski's green contact lenses. He and Amanda had blamed Charlene for their wild, near-death simulator ride in DisneyQuest, but a film had been playing in Finn's memory: Luowski bumping into Charlene and helping her to pick up the virtual roller coaster tickets off the floor when she'd dropped them. What if Luowski had substituted the killer ride for the one Charlene had designed for him and Amanda?

"But it's over, right?" Dillard said, bringing Finn back. Dillard sweated as he labored to keep up with the fast-walking Finn. "You guys vanquished them."

"'Vanquished?' That is so Gate Crashers," Finn said, referring to a popular video game.

"The Disney villains . . . they took care of the witch and the thing."

"Villains? Rumors. All rumors."

"So, you are hurrying because . . . ?"

"I've got to catch a city bus. I got a text from Philby," said Finn.

"Philby."

"Yeah."

"You two are tight."

"I suppose. He's a good gamer. You'd like Philby."

"Who'd win, do you think, at Sudden Disaster? Me or Philby?"

"We'd have to find out," Finn said.

"What kind of dumb answer is that?"

"My kind of dumb answer, I guess."

"Hey, could we slow down some? I'm soaked," said Dillard.

"You gotta keep up."

Dillard stopped short, beads of sweat flying off him and spraying Finn, who also stopped.

"I could keep up if I wanted," Dillard said.

"I know that. I'm sorry. I can slow down if you want."

"Why don't you go do whatever it is you've got to do. I'll catch you later."

"Don't be like that."

"Like what?"

"Oh, no," Finn said. "Get down!" He pulled Dillard to a crouch behind a parked car.

"Luowski?" Dillard said, looking that direction. "You and Luowski? I got nothing to do with that."

Luowski jaywalked, crossing the street to the other side.

Finn couldn't believe what he saw. Since when did Luowski give him a free pass?

"He's following me," Finn said.

"Like, spying?"

"Yeah, like that."

"Why?"

Finn thought back to the confrontation in the boys' room before lunch. He thought back to the photograph with the Evil Queen.

"It's . . . involved," he answered. "The question is: Do I dare test it?"

"Test, as in . . . ?"

"I'm going to go over there," Finn said. "If he

beats up on me, I may need you to rescue me."

"Me? And Greg Luowski? Right."

Finn handed him his phone. "Threaten to call nine-one-one."

"Seriously?"

"I'm not saying to do it. Just threaten it. Luowski's stupid, but he's not dumb. He won't want to mess with the police."

"He might want to mess with me," Dillard said.

"It's your call," Finn said.

"Yeah, okay, I'll do it."

Finn patted him on the shoulder. "Thanks."

Finn stood and hurried across the street. "Greg!" he called out.

Luowski appeared to panic. He spun around, then reconsidered and turned back to face Finn. He seemed uncharacteristically perplexed.

"Whitless." Luowski had been born mean. He was the kind of kid destined to be a serial killer, the kind of kid who burned down garages, who dropped rocks off highway overpasses. The kind of kid who deserved a "Go Directly to Jail" card in Monopoly.

"Are you following me?" Finn said.

"As if."

He was a bad liar.

Luowski turned his head slightly, and Finn saw

the green contact lenses. Instead of looking silly, they gave him a chill. Was it possible Luowski and other students (how many, he had no way of knowing!) had been put under a spell by the Evil Queen? That the green contacts were a way for them to identify each other and to intimidate the Keepers? How many had the Queen recruited? Did the spread of the Overtakers extend beyond their own school? If so, how many did the OTs now control? And why? It was enough to make Finn wonder why he'd so eagerly crossed the street to confront Luowski in the first place.

"You don't get it, do you?" Luowski asked.

"Apparently not." But *something tells me I'm about to,* Finn thought.

"The trouble with you, Whitless, is you think you're so special. You and your friends."

There were times that Luowski tried to act tough. Then there were times when he looked like a lightbulb screwed into the socket wrong—a sparking, problem-ridden, butch-cut, ex-Marine in a sixteen-year-old's body.

Finn warned himself to settle down. If he could manage a few seconds of *all clear,* Luowski wouldn't be able to hurt him. But at the moment the space between him and *all clear* was about as wide as the Grand Canyon.

Luowski was like a force field, and Finn a metal particle nearby. Worse, Luowski was relaxed. He didn't have a care in the world.

"Why would you want to follow me? That's what I'm asking myself," Finn said.

"You're confused. You are so naïve."

Finn studied the green-eyed kid. A word like *naïve* had no place coming out of his mouth.

"You must have had Language Arts today," Finn said.

"Take off," Luowski said, "before you fall down and get hurt."

"What did she promise you?"

"Don't know who you're talking about," Luowski replied.

Finn decided it was worth the risk. He pulled the photo out of his back pocket.

"Her," he said, showing the picture of Luowski and the Evil Queen.

"You Photoshop that or something? I don't even know who that is."

He sounded so convincing that Finn nearly believed him.

"I didn't Photoshop those contact lenses."

"The trouble with you, Whitless, is your mouth runs like a faucet."

"Language Arts must have been a block class today."

"See what I mean?"

"Don't believe her. She'll eat you up and spit you out," Finn said.

"Is that right?"

"Yes. That's right."

Luowski grabbed Finn by the shoulders. His hands felt like metal clamps.

"Listen to me carefully, Whitless." His breath was sour, his voice dry and raspy. The contact lenses made his eyes look like doll eyes when close up. Like dead eyes. "Some of us don't believe in magic."

He pushed Finn back, lifting him off his feet and sending him to the sidewalk. Luowski was strong—maybe the strongest kid in the entire high school, not just ninth grade—but it had been more than strength that had lifted Finn off his feet.

"I'M GOING TO CALL NINE-ONE-ONE!" came a girlish-sounding threat from across the street.

Dillard waved the phone. He shouted the warning again.

Luowski glanced in that direction, unfazed. "You're pathetic," he said, turning his back on Finn.

And you're strong, Finn was thinking. Supernaturally strong.

117

Crazy Glaze was a paint-your-own pottery shop owned and operated by Maybeck's aunt and legal guardian, Bess, or "Jelly," as everyone called her. They lived in the apartment above the store; he worked afternoons and Saturdays helping out. Sometimes she paid him, sometimes not, depending on how well business was doing.

Finn liked the smell of the glaze and wet clay.

By the time he got there, the other Keepers had already arrived, though not Amanda and Jess. Jelly had given them the back room all to themselves, the door closed to the outside noise and chaos of kids doing after-school art projects.

The collective mood felt highly charged with anticipation.

Finn sat down and caught them up on his encounter with Luowski. Philby related his story about feeling watched. Willa and Maybeck had similar stories to tell, but neither had connected the events at their school with the Overtakers until they heard Finn and Philby voice their suspicions.

"What does it all mean?" Charlene asked.

Philby spoke up. "It means the Evil Queen has found a way to recruit kids in our schools to watch us."

"It means we're outnumbered," Maybeck said, "and

outflanked. That we can't trust anyone."

"But the contact lenses," Charlene said. "They give themselves away as OTs in training, or whatever. Right? I mean, why do that?"

"Intimidation," Maybeck said. "Is there some other explanation?"

"Agreed. It's the fear factor," Finn answered. "Maybe they think we can all go *all clear*, and want us nervous and on guard to keep us from doing that."

"And it makes them feel special," Willa said. "It makes them important and part of a bigger group."

"It is unusual to make your spies known to the enemy," Professor Philby said. "Let's assume they're planning some kind of jailbreak. Remember, the OTs are characters. That means they're confined to the Parks—and it's entirely possible Maleficent and Chernabog aren't being kept locked up in any of the Parks. They could be in jail anywhere! That might make it necessary for the OTs to have field agents—people on the ground to do stuff for them. The Queen puts spells on a few kids—that would explain Luowski's bizarre strength—and tests them out with some assignments, and then moves them like pawns to do her dirty work."

Finn spoke first. "I hate to say it, but it makes sense. No one is going to stop Luowski with that kind of strength. If there are five or six of them like that, they could easily overpower a bunch of guards."

"Or us," Maybeck said, ominously. "Maybe, when the time comes, their job is to keep us from interfering with the Evil Queen's plans. We've messed things up a lot for them in the past."

"Good point," Willa said.

"Oh, my gosh!" Charlene said. "I just got it!" She was fixed on Maybeck. "You were trying to kiss me to bring me out of the spell! In Epcot. At ice cream!"

"Can we stay on topic please?" Philby said.

Maybeck said, "You missed your big chance."

"How long had you guys known? About the spell, I mean?" Charlene said, ignoring Philby's request.

"We can do this later," Philby said. "The point is, you're back."

"Jess showed me a sketch today," Willa said, changing subjects, "at school."

Finn recalled Jess drawing on a napkin at the ice cream parlor.

"And?" he asked.

"She said it had just come to her when we were in the Parks."

"AND?" Finn repeated anxiously.

"It was this military guy. Like a general. Or maybe a police officer or something."

"What kind of officer?" Philby asked.

"How would I know? They all look the same to me. Just a guy, a grown-up, in a uniform."

"I'd like to see it," Philby said, wondering if it had something to do with Wanda being locked up. According to Finn's mother, she was supposed to have been released earlier that day.

Finn nodded.

"So, you can ask Jess," Willa said.

"What are we supposed to do?" Maybeck asked. "Spy on their spies? That could be awkward."

"So what can we do about it?" the ever-practical Willa asked.

"Can you stop what happened to me from happening again?" Charlene asked.

"It shouldn't have happened to you in the first place," Philby said.

"That doesn't exactly answer my question," she said.

Philby said, "I can monitor the traffic. Set a data alarm. If there's another surge of data, high bandwidth usage, I should be able to detect it."

"That doesn't exactly sound promising," Maybeck said.

"I'm open to suggestions," said Philby, knowing he was the only one who understood any of what he'd just said.

"I'd like to gang up on one of these imitation-flavor Overtakers and have a little talk with them about what they're up to," Maybeck said. "I wonder how strong they are when it's three against one."

"I hate to say it," said Willa, "but it might be better—safer—to try a girl first."

"Sally Ringwald," Finn said. "She was in the photo with Lady Evil, and Amanda said she's now wearing green contacts."

"Can you or Amanda get her alone with us someplace?" Maybeck asked.

"Listen to you!" Charlene said, chastising them. "You're going to hurt some girl without even being sure she's part of this?"

"Of course you'd defend her! You were working for the Evil Queen yourself! Besides, who said we're going to hurt her?" Maybeck said. "Scare her a little, maybe? Sure. It's not like the OTs don't scare us. Am I right? You bet I am. It's time we return the favor, is all. If those guys are spies, we need to know it before it's too late."

Heads nodded in agreement.

"I was apparently a spy for them and I didn't even know it," Charlene reminded in a somber voice.

"We'll keep that in mind," Maybeck said. But it didn't sound as if he meant a word of it.

# 4

PHILBY'S CAT, ELVIS, was a plump, lazy cat. The kind of plump that might get him mistaken for a pet raccoon. The kind that scared off small dogs. Elvis, like all cats, enjoyed warm places to sleep. On the couch, nestled between pillows. Curled up in a shirt that had been tossed on the floor.

Philby's laptop computer ran hot. Its internal fan emitted a pleasant, catlike purr.

Elvis jumped first to the empty office chair, then up to the desk, and lay across the purring keyboard, luxuriating in its warmth.

At desk height he was nearly level with Philby, who slept soundly in his bed across the room. Elvis got up and circled once, unable to find the perfect position. His back paws hit several keys at once. On the screen a window closed. Then another. Elvis took no notice; he'd found the perfect spot to sleep.

He had no idea that he'd just closed the data traffic monitoring program Philby used to police the DHI server. No idea he'd turned off Philby's data alarm.

Instead, he settled his formidable self over the

keys, wiggling until gravity claimed various parts of him. He placed his considerable cat chin down gently onto his crossed paws and closed his eyes.

Behind him, the laptop timed out and went into sleep mode along with him. The boy in the bed knew no different.

* * *

Willa slept with a bear. Not a real bear, a stuffed bear; but no normal stuffed bear, either. A sizable bear. A gargantuan bear of proportions nearing those of a small child. She slept with it alongside of her, its head on a pillow, or sometimes rocked up on its side with its black button eyes looking right at her as she drifted off to sleep. And sometimes, at the same magical moment of finding sleep, she would sling an arm around it and pull it in close, subconsciously enjoying its fuzzy fur as well as the comfort of having something so wonderfully close.

She dozed off, dreaming of school that day, of meeting the Keepers at Crazy Glaze, and of a particularly disturbing exchange of texts with Philby. They'd been texting a lot recently, which she didn't mind at all. But when she found out that Philby, not Maybeck, had kissed Charlene to break the spell, she'd felt the tug of jealousy. Charlene, with her athletic ability, her incredible looks, and her class-A flirting—if she turned on the charm, a fire hydrant would agree to go to the mall with her. Why had Philby been the one to kiss her and not Finn? Why had his recent texts felt more normal and less crushy? Mr. Totems brought her comfort, but her mind wouldn't stop churning.

Willa's dream became intensely realistic. Suddenly, she was laying beside a lake, while clutching tightly to Mr. Totems, her bear. Across the lake—rising out of the water—was a green dinosaur. A brontosaurus, she thought, though she was no expert. It was not daylight, but it was not exactly night either. There was an eerie quality to the color of the light, everything around her was glowing. She let go of Mr. Totems, noticing the familiar shimmer to the outline of her forearm and hand. She held her hand out in front of her, admiring the translucent quality of her skin. Then a breeze blew across her and she shivered. And she gasped.

It wasn't a dream at all: she was a hologram. A DHI. She had crossed over in her sleep.

It wasn't supposed to have been able to happen. They had talked about avoiding crossing over until they knew more, until they knew it was safe. Philby would have told her if he'd planned this; otherwise it must be an extreme emergency, she thought. Something that couldn't wait.

And here she was: in her pajamas with Mr. Totems, somewhere in Disney World. At least her Justice pajamas weren't too embarrassing—red pants, and a long-sleeve top with a panda bear and fireworks that glittered. Not exactly what she wanted to be seen in; but better than a nightgown, which was what Charlene typically ended up in.

But which Park was it? Willa wondered as she took her bearings. She faced a street—not much of a clue. Some buildings surrounding an open plaza—again, not enough to tell her which Park it was. She sat on a raised platform; it was nearly pitch-black above her, except that she could just make out a patch of nighttime clouds swirling directly overhead in a doughnut of black.

Her lack of familiarity with the place told her two things: one, she wasn't anywhere in the Magic Kingdom or the Animal Kingdom—she knew both Parks too well; two, by process of elimination, that left only Epcot and Disney's Hollywood Studios.

Epcot had streets in the various World Showcase attractions, but none as wide, as real-looking as what she faced. A moment later, she had it: she was sitting beneath Mickey's Sorcerer's Hat. Now it made so much sense, she felt stupid. Disney's Hollywood Studios. Of course.

She heard a rhythmic *clomp, clomp, clomp*, reminding

her at first of the sound of the football team crossing the running track as they ran out onto a field before a game. The sounds rang of men and equipment. She sat up, only to realize she was clutching tightly to Mr. Totems. She held Mr. Totems to the side so she could see, and there, coming up Sunset Boulevard was a group—no, she thought, a *troop*—of soldiers. They were so hard to see that she thought they must be wearing camouflage. But as they drew closer—*clomp, clomp, clomp*—she saw it wasn't camouflage. They were a solid, dark green. They were the Army Men from *Toy Story*, but they weren't toys at all. They were life-size, and they were coming right at her.

Willa grabbed Mr. Totems and scrambled to her feet, heading away from the Army Men, keeping in shadow until she fled down a set of steps. She sprinted once she reached the plaza, running down Commissary Lane and putting some distance between herself and the troop.

Arriving at the end of the street, she heard more of the organized marching up ahead. She turned left, past some landscaping, and kept running, the sounds of marching soldiers all around her.

Forced by the sounds to move to her left, she now faced Echo Lake. Willa squeezed Mr. Totems all the tighter. This wasn't going well. To either side of the lake were more Army Men, enough to block her way. Behind her, the two squads arrived, now merged as one large unit.

"Mr. Totems, it's time to get out of here. Any suggestions?"

Mr. Totems didn't answer. His expression didn't change. Willa wondered if something like this had happened to Charlene the night before. Was she under some spell she didn't know about? What did they want with her? She recalled Maybeck wanting to scare the truth out of one of the green-contact-lens kids. She hoped that wasn't what was intended for her: if so, it was already working.

She needed to get to Epcot. She needed the Return.

"Close zee ranks!" came a heavily accented Frenchman's voice. Willa didn't see him at first; she was far more concerned with the circle of green Army Men tightening around her.

Then she spotted him: a man in a red velvet dinner jacket, beneath which was a frilly white shirt and a bizarrely large black bow tie, the tails of which disappeared into the velvet. His pants were three-quarter length, tight around the calf, and puffy on his upper legs, with hook-and-eye laced brown leather boots spit-polished to gleaming. He had long curly hair—a wig perhaps—beneath an exaggerated hat like those worn by the Three Musketeers. Judge Claude Frollo from *The Hunchback of Notre Dame.*

It took her another few seconds to figure out what he was doing here in the Studios—that he was part of the Fantasmic! show. The soldiers continued to close around her.

"You have to understand, my dear," Judge Frollo said. "I have no patience for young children. As a judge that is. My verdict is a simple one: guilty! Of having too much fun: guilty. Misuse of time: guilty. Irresponsible, unacceptable behavior: guilty. So it's nothing personal, you understand? It comes down to this: It has fallen upon me to determine what your friend showed you at school. I'm told it is a drawing, and that it was drawn upon a small, square tissue." He stroked his chin, a nervous habit. "What is the subject matter of this drawing, if you please?"

"But I don't . . ." she said.

"*Excusez-moi?*"

"If you please," she said. "I don't wish to tell you."

Perplexed, he cocked his head, considering her. "I would be careful, my dear. My politeness is but a formality, an inescapable part of my egalitarian French upbringing. So civilized, the French, don't you think? But make no mistake—I would just as soon direct my minions here," he said, gesturing toward the hundred soldiers, "to test the water, as it were. To send you bottom-fishing. To *drown* you, my dear. Did I caution you that I'm not a patient man when it comes to children?"

"I can't tell you what I don't know," she said, lying, though lying well, she thought.

"But you were seen. Witnessed. It was reported."

Her head swooned. Which was it, witnessed or reported? One way would put the event in her school hallway; another inside the private meeting with the other Keepers. The source of the leak was of vital importance to her. She thought of Philby and what he'd do in her position.

Gather intelligence, she thought. Gain enough data, enough information to form an exit strategy, an escape plan. Finn would have schooled her to rely upon her DHI status—to maintain *all clear*. But she was so scared her teeth would have been chattering had she not been biting down on her tongue. If she were fifty percent DHI at the moment she'd be lucky. The thin blue outline that should have been surrounding her arms had dimmed to nearly nothing. *All clear* was not an option—not at the moment, anyway.

Judge Frollo smiled, a snarl of gnarly teeth and a twist of lip that turned her stomach.

"If it please the court," he said, then guffawing (since he *was* the court), "I will ask the defendant again: What did you see drawn upon the tissue?"

"It was a napkin, Your Honor," she said, trying to appeal to his sense of importance. "A tissue meant to catch crumbs in your lap. It is not something one writes upon. That task is better served by a pad of drawing paper, or notepaper. There may have been a logo, or business name I was meant to take note of. I'm sorry to say, I don't happen to remember."

"You do, however, recall what it is I intended to do to the infant boy in the animated motion picture that bears, in part, the name of a certain famous Parisian cathedral?"

"Notre Dame."

"The same!"

"You were going to kill him," she said. "Quasimodo."

"Your memory is not so bad after all, I see! Excellent. Now, try again—one last time—what was drawn upon the . . . napkin—the crumb-catching tissue?"

"And again, as much as I'd like, I can't describe something that wasn't there," she said, trying to speak somewhat like him, trying to befriend him.

"More's the pity! My lack of patience is something I must improve upon. Very well. Seize her! Into the lake with her. A wet nap. A swim with the fishes. DROWN HER!" he roared, waving his hand like a ballet dancer's toward the lake.

Strangely, she thought only of Mr. Totems. If they drowned her, what would it mean for Mr. Totems? Would they tear him to pieces? As much as she loathed the idea of leaving Mr. Totems behind, a plan began to form in her mind. The soldiers were about to pick her up and throw her into the lake. If, at the exact moment, she could substitute Mr. Totems for herself . . .

She couldn't feel sorry for Mr. Totems. She had to think of it as Mr. Totems sacrificing himself for her. Maybe she could come back and get him later. Who knew? They'd come through a lot together: bubble gum stuck in his fur; the replacement of one of his button eyes; a torn seam that left him spewing stuffing, tiny plastic balls that smelled something like fish.

If she charged the line of Army Men, they would simply catch hold of her. No, the answer was the water itself: give them Mr. Totems and then dive in and swim for the opposite side, hoping to beat the cloddy soldiers.

With a second dismissive flick of his wrist, Judge Frollo signaled the green soldiers to close around her. Willa felt light-headed. She held Mr. Totems tightly.

Three . . . two . . .

A soldier reached for her.

She stuffed Mr. Totems into the soldier's open arms, pushed Judge Frollo into the others, turned, and ran five steps to the lake's edge.

"SHOOT HER!" she heard.

She dove.

White lines raced around her, bullets zooming through the water. She couldn't surface without being shot. Down, down, she swam, pulling against the water and traveling deeper and deeper. She had thought Echo Lake was only a few feet deep, but suddenly it was much deeper. The bullets weren't reaching her now, but—as she looked up—they were zooming overhead like shooting stars.

And there, in silhouette, was Mr. Totems floating on the lake's surface. Snow was falling all around him as bullets riddled his body. Not snow, she realized, but his stuffing. Mr. Totems had given his life for her.

Willa screamed underwater, bubbles rising above her like silver Christmas balls. She was smart enough not to breathe in, to avoid inhaling a fatal lungful of lake water, but she was sinking now, her lungs aching. She felt light-headed.

Something up ahead . . . A dark, flowing shape interrupting the light on the surface: a fish the size of a porpoise or a shark, yet even more graceful. It grew larger with its approach.

Her lungs about to burst, Willa saw a flash of green, a glimpse of rust-colored seaweed. No, she realized, not seaweed but *hair*. It was a mermaid.

It was Ariel.

A girl's long fingers reached out for her. Willa took hold. Ariel pressed her face close to hers and blew bubbles in a steady stream into her lips, and Willa drank them in. The pain in her lungs subsided. The two swam side by side, Ariel stopping every few yards and blowing another stream of bubbles for Willa to inhale.

Ariel led her across the lake and they surfaced together on the far side of a large white ship tied up to shore. Willa sucked in the fresh air, and Ariel held a finger to her lips, silencing her.

There was much shouting and yelling from Judge Frollo, and the sound of the soldiers' feet pounding the pavement as they surrounded the lake. Ariel pointed down, signaling for them to go underwater again. Willa was reluctant but nodded her consent.

Where had Ariel come from? Were there more Characters like her willing to help the Keepers?

They dove. Ariel led her along the tank wall—the lake was nothing more than a giant swimming pool—until they reached a large hole, the end of a pipe. Ariel filled Willa's lungs with air and smiled beautifully, and Willa knew it was going to be okay. Ariel swam into the opening first and Willa followed.

The pipe grew increasingly darker. Unable to see, Willa felt outward and caught Ariel's hand. Suddenly the powerful tail propelled them. Willa had never moved so fast in the water. Twice Ariel stopped to charge Willa's lungs in the dark. Twice Willa drank in the air, only to feel herself whisked away into the darkness again. Ariel pulled her upward. Willa's head broke the surface. Again, she gasped for air, marveling that she was still alive.

They were in a large tank with a ladder and a metal platform. She spotted a sign on the wall that read, VOYAGE OF THE LITTLE MERMAID—BACKSTAGE ENTRANCE. An arrow pointed to a door. Ariel focused on the door, then eased Willa toward the stairs in the water.

Willa shook her head. "I can't thank you enough for saving me. But if the soldiers saw us they will come looking. They will start here," she said, pointing to the sign. "I need to get to Epcot . . . My friends and I—"

"The Keepers," Ariel said in a beautiful, lilting voice.

Willa coughed. "You know about us?"

Ariel blinked and smiled at her. "My dear girl, *everyone* knows about you. You are our saviors."

*Our* saviors? What did she mean by that? Willa wondered. *Are there more of you?*

"No, no, no. We're just kids. We're nobodies, believe me."

"I'm afraid no one would believe such nonsense,"

said Ariel. "We know who you are. We are most grateful for what you are doing. We all—any of us—will do whatever we can to keep the magic. The magic is what feeds us."

*Us!* There it was again!

"It isn't safe here," Willa said. "I don't want to leave you. Please don't think me rude, but I don't want to get you in any more trouble than you're already in."

"You are shaking," Ariel said.

"I'm cold."

"One last swim," Ariel said. "I know a place. The perfect place. Warm. And I can be with you without concern."

"I couldn't ask that. You've done enough."

"It's okay, dear girl—"

"Willa."

"Ah! You are the Willow!"

"Will*a*," she corrected.

"Yes, I know. Of course. And Shirley—"

"Charlene . . ."

"Of course. I know. You ask nothing. It is after hours. I can go back and forth, tail or legs, as I choose. I am happy to help you. Come, please swim with me."

"A short distance?"

"I promise."

Willa didn't want to use that backstage door. She

nodded. Ariel dove. Willa followed and grabbed her hand. Again the water was dark. Ariel's powerful tail drove them left, right, and up—straight up. Harder and harder the tail pushed. Higher they swam.

Willa didn't understand how it was possible. When they'd started, they couldn't have been more than ten or fifteen feet underground, yet now it felt as if they'd climbed fifty feet or more.

Ariel had not fed her any air. Her lungs were bursting as they broke through the surface. She coughed and gasped for air.

They found themselves in a much bigger tank. Again, a metal ladder ran down below the water's surface, stretching high above them to a circular catwalk surrounding the tank.

As Ariel pulled herself up the rungs, Willa watched as her mermaid's tail changed into a girl's long, bare legs and bare bottom.

"I keep these handy just for this transition," Ariel said once they'd reached a steel catwalk at the top. She had her back to Willa as she slipped on a pair of bikini bottoms that she'd had cleverly wrapped around the back strap of her halter top, hidden by her long hair.

She led Willa out a heavy metal door and onto another catwalk. Willa nearly screamed as she reached to steady herself. They were a hundred feet above ground, high up on a catwalk balcony surrounding the Park water tower. But Willa, like Philby, was a climber, and had no trouble with the height once she realized where she was. Ms. Cheerleader, Charlene, could do some climbing too, but more of the gymnastic variety. Willa and Philby were the Keepers who did the rope courses and climbing wall as after-school activities. It was where she'd first started liking him.

"It's . . . beautiful," Willa said.

"Yes. I love it up here. There's a lot to be said for being human."

"You saved my life."

"Mermaids," Ariel said, interrupting, "have a long-standing tradition of rescuing sailors at sea. It would seem that is about all we're good for. That, and exciting homesick sailors in the first place."

"In my house, you're known for your singing."

"Yes, well . . . that came later."

"What do we do now?" asked Willa.

"I am not sure. I only know that no one will find us here. No one will see us. I often spend time here— overlooking the Park, watching the guests, playing the occasional prank. Did you know that mermaids like to make practical jokes?"

"First I've heard of it."

"Yes, well, how would you feel if shipbuilders were constantly carving sculptures of you on the front of their ships from the waist up? It's undignified. Such things deserve practical joking."

"Can I ask you something?" Willa said.

"You just did."

Willa giggled. "You said you knew of the Keepers."

"Of course."

"Are there . . . *others* who would consider helping us?"

"I told you: You have many friends here. You might be surprised to discover how many stand with you. Here in the World, and in the Land as well, we lack only a leader. We assume that is why you and the others have come. To lead us."

Willa's head spun. Finn had often talked about Wayne making reference to leadership. She'd always thought of it in terms of the Keepers—never the Disney characters themselves. Willa had never considered that she and the others were there to lead a movement. She doubted Finn or anyone else had, either.

"My father, King Triton, says a kingdom has room for only one ruler," Ariel said.

"Our group is more of a democracy," Willa said. "But maybe we're here to help you find a leader. What about Mickey? Isn't Mickey your leader?"

Ariel locked into a distant stare. She'd gone

somewhere far away. "We can discuss this another time, I think." Her entire demeanor had changed.

Willa filed the information away for later. Why had mention of Mickey closed off Ariel?

Willa said, "Let me ask you this. If you're here . . ." she reached over and touched the beautiful girl, "does that mean Ursula's here, too?"

"Of course. Everyone's here. Aren't they? There are so few you can trust here, believe me."

"We need a plan," Willa mumbled.

"Or a script. There's always a script to follow."

"Not always, I'm afraid," Willa said. "This is one of those times. We need to write our own script."

Willa looked out on the empty Park. Occasionally she caught movement from a particular direction, but by the time she turned to look in that direction the street would be empty, the Park a ghost town.

Willa recalled with some dread Judge Frollo's eagerness to drown her. How the soldiers had appeared so well organized.

They had been waiting for her to cross over. They had wanted her to describe the sketch Jess had shown her at school. It meant only one thing: someone had told them about Jess showing it to her.

The spies were real.

"Something's going on here," she allowed to slip out.

"Oh, there's a great deal going on, dear girl. We just so seldom see it."

"We're in danger."

"Yes." It was as if this was old news to Ariel.

"I need to get to Epcot." To the Return, she was thinking.

"But you just got here!" Ariel complained.

"My friends and I want to help," Willa reminded. "But we can only help if we're together. Like a team."

"Friends? A team? My friends are a crab and some fish. I'm all alone here," Ariel said, wistfully.

"Not anymore you're not," said Willa. "You're part of the team now."

# 5

WHILE WILLA WAS SITTING with her feet draped over the catwalk surrounding the Disney's Hollywood Studios water tank, Finn was awake contemplating a text message he'd received from an unidentified sender. It wasn't that he didn't receive text messages; of course he did—hundreds a week, maybe more—but this particular message held more interest than most:

www.thekingdomkeepers.com/key

Beneath the URL was the title of the book and a page number—a book Finn knew all too well. A book written about him and his friends. Underneath the title of the book, a single letter:

**W**

It was that *W* that had held his attention for the past hour or so. That letter and all it represented. Philby had been contacted by Wayne at school. He'd sent them on the Kim Possible adventure.

Now this.

Wayne was becoming involved again.

Finn's first instinct had been to find the book and go to the Web site. That was why the book was sitting open to the right of the keyboard, and why Finn was sitting in the chair in front of his computer. But for the longest time he couldn't bring himself to do it. He just didn't completely believe Wayne had sent the text—even though Wayne had given him and the others their phones and therefore would know how to text him. Even though he was eager to connect with Wayne. The problem was this: Wayne never made it simple. Finn couldn't think of a time that Wayne had given them something easy to solve or easy to do. The method he'd used to contact Philby supported that notion. Why hadn't he just texted Philby if he thought texting was safe?

Wayne had a tendency to surprise: arriving uninvited in a chat room or interrupting a Skype session. A straight text seemed so unlike him.

But that *W* was like a finger drawing Finn closer to his keyboard. The longer he stared at it, the more tempted he was. Finally, he webbed the fingers of both hands, cracked his knuckles by bending them backward, and placed them upon the keyboard. He typed the address into his browser.

The page loaded, and he was instructed to hold the particular page of the book up to the computer's internal video camera. He pushed the laptop back a few inches and hoisted the book. He hit ENTER. The computer *bonged* and the screen changed color.

*SUCCESS!* the screen declared.

For a moment there was no change. It was late, and he was tired. All that anticipation had been coursing through his veins for the past hour like caffeine from a soda. With nothing happening, a wave of fatigue overcame him. He felt like a pool toy losing its air, a condition that left him wholly unprepared for what happened next.

Wayne appeared on top of his desk, just in front of the keyboard. A small hologram of Wayne, no more than four inches tall, impossibly real-looking. Finn waved his hand through the image just to confirm it was what it was.

"Whoa!" Finn said aloud. "Can you hear me?"

"Hello, Finn."

It was Wayne's voice—there was no mistaking the scratchy quality. But, maybe because of the projection or the transmission, the words sounded somewhat artificial, almost glued together, the intonation wrong.

"What exactly . . . ? Where . . . ? Is that really you? Where are you?"

"Come down . . . lower . . . Finn. Look at . . . my face. I should see . . . you . . . better."

Finn had heard Philby talk about augmented reality apps—AR—baseball cards that came to life as holograms on your desk, maps that did the same thing. The Keepers had heard rumors that Disney was considering making Kingdom Keepers playing cards with an AR component, allowing them to appear as 3-D images just as Wayne was now appearing. Some augmented reality could even be animated—a baseball player swinging a bat, a dancer spinning on her toes—but he had never heard of an AR element projecting in real time the way this one was. It was like a 3-D video chat, and Finn found it captivating.

He backed up his chair and lowered his head as instructed in order to look directly at Wayne's small face.

Somewhere in the far reaches of Finn's mind, a warning light went off. The choppiness of Wayne's voice could be a transmission problem, as he suspected—but why would the hologram be so clear and the audio be so choppy? That didn't make sense. The audio sounded edited—words cut and pasted into sentences.

As he lowered himself toward Wayne's small face, Finn simultaneously cleared his thoughts and pictured a dark tunnel with a pinprick of light showing far, far in the distance. He allowed that light to grow closer, allowed himself to sink not only toward the desk, but into a peaceful, blissful state. *All clear*.

"That is . . . better," said the hologram.

Then, as Finn looked at Wayne, the face transformed, no longer a man with white hair, but suddenly the stern face of a beautiful woman. The Evil Queen's mouth was already moving, her voice both haunting and musical.

> *"As soft as a whisper*
> *No one will tell*
> *The curse, reversed*
> *Seen by the sister*
> *When kissing Jezebel"*

Finn's fingers and toes tingled. With the mention of kissing Jezebel—the name Jess had gone by a few years earlier—he panicked, and he slipped out of *all clear*. The Evil Queen repeated her message:

> *"As soft as a whisper*
> *No one will tell . . ."*

Finn was caught in a state of partial *all clear*, a dangerous place—mentally alert but with tingling toes and fingers. Part mortal, he was real enough to be wounded, yet enough *all clear* to believe he was safe.

In this interim state, he managed to reach forward, move the mouse, and click the "back" button on his browser. The computer screen showed an Algebra 2 Web page he'd been using for homework.

The Evil Queen hologram sparkled and vanished. Finn sat back into his chair feeling . . . different.

The page-forward button on the browser flashed as if he'd clicked it with the mouse, which he had not. *Thekingdomkeepers.com* page reloaded. The Evil Queen hologram reappeared.

Someone was controlling his computer.

The Queen began reciting the verse again. Finn pulled the power plug on his computer, but the laptop, being battery-powered, continued to run. He shut the lid, and the computer went to sleep.

He focused at that space in front of his keyboard where the Evil Queen had stood. No matter how he fought against it, he could hear her.

> *"As soft as a whisper*
> *No one will tell*
> *The curse, reversed*
> *Seen by the sister*
> *When kissing Jezebel"*

Kissing Jess? He spat on the floor before he knew what he was doing. It wasn't that he didn't like Jess, of course he did. But not in *that* way.

Why Jess? Why would the Evil Queen want him to do that? Was it simply a matter of making Amanda jealous—dividing the "sisters"? What would that accomplish?

He would have to reboot his computer in safe mode and run a virus check. There was work to do before he could attempt a chat session or e-mail. He put the machine to work, searching for the backdoor or bug that had allowed it to be controlled remotely. He knew he should have probably allowed Philby to look at the machine first, should have given Philby a chance to trace the infection back to whoever had caused it, but he had no desire to share the stupid verse with anyone. Just the mention of it could have the desired effect: anger, jealousy, confusion. He had to think this through.

He relived the incident, convincing himself he'd been *all clear* at the time the verse had been recited. Nothing to worry about. If it was a spell, it had not reached him. It didn't occur to him for even a split second that such denial might be part of the spell, that by not doing anything, he was already doing something.

*Stone stair-steps.* At least they looked like stone stair-steps leading up to a box. Or possibly a door? Jess moved slowly, like she was trying to walk through Jell-O.

Finn was there. Practical Finn. Organized Finn. Amanda's Finn. Jess preferred boys like Kaden Keller, more on the unpredictable side. More wild. But Amanda was crushing—no doubt about it. And Jess liked Finn a lot, so she was happy for Amanda.

So why, she wondered, was she just standing there as Finn walked up to her with that look in his eye—a look any girl knew. A look that said he was going to kiss her. And why, she wondered, was she going to allow it to happen when she knew how it would hurt Amanda? He took her by the shoulders, closed his eyes, and pressed his lips to hers. And he stayed there like that. A real kiss that flooded through her like a sugar rush, lips to toes. By the time she awoke and began to sketch in her diary, she knew full well it had been only a dream. But with her dreams came a connection between now and then, between here and there, the present and the future. Only later could she ever make full sense of such a dream—a day, a week, a month. Adults had labeled it a power; Amanda called it a blessing; Jess often thought of it as a curse.

She knew some piece of the dream would happen,

but not when, or why, or how it might change things. Upon seeing her sketches, the Keepers often looked for answers she didn't have. She could see the future; she couldn't interpret it.

But the kiss lingered on her lips. It had felt real—incredibly real.

She adjusted her pillow and continued to draw. She started with the background first—the five uneven steps seen in profile, rising to a landing. She loved the sound of the pencil lead scratching the paper; she felt no fatigue. She enjoyed these visions. They no longer came as often as they once had. As a child, she'd had several a week. She'd seen a flood, a car crash, a fire. She'd made the newspaper with the prediction of the fire. That was when the doctors had started hooking up wires to her, when the military men had begun asking questions. When she'd been taken from her original foster parents and moved in with the Fairlies.

Before she and Amanda ran away.

The visions came much less frequently now, a secret only Amanda knew. Sometimes in groups—three or four in a week and then none for months. Sometimes a piece of a dream, but not enough to stick with her, not enough to draw. Being in the Parks, hanging with the Keepers, seemed to increase their frequency and intensity.

She drew the scene of the kiss as best she could, her artistic abilities having improved over time. She not only caught the angle of their heads correctly, but the profile of the boy really looked like Finn, and though the girl was less obvious, she knew it was her.

It was one dream she would never allow to happen, would never do this to Amanda. Had no interest herself. If Finn wanted it, too bad. Not ever!

She heard Amanda stir in the overhead bunk, so she switched off the small light, and covered the drawing with her hand in case Amanda leaned over, curious. But Amanda only rolled over. Jess switched the light on and finished drawing the kiss.

She studied the girl's face more carefully. She couldn't be absolutely sure it was her. But she knew what she'd felt. She knew what was going to happen.

* * *

"Please," Charlene said, appealing to her mother over the breakfast table. "It's no big secret that I like him." Her mother's one soft spot was her daughter's love life. There were times that Charlene felt as if her mother was trying to be her same age again, which was so random it pained her to even consider it. But the fact was, her mother had been a high school cheerleader, had been pretty, and, according to her, chased by all the boys, and she seemed to want all that for Charlene as well.

"You don't want to be the one doing the pursuing," her mother cautioned. She advised Charlene about her interest in certain boys as if she were coaching a chess match.

"I'd just be visiting Winter Park for a day."

"That's his school."

"Ah . . . yeah."

"Which will be seen as you pursuing him."

"I have friends there, too, Mom. Do I want to hang with him at lunch? Yes. Of course. But it's not like I'm going to follow him down the halls or something. It's *one* day." She and Amanda had plans, but she couldn't go there. Her mother understood boys. Charlene knew which buttons to push. "I can spend time with my friends after school. I never get a chance to see them anymore." With graduation from middle school, some kids had gone to different high schools because of redistricting. Her mother knew the situation; they'd talked about it often enough.

"I know, I know," her mother said.

Charlene heard the change in tone; she'd won.

"All we have to do is have you sign me in at the office. It'll take two seconds."

"And you'll call or text me when school's out?"

"Promise."

Her mother smiled. "You must like him a lot."

"You have no idea," Charlene said.

* * *

As the buzzer sounded leading into the lunch period, Charlene, wearing her visitor tag, waited by the water fountains in the west hall, as arranged in a hasty meeting with Amanda earlier. She peeled off the tag and stuck it inside her shirt so it would remain sticky but not be seen. She pulled out the section of panty hose from the pocket of her jean shorts and kept it scrunched in her hand. Her heart was beating the way it did before a gymnastics competition.

Amanda appeared among the mass of students crowding the hallway, wearing a look of fierce determination. Charlene knew what they were about to do went against everything Amanda held dear. Knew that for Amanda this was about friendship and loyalty and her dedication to Finn and the Keepers. Knew that she was, like Charlene, dying inside with anticipation.

"Follow me," Amanda said, all business.

Charlene stepped into line behind her. Amanda made her way to the stairway. They held close to the banister and hurried down, passing other students. They reached the ground floor and continued down to the basement level.

"It's all about timing," Amanda said, over her shoulder. "You remember your assignment?"

"Yes. Of course."

"You have the stockings?"

Charlene held up her balled fist.

The basement level was far less crowded. They walked together down a hallway and turned to the right.

"She'll be coming by here any minute," Amanda said, pulling open a door. "Band room. Empty this period."

"Okay," said Charlene.

"We'll be expelled if we do this wrong."

"I know. So let's not do it wrong."

"I'm in the hall. You're inside, but out of sight," instructed Amanda.

"I remember."

"I'll cough."

"I know."

Charlene turned into the darkened room and tucked around the corner, her chest ready to explode. There was a bass drum on a metal stand. Risers with chairs and music stands. An upright piano. She left the lights off, bracing herself for what was to come. She pulled the piece of panty hose down over her hair and head, obscuring her face.

Amanda wore the section of rolled panty hose on her head like a winter cap, kneeling with her face to the wall, her hands in her computer bag, digging around as if looking for something.

Sally Ringwald came down the hall with two girl-friends. Now came the tricky part.

Without turning, without showing her face, Amanda said, "Hey, Sally, got a minute?"

"I'll catch up," Sally told her friends.

As predicted, the two girls turned up the stairs. Amanda had chosen this spot for a reason.

"What's up?" Sally said to Amanda's back.

Amanda coughed and pulled the stocking down over her face and turned around, looking like something from a slasher movie.

"What the—"

But Sally didn't have time to complete her exclamation.

Amanda lifted her hands and *pushed*. Sally lifted off her feet and flew backward through the doorway, skidding on her bottom across the floor. Amanda stepped through and Charlene pulled the door shut.

When Sally jumped off the floor, she wasn't even human. She sprang like a mountain lion, crashing into Amanda, her green eyes flashing in the dim light. She and Amanda smacked into the wall by the piano.

Charlene came at her from the side, grabbing an arm. Sally tossed her off like she was a stuffed animal. Charlene landed hard.

Amanda *pushed* for a second time. Sally lifted off her feet and crashed into a music stand, taking it down as she knocked some folding metal chairs out of the way, landing in a heap. Amanda pushed again. Sally slid on her bottom and was pinned to the riser. Amanda held her there, still pushing, arms extended.

Charlene crossed the room and was slammed to the floor as if a ninety-mile-per-hour wind had struck her. Groaning, she rose, and with Amanda still pushing, Charlene wrestled Sally's arms behind her back and tangled their legs together, keeping Sally down.

Amanda released her push.

The three girls were panting, out of breath.

Charlene said coarsely, "What do they want?"

Sally wrestled, but couldn't get free of Charlene's hold.

"Power," Sally said through clenched teeth. "What's anybody want?"

"From us?" Amanda said.

"You're insignificant. Don't flatter yourselves."

# GIFT RECEIPT

Barnes & Noble Booksellers #2367
800 Settlers Ridge Center Drive
Pittsburgh, PA 15205
(412) 809-8300

STR:2367 REG:005 TRN:8300  CSHR:Matt B

BARNES & NOBLE MEMBER    EXP: 10/10/2012

Power Play (Kingdom Keepers Series #4)
   9781423138570        T1
   (1 @ RZ.RH)                    RZ.RH G

Thanks for shopping at
Barnes & Noble

101.27B              12/05/2011  12:22PM

CUSTOMER COPY

...permitted.

Magazines, newspapers, and used books are not returnable.
*Product not carried by Barnes & Noble or Barnes & Noble.com will not be accepted for return.*

*Policy on receipt may appear in two sections.*

## Return Policy

With a sales receipt, a full refund in the original form of payment will be issued from any Barnes & Noble store for returns of new and unread books (except textbooks) and unopened music/DVDs/audio made within (i) 14 days of purchase from a Barnes & Noble retail store (except for purchases made by check less than 7 days prior to the date of return) or (ii) 14 days of delivery date for Barnes & Noble.com purchases (except for purchases made via PayPal). A store credit for the purchase price will be issued for (i) purchases made by check less than 7 days prior to the date of return, (ii) when a gift receipt is presented within 60 days of purchase, (iii) textbooks returned with a receipt within 14 days of purchase, or (iv) original purchase was made through Barnes & Noble.com via PayPal. Opened music/DVDs/audio may not be returned, but can be exchanged only for the same title if defective.

After 14 days or without a sales receipt, returns or exchanges will not be permitted.

Magazines, newspapers, and used books are not returnable.
*Product not carried by Barnes & Noble or Barnes & Noble.com will not be accepted for return.*

*Policy on receipt may appear in two sections.*

"So insignificant that you're spying on us," Charlene said, pulling the girl's arms back harder to make her point. "What's that make you?"

"Busy," she said, snickering.

"Who . . . are . . . you?" Amanda asked, for the girl's eyes were wide and evil-looking.

Sally Ringwald laughed. But it wasn't a girl's laugh. It was a woman's. "The future," she said.

"Not my future," Charlene said, gasping. It was taking all her considerable strength to restrain Sally's arms. Both she and Amanda feared what Sally might be capable of if she could get free.

"There is no yours or mine where the future's concerned. It's *ours*. You can either be on the right side or the wrong side," Sally said.

"There is no side to the future, only to the things we do with it, the choices we make," Amanda said.

"What do you know? The future always arrives before you can stop it," said Sally. "Talk to me Saturday morning."

To Amanda it sounded like a recruiting line. She felt slightly light-headed. The pushing had drained her. Charlene looked as bad as she felt. They were out of time.

"How many of you are there?" This had been the question Philby most wanted asked.

"More each day," Sally answered. "More than you can possibly imagine."

"We have big imaginations," Charlene said, increasing her hold, and winning a wince of pain on Sally's face.

"Your kind think 'dreams really do come true'? Then dream on."

Charlene flashed Amanda a look—her signal she couldn't hold on much longer. Amanda had been expecting it. She nodded.

"Now!" Amanda called out.

Charlene let go and rolled.

Amanda pushed, sending Sally into a back somersault and into another music stand and more chairs. She and Charlene ran for the door. They got into the hall, and both girls grabbed the door handle together and held on.

The door was struck from the other side by what sounded like a truck. The entire jamb dislocated in the masonry wall.

"On three," Amanda said. "One . . . two . . . *three*!"

They let go of the door handle, stripped off the panty hose masks, and ran as fast as they'd ever run for the stairway. They heard an enormous crash behind them as they climbed the stairs out of breath.

Reaching the mob scene of students, they slowed,

hooked elbows, and walked calmly into the surge of bodies. They heard footsteps flying up the stairs behind them, but never looked back. They were deep enough into the mob that their clothes could not be seen to be identified. They turned into the lunchroom packed with other students.

Amanda looked around for Finn.

He wasn't there.

# 6

FINN SAW GREG ŁUOWSKI down the school hallway standing at a locker, and recalled their strange
encounter on the street. An agent for the Overtakers?
Was it possible? Did Wayne's Kim Possible message
about friends turning their backs on you have something
to do with Luowski, or only Charlene's erratic behavior?
Luowski could never be considered a friend to Finn, but
did Wayne know that?

Next he spotted a woman, wearing a visitor's sticker,
down the hall. She was staring at him, her face vaguely
familiar yet unknown to him. The way her gaze locked
onto him he had no doubt she was there to see him.
Worse, she was upset. Any kid knew that look on the
face of a grown-up.

That was when he realized how a stranger could
look so familiar: behind the crinkly eyes and puckered
lips, Willa looked back at him.

The woman started toward him at the same time
Luowski caught Finn staring. Luowski's menacing
expression seemed to say, "You want something?"

Finn looked away rather than provoke the

bulldog. He didn't need Luowski in his face.

"Finn Whitman," the woman said, now upon him. "I'm—"

"Willa's mom," Finn said.

"Yes. We've met before but it was some time ago. I need a word with you."

Perfect! What had he done now?

"You have a class in five minutes, so it needs to be now. Right now. That, or we can do this with your parents after school."

His father? No way! "Next period's my lunch period," Finn said. "I'm okay." Anything but his father.

"Is there someplace we can talk?"

*Gulp.*

Finn checked out a classroom. Then another. He held the door for her, hoping it might score some points. They entered.

She studied the classroom as if making sure they were alone.

*Double gulp.*

She ran her tongue into her upper teeth. When his mom did that it was to bite back her words, to keep herself from saying the first thing that came to mind.

"I don't know where to begin," she said. "Whatever's going on, young man, whatever you're up to, you had better stop it, you had better fix it right now."

Finn's heart beat so powerfully that it occupied his entire torso. He was having trouble breathing. He could tell she was just getting warmed up. He held back the wisecracks, wondering why they always came to mind when he found himself in trouble.

"Don't pretend you don't know what I'm talking about. I'm in no mood to play games."

She'd been crying. He understood that now. Red eyes. Fatigue.

"Say something!" she insisted.

He shrugged. She hadn't left him many options: he had no idea what she was talking about, but had warned him not to say so.

"Willa is not in school today, in case you haven't heard." Her eyes had narrowed to little lasers.

"I didn't know," he said.

"No, of course you didn't," she said sarcastically, making him feel like a liar. His parents did this all the time—answered their own question before giving Finn a chance to speak.

"She doesn't go here," he reminded her. How was he supposed to know that Willa had skipped school? Why was he suddenly responsible?

"She's in bed. Asleep." Willa's mother puckered her lips as if about to cry. "Asleep, as in unable to wake up. Like Terrence Maybeck that time. You all have a name for it, I believe? Sleeping Beauty? Something like that."

He felt like he'd been punched. "The Syndrome," Finn croaked out. "Sleeping Beauty Syndrome." It *had* to be something else—*anything* else. The flu? Food poisoning? The panic started in his legs as a painful chill and ruptured through the rest of him. *THE SYNDROME?* Did Willa's mom have any idea of what she was suggesting? For Willa to be in SBS, Philby would have had to cross her over. For Philby to cross her over, he would have at least told Finn, if not all the Keepers. Philby had not told Finn. So either Philby had turned traitor—he recalled Wayne's Kim Possible warning!—or *someone else had crossed her over*. Exactly as had happened to Charlene. Both considerations were . . . terrifying. Which only drove the cold all the deeper into his bones.

"Now, you listen to me, young man."

Finn felt himself go rigid.

"The Imagineers supposedly repaired the DHI program. They met with us—the parents—and told us that this kind of thing—this crossing over, or whatever you all call it—couldn't happen again. Wouldn't happen again. But now it has—to *my daughter*—and I want some answers." She sniffled back some tears. "I want Willa back. She's always said you were the leader. I have several options: the police, the Imagineers, the hospital. Willa made me promise that if anything like this ever happened I would come to you first. So I have. She told me that the Imagineers couldn't help Terrence, and doctors only made things worse for Dell Philby. So before I take the next step—here I am, awaiting your explanation."

Finn could barely believe what he was hearing. What if other Keepers were in the Syndrome and he didn't know about it? What if he was the only one *not* in the Syndrome? He hadn't even seen Amanda this morning at school. The cold panic owned him.

"Well, young man?"

"I . . . ah . . . The thing is . . ." What was he supposed to say? He had more questions than she had. All he wanted to do was start texting—but he had Willa's mom to contend with, and texting was illegal in school. He looked around, considering leaving her standing there and skipping out of school. He muttered, "Yes, it's true they . . . the Imagineers . . . fixed the DHI server." At least he thought they had. "But there've been some glitches in the past couple days. A week, maybe." His mouth uttered the explanations but his mind was elsewhere—Wayne's warning, the photo of the Evil Queen with Luowski and others. Did she have the kids working for her? A spell would explain Luowski's supernatural strength.

He continued, "The Imagineers—Wayne—warned Philby that stuff was happening. If you contact them—the Imagineers—they'll back that up. As for stopping it? If she's really crossed over—"

"If? Are you calling me a liar, young man?"

"Oh, come on!" Finn said, suddenly annoyed. He was half-crazed with a mind that couldn't stop thinking about a million things at once. Why wouldn't she just go away? "Listen: the same thing happened to Charlene two nights ago. We have *no idea* what's going on." That came out wrong. "We got Charlene back. We can get Willa back. But this is not *us*. Okay?"

She crossed her arms defiantly. "If you think I am going to stand idly by while my daughter is in a coma, you are *gravely mistaken*."

He'd seen his own mother this way. Unpredictable, terror-ridden. Poor Willa! he thought. Stuck in some Park, not knowing how she'd gotten there. Did the Overtakers have her? Why? What did they want?

*Just go away, would you?* he felt like shouting.

"I will cross over tonight and find her. I'll bring her back. Promise." He was promising something he couldn't necessarily deliver, and he thought they both knew it. *The police?* That had been mentioned as her first option.

He thought about Wanda being arrested, and now

it made so much sense: if the Overtakers wanted to eliminate the competition, where would they start? With Wayne. With Wayne's daughter. And then, one by one, the Keepers.

He thought about the photo—the green-eyed students with the Evil Queen.

He felt a shiver down to his toes. They *were* under attack. He'd said that to her, but only now did he fully grasp his own words. It was all-out war, and the Keepers were late to the party.

He needed to settle down, to project confidence. Instead, he felt paranoid. Terrified. Spooked. But he had to keep her from complaining to the police, or even to the Imagineers. The Syndrome was nothing to mess with—not even the Imagineers understood it the way the Keepers did.

He tried to explain: "If you go to the Imagineers, the first thing they'll do is shut down the DHI servers in each Park. That's why she told you to come to me first. If the servers are shut down she's done." *Was that what the OTs wanted?* he wondered. *To take the Keepers out of the picture by getting the entire DHI system shut down?* "She's in the Syndrome. She wanted you to come to me so that we'd go get her. Let me do that. PLEASE! It's what she wants to happen."

"Do not tell me what my daughter wants," she said,

though he could see her processing everything he'd told her. She appraised him with a searching, skeptical eye. She said, "You have one night. Understand? After that, it's the police, the Imagineers, and the doctors."

"Okay," he said. "Thank you."

"*One night*. And I'll tell you something: this is going to be the longest night of my life."

Tears ran down her cheeks. Her lips trembled. She looked so afraid.

"For what it's worth, she's gonna be okay."

The woman sobbed.

"Go to lunch," she said, in her motherly way.

*Lunch?* Finn thought. "Right," he said, knowing he would head straight to his locker and start sending texts.

* * *

Wlla=SBS Return her asap

Phones weren't allowed in class, but you could use them outside once school was dismissed. The work-around for the students was to keep their phones on vibrate in their lockers, where they would check them between classes without being seen. For the ten minutes between classes, the hallways were now less crowded. Instead of mass confusion, a hundred kids had their faces planted inside their lockers as they sent and received texts. Bullies and jocks would take plastic rulers and run down the hallway slapping bottoms, an unpleasant but tolerated punishment for the right to communicate. If a teacher approached, the phone was replaced by a textbook, and the locker was closed. It was almost impossible for them to bust a kid.

When Philby read Finn's text, he believed it a mistake, or worse, a prank sent by one of the green-eyes. He'd double checked the number: it was Finn.

Willa couldn't be stuck in the Syndrome because, like Charlene, he'd never crossed her over. More to the point: he'd been monitoring the server's bandwidth. He had an alarm set. There had been no alarm last night—therefore, Willa had not crossed into the Parks as her hologram. But then he remembered finding Elvis asleep on his laptop. Late for the bus, he'd pushed Elvis off and had shut the laptop's lid, scooped it off his desk, and stuffed it into his backpack without a second thought.

He felt sick to his stomach. When he'd reopened the laptop at school had the DHI monitoring program been open? He couldn't remember. He was the last line of defense against the Overtakers. Had he messed up? Had he failed Willa, of all people?

He raced down the hall to Hugo's locker, his head ready to explode. *Willa?*

"I've gotta borrow your laptop," he said. He wasn't asking.

"No, you don't," Hugo said. "I need it for science." Hugo didn't even look like Hugo. Something was different about him. But everything looked different: The school hallway seemed about two feet wide. Philby's world was all backward.

"I'll trade you. You can use mine," he offered. "You have a data card. I don't. I need Internet access. I can't be on the school server. Please!"

"What's up?"

"Keepers stuff."

"Such as?"

"Later. I gotta do this now. I've got a class. Please." Hugo exchanged laptops.

Philby hurried into the boys' room, locked himself in a stall, and set up Hugo's computer on his lap while sitting on a toilet seat. He used Hugo's wireless data card to connect to the Internet, entered the URL for the back door into the DHI server, and typed his log-in password.

He navigated to the page where he could manually cause a Return—the same set of instructions that were used for the fob when inside the Parks—and typed from memory Willa's twenty-six-character ID string.

The window flashed. He'd lost the handshake.

He double-checked the data card connection—all was good—and reentered the URL, ready to start over. He reached the log-on page and reentered his password.

INCORRECT PASSWORD: ACCESS DENIED

Believing he must have typed too fast, he tried again.

INCORRECT PASSWORD: ACCESS DENIED

Now he had real problems: a third failure in a row would mean he'd be blocked from trying to enter a password for twenty-four hours. Willa didn't have twenty-four hours. Wondering if it might be a problem with Hugo's data card, Philby decided that the only thing to do was to get to the DHI server in person and make an attempt at the password from there.

He texted Finn:

major problems. password not workin. call emergency meeting

The rest of the school day dragged on impossibly slowly. Several times Philby debated skipping, but he'd never done that in his life and he had no desire to be caught and grounded for eternity. That would make matters even worse for everyone. Especially him. He traded back computers with Hugo before seventh period, thanking him.

He and Finn, Maybeck, and Charlene met at the Marble Slab ice cream shop. Charlene told them about the confrontation with Sally Ringwald. She'd been too hyper to catch every last word, but she gave them all she could remember. "Amanda will have the full four-one-one," she said, "but what's important is that Sally is definitely under some kind of spell, there's lots more where she came from, and something big is going down on Saturday. For what it's worth."

"We've got to move on," an anxious Philby said. "Willa . . ." It came out as a moan. "The point is, the server password's not taking," he explained. "Basically, I'm going to be locked out of the server if I try it remotely again, so I've got to make it count."

"Why wouldn't your password take?" Maybeck asked.

He was met with three blank faces—one of them with strawberry ice cream on both corners of her lips.

"If it's the Imagineers' security kicking in," Philby said, "it's not so bad—maybe someone would help us. But somehow I doubt it with everything that's been happening. I've been thinking about it all day. I lost the connection after I first logged on. I thought it was the data card—you know, like a cell phone dropping out. Happens all the time. But it's possible . . . maybe not probable, but possible . . . that my keystrokes were captured. It's possible that the system was reset right after I'd logged on in order to break my connection. By the time I was back on, my password had been removed, my back door closed."

"The OTs," Charlene said.

"Yeah. They could have been waiting for me."

Finn quoted the Kim Possible mission: "'Everyone needs a server now and then.' You think Wayne was trying to tell us the OTs had hacked the server?"

"They didn't like that you came and got me," Charlene said. "They aren't about to allow that to happen again."

"So they ambushed us," Maybeck said.

"Without access, without control of the server, we can't cross over," Philby said. "The only way we can help Willa is to Return her. We've got two choices: we can either hack back into the server, or we can go into the Parks, try to find her, and then use the fob to Return her."

"Good luck," Maybeck said. "We don't know which Park. We don't know where she is in whatever Park she's in. That could take years."

Maybeck's DHI had been locked up in a maintenance cage inside Space Mountain. He might never have been found there.

"If I hack the server, we'll know which Park she's in," Philby reminded. "The activity log will tell us."

"But," Finn said, "in order to see the activity log we—*you*—have to hack the server. So we have to get to the server as us. Not DHIs. Right? I mean, we can't cross over because we've lost access to the server, which is the whole point."

"Right," Philby confirmed. "We go in as us. Hopefully, I get us back online. After that we can cross over, if that's what we have to do."

Maybeck cursed and pushed away from the table, disgusted. "This rots," he said. "We've got to get her back. What are we waiting for? We can use our employee passes. We get Philbo into the server room and let him do his thing. If the Return doesn't work from there, we go into whatever Park and we get her back. I've been there—in the Syndrome. So have you, Philbo. It sucks. We've got to do this."

Wayne had supplied them with employee cards that allowed them to enter the Parks as Cast Members. They rarely used them, keeping them for this kind of emergency.

"My mother expects me home," Charlene said. "I

have an orthodontist appointment this afternoon. I could sneak out later, but if I miss that appointment she might start calling your parents."

"Jelly will cover for us," Maybeck said. "She knows what it's like to have a kid stuck in the Syndrome. Trust me, she wouldn't wish that on anyone. You can all tell your 'rents you're coming to my place to study for an exam."

"We aren't in exams," Philby pointed out.

"Yeah, okay. I got you. But you think your parents know that?" Maybeck said.

* * *

Ariel had come and gone, but basically stayed through the night with Willa on the water tower. With the sunrise she moved Willa through water pipes to what she called "the grotto." As a DHI, Willa was stuck in her pajamas, which was going to make it a problem to blend in. She spent the day in hiding, hatching a plan.

If she were going to Return, she needed the all-important fob. But the fob was currently hidden in Epcot, and she'd been sent into the Studios. Between the two Parks was a sea of DHI shadow—an area that lacked DHI projectors. This would be to her advantage: DHI shadow meant she'd be invisible for most of the path that connected Epcot to the Studios. As long as she could get out of the Studios without being spotted, this was doable. She'd get over to Epcot, find the fob, and Return. The nightmare would be over.

"I can do this," Willa told herself. She'd leave the Studios at sunset when the light was soft and her DHI qualities more difficult to spot. The occasional sparkle. The blue outline.

Home. Her bed. Her mom. Almost too good to be true. She couldn't wait.

The Parks experienced a big turnover around dinnertime: kids got tired; adults got hungry. Epcot was an evening favorite—terrific food and a spectacular fireworks display. Entering Epcot would not be easy: she had no pass or ticket, no money, and worse, she was a hologram wearing pajamas.

"I'm leaving," she told Ariel. "I'm going to try to get out of the gates without being seen."

"I can help you."

"You've done so much for me already. I'll be fine."

"I can pose for photographs and autographs, provide a distraction. A diversion, I think Eric calls it."

It was the first time she'd mentioned Eric.

"So he's . . . real? I mean, as far as characters go."

"Eric?" Ariel blushed. "Oh, he's very real. As real as real can be. But they keep him in the Magic Kingdom.

He's part of the stage show there. In front of the castle. We rarely see each other."

Willa wondered if there was another Ariel in the Magic Kingdom, or if that one was only a Cast Member. Wondered if Eric had all the mermaid company he wanted, while she sat here pining for him.

"A diversion might help."

"Consider it done."

"Don't you need a handler to make an appearance? Someone who takes care of you?" Willa asked.

"The handlers come and go, dear girl. Who's the one who's been doing this all these years? I think I can manage."

"But won't you get in trouble?"

"That's the idea, isn't it? The more trouble, the better the diversion."

"I can't let you do that for me."

"Actually, you can't stop me," said Ariel. She was beaming. "I haven't had this kind of fun in . . . well . . . probably longer than you've been alive."

Willa looked at her—Ariel was maybe sixteen or seventeen. "You never get any older." She hadn't thought of what it was like to be a character, not a Cast Member. The characters didn't change, while the Imagineers, handlers, and staff came and went. Year after year, it was the same shows, the same posing for photos and signing autographs. It had to drive the characters half-crazy. No wonder the Overtakers were rebelling.

Ariel hung her head, clearly saddened by the reminder.

"No," Ariel said. As she looked up, a coy grin played across her face. "Not older, but I do get wiser."

* * *

Ariel's appearance at the front gate did the trick. Excited guests encircled her, winning the attention of Security guards. Willa joined the mass of departing Park visitors and left the Park unnoticed.

Soon she was walking in the direction of Epcot. Most everyone else rode the monorail or the buses. Only she and a few others walked. When Willa noticed her hand and arm sparkling, she stopped to let others pass. She had reached the edge of the DHI projection coverage. A few more yards and pieces of her image would decay, leaving holes in her, or missing limbs. She would be human Swiss cheese, and would likely have guests either lining up for autographs, or calling 911.

So she moved up into the flowers and shrubs that hid a cyclone fence. Remaining amid the plants, she continued on, paralleling the sidewalk. Her elbow and part of her shoulder disappeared. Her left leg, from the knee down, vanished. For a moment, she was a set of headless pajamas. Finally, she vanished completely.

DHI shadow was a weird state: she could hear, though not touch. She could see, though narrowly, as if though a camera lens. Whatever this state was technically, it wasn't perfect. Once while in DHI shadow she and the others had been able to pick up sand from the floor of a tepee. There seemed to be exceptions to the physical laws of nature. Philby explained these as having to do with the survival instinct, comparing them to a mother picking up and moving a car that pinned her child, or a father heaving a slab of concrete aside as if it were Styrofoam.

Back on the sidewalk now, in full DHI shadow, Willa picked up the pace, walking faster. She approached a family coming at her and moved into the grass to avoid them.

One of the two young kids, a girl no older than eight, let out a yip.

"Ghosts, Mommy! Ghosts! I heard a ghost!"

"Oh, shush, Ginny," the woman said. To her husband she complained, "I told you that ride would scare them!"

He mumbled something as they continued on.

A chill passed through her. How many times as a child had she felt a ghost in the room? How many times, when taking the trash out at night, had she felt someone watching through the dark? For how long had DHIs been around? she wondered.

Her hologram began reappearing as she neared the BoardWalk. Her image sparkled and sputtered. Some kids pointed at her, making fun of her pajamas. A couple of girls recognized her as a Disney Host Interactive from the Magic Kingdom. They approached her for her autograph. Willa explained DHIs couldn't sign autographs, and allowed the girls to wave their arms through her.

Free of fear and still in her DHI state, she strayed off course a few minutes later and walked through a fence, joining a roadway behind the Eiffel Tower.

It was only a matter of reaching the fob now. Dusk had settled. It would soon be dark. She was perhaps a quarter mile from the fountain plaza. From the Return. From home.

She set off in that direction in determined strides.

W<small>ITH ONLY AN HOUR TO GO</small> before the Magic
Kingdom closed for the night, Finn, Philby, and
Maybeck used the employee passes to enter, which
didn't register on the computer system and allowed
them to avoid the front gates. Operations Management
prohibited them from entering any of the Parks as
themselves without prior approval, and now they risked
being spotted. For camouflage, all three wore as close
to the same clothes as their projected DHIs wore. This
way, they'd be mistaken as their own Disney Hosts. But
they weren't perfectly identical costumes: Maybeck had,
for some reason, chosen a pair of dark socks; Finn no
longer owned the running shoes he'd worn when modeling for his DHI so he was wearing the black ones he'd
colored with a Sharpie.

They walked slowly, side by side, behind the buildings on Main Street in the direction of Cinderella
Castle. They appeared relaxed and self-confident, never
a problem for Maybeck.

As they happened past other Cast Members they
heard comments trailing behind them like, "Can you

believe how real those things look?" The three fought to keep smiles off their faces.

The Magic Kingdom had been built atop a series of interconnecting tunnels called the Utilidor. Through these tunnels passed Cast Members and electric golf carts that served as small trucks. Control of the Park's technology was handled from offices in the Utilidor, which included a massive computer server room, the brains of the Park. This was the Keepers' destination.

Multiple backstage Cast-Member-only entrances to the Utilidor existed throughout the Park. As the three approached the entrance just behind the Main Street ice cream parlor, Maybeck blocked Finn and Philby, pushing them back against the wall.

"Pirates!"

Finn and Philby spotted them: a pair of pirates casually talking in front of a double doorway up ahead.

"That's the door to the Utilidor," Professor Philby said.

"Overtakers?" Finn said.

"Must be," Maybeck agreed. "They're guarding the entrance, just in case we come along to spoil all their fun."

"We could try the entrance by Splash Mountain," Finn suggested.

"We'd have to cross the entire Park to get there,"

Philby said. "And if these guys are guarding this one, others are probably guarding that one, too."

"We need another way in," Maybeck said.

"How do you guys feel about getting filthy dirty?" Finn asked.

He led them through the crowded parking lot, staying as far away from the pirates as possible. As they neared a full-length mirror at the Cast Member entrance into the Park, a foul smell overpowered them. A message on the mirror read *Make it a magical day for our guests!*

\* \* \*

"What the . . . ?" Maybeck said. "Stink . . . eee!"

"Shh! Keep your voice down," said Finn. But the constant roar to their right covered their voices. He led them toward that noise: an area just before Cast Members entered the Park, tucked behind a plywood screen with empty cardboard boxes piled in a corner and a large pipe, three feet in diameter, sticking out of the concrete.

"Brilliant!" said Philby as he realized where they were.

Maybeck focused on the pipe. It had a weighted lid and was surrounded by warning signs. "No way," he said. "You are not getting me down there."

"That'll work," said Finn. "We need you to stand guard. We all have our phones."

"I wouldn't count on ours working down there," Philby cautioned.

"Macbeth," Finn said, trying to get back at Maybeck for all the nicknames he called him, "will stay up here to keep an eye on the pirates. You'll text us if you see any change in them, because it may mean trouble for us. Philby and I will try to get to the server room."

Maybeck said, "So I text if I see something awkward up here. Is that all?"

"No," said Philby. "You see this red stop button?"

"Kind of hard to miss," Maybeck said. The plastic emergency button was huge.

"If you hear the system restart, then you hit that button."

Finn added, "We'd rather not get sucked through the system and spit out into the compactor. It's up to you to see that doesn't happen."

"Could be bad for our health," said Philby. "As in, *fatal*. The wind generated to suck the trash out of the Park reaches sixty miles an hour in the pipe. That's almost hurricane speed."

"Got it," said Maybeck. "Hit the red button. Kill the wind."

"Seriously," Philby said.

"Red button. Easy enough."

"Okay then," Finn said to Philby. "Ready?"

"As I'll ever be," said Philby.

Finn punched the red button. The roar ground to a stop.

Philby lifted the heavy lid and the smell intensified.

"Glad it's you guys going down there and not me," Maybeck said, pinching his nose.

"We won't have long," Philby warned. "Engineering Base over in the Studios will see a warning that the system's down. They'll try a restart before anything else."

"So . . . I'll go first." Finn's only other time in the trash system had been a long time ago. Maleficent had been chasing him. He'd been terrified.

He climbed over the sticky edge into the steel pipe, while Philby and Maybeck held open the lid. Maybeck's face was puckered in disgust as the putrid odors of rotting trash wafted up.

Finn let go and dropped. He fell a few feet, landing in some wet slop at the bottom of a similar-size steel pipe that ran parallel with the surface. A tunnel within the tunnel.

"Out of the way!" Philby said.

The pipe was too small to crouch and stay on two

feet. Finn was forced to drop to hands and knees amid the sticky, disgusting goo of old garbage.

He called back coarsely, "You might want to get your flashlight out *before* you put your hands in this stuff."

Philby dropped in behind him, flashlight on. Finn's shadow spread before him amid the garbage and debris that adhered to every inch of the pipe—wrappers, crushed cups and cans, chewing gum, rubber bands, grotesque rotting remnants of former meals, banana peels, turkey leg bones, and every kind of plastic container ever made, most of them unrecognizable. The smell only grew worse the farther they crawled. Finn held his breath for as long as possible, but an inhale was inevitable, and when it came, it tasted like he was eating trash.

"I think I'm going to puke," Philby said from behind him.

"Go ahead. It might improve the smell."

"By now Base has tried to reset. That'll take a couple of minutes to be in effect. When Maybeck pulls a second emergency stop they'll send a team to investigate. We need to be out of here by then. This thing is basically a wind tunnel."

Philby could recite the statistics, but Finn had experienced the trash pipe. What Philby didn't seem to grasp was the power of that suction. If the trash bags were moving at sixty miles an hour, the two of them would be also. Some things were better left unsaid. He picked up the pace, though it wasn't exactly fast going. The slime coating the tube was the consistency of tar. His knees and the palms of his hands stuck to it like a fly to flypaper. Each movement made a sucking and slurping noise.

"Hurry it up!" Philby said.

"I'm trying."

"It smells like my father's beef-jerky farts."

"TMI."

Finn paused at the first intersection—a pipe ran off to the left. Professor Philby had to take a closer look himself. He shined the flashlight at the walls of the connecting pipe.

"Hair," he said, pointing out clumps of what looked like steel wool stuck to the surface. "The beauty parlor is close by. The server room is up ahead at the next intersection. It should be a recycling station."

Finn was going to ask why a recycling station would be connected to a trash system, but he knew better than to challenge Philby. For one thing, Philby's explanations could run on the long side. Finn slogged ahead, so disgusted with the ooze that he began walking on his elbows rather than sinking his hands into it.

"We're too slow. We're taking too long," Philby warned. And just like that, a *clunk* was heard, like a grumbling in the belly of a beast. The system was restarting.

"Okay, that's what we expected." Philby tried to sound calm. His hair stuck to the goo on the walls. "Now, all that needs to happen is for Maybeck to trip the emergency stop again."

Finn considered trying to send a text, but looked at the layer of tarlike goo on his hands—something they hadn't considered. Nonetheless, he reached into his pocket for his phone as the wind lifted the hair off his head.

Zero bars: no service.

"Oh, perfect," he said.

* * *

Maybeck understood his assignment: keep an eye on the two pirates; stop the system if it restarted. Piece of cake. What Philby had only vaguely mentioned was that on-site engineers might seek immediate answers to their trash system shutting down. Despite the casual, playful, magical impression the Parks had on visitors, in truth they were run more like a NASA mission. There were teams of experts to tackle and instantly solve any kind of problem—from the lettuce in a restaurant going brown, to the intricacies of staging the three o'clock parade each day; the evening fireworks; the street bands; the stage shows. There were enough maintenance employees to form a small army. Two of these men were radio-dispatched by Engineering Base to investigate an emergency stop at URS-3—Utilidor Refuse Station #3.

Luckily, Maybeck heard them coming before they saw him. They were complaining to each other about what kind of knucklehead would pull an emergency stop on the trash system. They were just on the other side of the trash area's plywood barrier as he heard them. He turned, dropped to his hands and knees, and burrowed deeply into the pile of cardboard recycling.

He stared out from his hiding place as the two maintenance guys inspected the door that sealed the trash drop, as well as the electronic box that housed the red emergency stop override.

"I don't see nothing wrong," said the shorter of the two. He was thick-boned and heavyset and had a voice like a dog growling.

Philby had said the system would be restarted the first time remotely from Engineering Base. He'd been wrong—a rarity.

"Nah," said the other, a taller, leaner man. "Some wise guy's idea of a practical joke."

The short guy grabbed his radio. "Good to go URS-three. Repeat: green light for URS-three restart."

"Roger, that," came a woman's voice over the radio.

A moment later, Maybeck felt a *thunk* underfoot.

The system had restarted.

\* \* \*

Willa, her DHI riddled with static, moved carefully through the backstage area behind France, taking care to screen herself behind trailers, vehicles, and pieces of staging. Hypersensitive about how she stood out wearing pajamas, she wanted to avoid being seen as much as possible. If kids recognized her, she'd be mobbed and she'd have to role-play as a Disney Host. Another Willa guide—dressed in lederhosen—was currently somewhere in Epcot, which could explain her own current projection problems. Willa's own hologram would likely improve once Epcot was closed and the regular DHIs were turned off for the night, but she didn't want to wait. She had a few hundred yards to cover in order to reach the pin-trading station by the fountain. The Return. The most direct route was to join the sea of Park visitors, but the idea terrified her.

She knew that if she looked scared and out of place,

she would appear vulnerable: If she looked confident and comfortable, despite the pajamas, she would fit right in. After all, newlyweds went around the Parks in mouse ears and bridal veils. On a scale of 1 to 10, pajamas barely registered.

She briefly hid behind a Food and Wine Festival station, gathering her courage. Then she stepped out and confidently joined the hordes. She was in a courtyard in France, the lake straight ahead. There were shops to her right and a French bakery. Benches to her left. Trees and raised islands of flowers in the center of the oblong, cobblestoned plaza. Music filled the air—pieces of the sound track to *The Hunchback of Notre Dame*. It had an inviting and calming effect. The music surrounded her and made her feel at peace. She loved the Parks when they were open and filled with families and brimming with happiness. Her toes and fingers tingled. Her blue line grew solid—she was pure DHI.

In her euphoria, she failed to look where she was going, and walked right through a raised flower bed, coming out the other side. Some kids recognized her immediately and approached, crowding her, asking for photographs and autographs. She had to agree or risk making an even bigger scene as visitors complained. She posed for some photographs, explained politely that as a hologram she couldn't sign autographs, and hoped to get away. Camera flashes blinded her. Kids bubbled with enthusiasm.

"Over here!" a mother called out.

Willa looked in that direction—toward the bakery. Above the woman's shoulder she saw a court jester in a green felt costume and clown makeup. The jester stared at her, but not in admiration. More like a policeman watching a suspect.

As she heard the organized sounds of synchronized marching approach, she knew she was in trouble. Epcot was not a place for goose-stepping soldiers. Twelve costumed cathedral guards appeared from around the corner. Judge Frollo's guards, she thought. *Overtakers*. They marched straight for her.

"Excuse me," she said to a group of kids, "but I have to go. I hear those guards will give you candy if you hold onto them and don't let go."

The kids squealed and took off, shouting at the guards.

Willa walked quickly toward the bridge leading to the United Kingdom. The rhythmic footfalls stopped as the kids assaulted the guards. Again, she heard her name ripple through the crowd as more people identified her. Things were going badly. What had seemed like such a short distance now felt like miles. Spaceship Earth looked so tiny and distant all of a sudden.

Behind her, a French-accented guard called out, "Clear the way! Clear the path!" Apparently, not all of the guards had been sidelined by the kids.

Disney visitors were too polite: they cleared a path behind her.

Willa glanced back; the guards were gaining ground.

The crowd ahead now grew thicker as the walkway narrowed. She dodged her way through pedestrians, but wasn't increasing her lead. Behind her, Frollo's guards continued their relentless pursuit.

Only as she lost her balance and bumped into a baby carriage did she realize the value of her being a DHI. A moment earlier she'd walked through the flower island; she needed to get to *all clear*.

She allowed the music to own her, let it carry her away to where she'd been only moments before; music was the elixir for her; music was her cure. The tingling of her fingers signaled her transformation, and she broke into a sprint, running *through* anything in front of her—people, strollers, it didn't matter. With her approach, startled guests jumped back, only to have her run right through them. Kids cheered. Adults shouted startled complaints.

But she left the guards behind. No matter how they tried, they weren't going to catch her. Twice more, she settled and focused on the music. Twice more, she went *all clear.*

Willa passed the Canadian pavilion, still a long way from the Return, but gaining with each step. Her confidence increased: she was going to make it.

The fountain and plaza came into view. Almost there! But then, appearing from around the fountain, a half-dozen Segways—not CTDs, but Park Security.

Her hologram's blue outline had faded slightly. She couldn't allow them to scare her, couldn't allow her DHI to weaken—to become even fractionally mortal. The path split just ahead: directly in front of her, the fountain; to the left, a pathway leading behind Innoventions West, with access to The Land and The Seas. She took this alternate route, hidden from the Security team.

From behind her came the steady *tromp, tromp, tromp* of the cathedral guards.

She reminded herself that she only needed to reach the Return. Willa cleared her thoughts and watched her blue outline grow more solid. If she could trust her DHI she could charge the pin-trading station, grab the Return, and send herself back. So close now.

She followed the path to the right, the pin-trading station straight ahead.

"You there!" a man shouted.

Arriving to the fob's hiding place, she jumped to reach into the intersection of support pipes.

*Empty!*

She tried the next steel support, realizing she must have the wrong post.

*Empty!*

"YOU!" another man's deep voice shouted. "STOP!"

She tried a third column. *Nothing!* The next.

The Segways rolled toward her.

The cathedral guards closed in from behind.

Her mind reeled. Where was the Return? Where had Philby and Finn put it? How was she supposed to get back without it?

She couldn't stay there bumming over it. She needed to hide. She needed . . .

Spaceship Earth. Its geodesic construction rose 180 feet into the night sky. Maybe inside the dome she'd find a place to hide, or maybe she'd turn out to be in DHI shadow?

She turned and ran, the men behind her calling after her to stop.

*Not likely.*

* * *

Philby looked back into the strong wind. A Park map landed on his face and wrapped around him like a veil.

Litter splattered him. As the wind tunnel restarted, the lightest items were lifted first, followed by increasingly heavier ones. Ducking the larger pieces of airborne trash was like something from a video game. Finn and Philby didn't dare turn their backs on the onslaught for fear of missing something really big and dangerous. So they faced into it, crawling backward as quickly as their knees and hands would carry them.

"Incoming," Philby announced. He flattened himself as a constellation of aluminum cans came down the pipe.

One struck Finn on the shoulder. "Oww!"

"Don't let one bean you," Philby warned. "It could probably knock you out."

Neither boy was amused. Now came plastic knives, forks, and spoons. Paper plates, more cans. The half-eaten turkey bones came at them like spears and arrows. Fruit and vegetable waste and all matter of wet stuff. Finally, they couldn't take it. They had no choice but to turn their backs to the steady stream for fear of having their eyes poked out.

The force of air grew stronger, ruffling their clothing and hair. The amount of loose garbage was overwhelming. It smashed into them, sticking to their clothing and bare skin. Finn slapped away a plastic fork that adhered to his ear. A sticky rain pelted them—ketchup, soda, cold coffee, and soup.

"Hurry!" Philby shouted, as a tumbling sound arose from down the pipe.

The first of the garbage bags. It sounded like it was rolling at the moment, but soon it would be lifted and carried by wind; soon it would be a missile headed for them.

"That's it!" Philby announced, shining his flashlight ahead of them, highlighting an intersection of pipe.

A bag crashed into Philby, careened off the pipe wall, and knocked Finn sideways, flattening both boys. They clambered to their hands and knees only to be bowled over by the next. And another after that.

Any chance of Finn going *all clear* was out. The situation was terrifying.

The bags felt like rocks when they hit. Each time Finn managed to get his legs and arms under him, another bag knocked him over. The pipe intersection just ahead seemed no closer.

"Where's Maybeck?" Finn called out. "We need Maybeck!"

* * *

Maybeck couldn't believe that the two Engineering guys would just stand there, hanging out by the trash dump. He could feel the rumble under his feet, knew the system was engaged. He could picture Finn and Philby like soda bubbles in a straw getting sucked toward the trash compactor.

He watched as the shorter guy grabbed his radio. "Awaiting instructions," he said.

"Roger that," came back a voice, thinly. "We're waiting on Base."

"Copy."

The two guys were obviously in no hurry—were used to waiting.

Maybeck eyed the red emergency STOP button, wondering what to do.

* * *

Willa ran up the long ramp leading into Spaceship Earth, out of breath. The Segways, ridden by Security guards, were only yards behind her. She slid like a baseball player under the chains blocking the entrance, scrambled to her feet, and took off running again. Behind her, the Security guards had to dismount the Segways, costing them precious seconds.

Behind them, the phalanx of Frollo's cathedral guards followed up the ramp. The Security men turned to face the marching unit.

"Stop!" one of them hollered, raising his out-stretched palm. He'd never been in this situation before.

*Marching guards?* He had no idea what to do. "This attraction is closed. The Park is closing for the night. Report back to Operations Management."

The guards stood there in formation, their eyes straight ahead like true soldiers. Not one of them said a thing.

"Did you hear me?" the Security guy said. "Fun's over."

The lead guard signaled his group forward. They marched toward the Security man.

"What the heck?" the Security man complained.

Willa hurried through the dark, crestfallen to look down and see her own feet. Spaceship Earth was not in DHI shadow.

The ride was running, though its seats were empty. The Park was closing down for the night. She climbed aboard the first car that passed.

First things first: she would hide until she came up with a plan. At their meeting they'd discussed why Charlene had been crossed over into the Park. Philby had thought it was to debrief her as a spy. But now a second, more insidious motive presented itself: by putting Charlene into Epcot and knowing she would try to escape, the OTs could follow her to the Return and steal it. Without the Return, and without Philby's back door on the server, any Keeper who crossed over would have no way back. Crossing them over one at a time made so much sense: when working as a team the Keepers had never failed, but as individuals they were far more vulnerable. They would be stuck in the Syndrome. Locked in a coma in their beds at home.

Not just overnight.

But forever.

* * *

The flashlight fell out of Philby's hand as the next bag of trash struck him down. In the swirling light, Finn watched a bulging trash bag approach at the speed of cannon fire. He ducked, and it flew overhead. The flashlight rolled at his feet. Finn lunged for it, but missed. Affronted by a windstorm of sloppy trash and deadly bags, he inched toward the intersection of pipes.

"Philby?!" he cried.

The wind in the tunnel was at full speed—hurricane force. Finn was sliding backward, clawing at the goop, trying not to lose track of Philby. Suddenly, a hand appeared. Finn grabbed it. He felt himself braked as he and Philby joined hands—Philby had caught on to the edge of the intersection. Together they strained to hold on, Finn repeatedly struck by flying trash bags. Then the wind all but stopped. He and Philby were in the adjoining pipe.

Light shone through a circular crack a few yards ahead.

Philby saw it, too. "That's the way out! The system has supplementary pressurization stations," Professor Philby explained. "There are dozens of extra fans along the route. All connecting pipes must be airtight."

"Maybe another time," Finn said.

Philby led Finn to the end of the short section of pipe. Together they managed to unlock and push open a maintenance door against the drag of the wind. Philby used a plastic bottle to jam the bottom of the door open. Finn climbed out first, down a metal ladder. Philby followed. They were behind heavy equipment, a cardboard compactor, in an alcove off the Utilidor.

The boys were disgusting—covered in a layer of stinking brown sludge from head to toe. "We cannot just walk out there like this," Finn said. "How are we ever going to pull this off?"

Philby's eyes ticked back and forth—the professor at work. He poked his head through a network of smaller pipes. "Got something," he said, crawling through. He returned a moment later with a small, greasy hand towel. They took turns cleaning each other's face.

"We're still a mess," Finn said, indicating his clothes. "I'm like a human booger."

"This is a cardboard recycling station."

"Yeah? So?"

"It's closing time. Everyone wants to get home. You think anyone's going to look twice at a couple of kids coming down the hall wearing cardboard boxes?"

"I like it!"

The boys snuck around to the side where dozens of collapsed cardboard boxes leaned against the wall. Philby sized up two of them, and the boys reassembled them, overlapping the flaps to make them square and sturdy again. Philby then tore sections out of the flaps: one for Finn's neck, and one for each of his legs on the opposite end of the big box. It was marked DORITOS. Philby's was SUN CHIPS. They got past the machinery, and Philby quickly helped Finn into his box so that it hung on his shoulders and ended just above his knees, making walking awkward. Philby climbed into his box, but had trouble getting the bottom flaps closed. Finn tried squatting but it did no good—he was just a big cardboard box. Finally, Philby gave up. His box hung from his shoulders with his head sticking out, but the bottom flaps hung down, moving with his every step.

With Finn walking awkwardly in the lead, the two boys moved out into the thirty-foot-wide Utilidor tunnel joining dozens of Cast Members. Philby had been right: no one gave a pair of moving boxes a second thought.

Twenty yards later, they reached a set of windows on their left. Venetian blinds drawn from the inside. They walked past.

"The server room," Philby hissed from behind.

Finn didn't need to be reminded. He'd been here more than once. The last time, a certain green-skinned fairy had been here as well.

Philby tried to get his eye to the window at the edge of the blind so he could see through, but the box was too big and it blocked him from leaning in close. He turned to the side, but again the box blocked him from seeing in.

Suddenly, the door swung open. Finn spun around and said to Philby, "Here, I'll fix it for you." He spun Philby and his box around, mainly to hide their faces.

Three Cast Members came out of the server room, saying good-night to each other. Two of them wished the other a good vacation, and the man thanked them. Finn turned back as the door was shutting. He got a look into the room, seeing no one. But then, reflected off the door's safety glass, he caught sight of a man at a desk.

"There's still at least one guy in there. At a desk over on the far side of the room."

"Well, we can't just stand around here. We've got to do something."

Finn said, "The smells coming out of this box are going to make me puke. We'd better keep moving."

The boys continued on toward an exit where people dressed in street clothes were leaving. Golf carts laden with everything from bottled water to Pirates of the Caribbean muskets streamed past. The Magic Kingdom was shifting into maintenance mode. Stores and restaurants would be restocked. There would be painting and carpentry, cleaning, and polishing carried out within the Park for the next several hours. The boys had to reach the server, gain access, determine which Park Willa was in, and launch a rescue attempt. Every second counted.

Behind them, the server room door opened and two men came out. The second one checked to make sure the door was locked, and the two said good-night.

"Can you manage *all clear*?" Philby asked.

"Maybe for a few seconds."

"Unlock the door and let me in."

Finn nodded. They stood in front of the door. Willa needed him, Finn reminded himself. He closed his eyes and pictured the train coming. When he opened them again, the blue line shimmered around his filthy sleeve. He stepped through the box and the closed door into the server room. The lights were off. No one was there. Good.

Ten seconds later, he watched the blue line fade

until it was gone. He reached out and unlocked the door for Philby.

A few minutes later, two cardboard boxes were discovered by a cleaning crew outside the server room. The cleaners picked up the boxes and carried them to recycling, while on the other side of the wall two nervous boys waited for them to pass.

"We're in," Philby said.

\* \* \*

Jess sat upright in bed. While dozing over homework, she'd had the kissing dream again. The same steps in the background. She shuddered, feeling guilty and somewhat creepy. Finn was a good enough guy, but she didn't think about him like that. She felt a little sick to her stomach. No matter how this went down, it couldn't be good for anyone.

Her reaction was automatic and immediate. Once again she reached under her pillow and came out with her diary. She switched on her book light and flipped through the pages to the earlier sketch. There were details about the stairs to add: they stepped down left to right and—here was the weird part—weren't equal in size. Bad perspective, she thought, or out of scale. She sketched in some planting that looked familiar to her, though she couldn't place it. She added some texture to Finn's face; he looked incredibly lifelike. Filled in his shirt with stripes. Modified the tailored shirt she was wearing in the sketch, only to realize it was a shirt she didn't like very much. She lent it to Amanda more often than she wore it herself.

Well, there's a solution, she thought. If she avoided wearing that particular shirt, then she wouldn't be wearing it in the future. If she didn't wear it in the future, then she wouldn't kiss Finn.

Relief flooded through her. So simple. It all came down to avoiding that shirt.

\* \* \*

"Here's something to think about," Philby said, standing alongside Finn, facing row after row of library-like shelving that held stacked computer servers, Ethernet routers, modems, power supplies, and wireless boxes, all blinking a constellation of colorful lights. "If the OTs are messing with this stuff, this is the time they mess with it: after the Park closes. We may not be alone here for long."

"Way to cheer me up. Thanks," said Finn.

Philby reached the DHI server, the electronic brains responsible for both generating their images and communicating those images to an array of Park projectors within the Magic Kingdom. It also tied to other DHI servers through fiber optic lines, in the Animal Kingdom, Epcot, and Disney's Hollywood Studios.

Philby pulled out the tray holding the server's keyboard and entered his back-door password. The system rejected the password.

"I thought it was a data transmission problem," he said, half talking to himself. "There's no attempt limit from the hardwired keyboard, only with remote access. I thought if tried my password from here I'd get in. But that's not working. What I know for sure is that if I tried remotely and failed three times in a row, remote access would be denied for twenty-four hours. An alarm would be sent up-line. Engineering Base over in the Studios would see the hack attempt and probably notify Security. I've got one more remote try, but I know it's not going to work. It's the OTs. They were waiting for me."

"You don't actually know that."

"You think it was the Imagineers? Wayne sends me a warning, then locks me out of the server? I don't think so."

"So what about Willa?"

Philby just stared at the screen, fuming. "The fob should still work for a Return—it's sent wirelessly over the cell-phone frequency, a whole different subsystem than a manual Return. But it's not going to be easy finding her."

"You gotta get us into this machine."

"Tell me about it. Okay. Give me a minute." He laced his fingers over his head and closed his eyes.

"I can help out," Finn offered.

Philby sat very still for several minutes. Finn grew increasingly impatient but said nothing.

"Okay," Philby said, standing and moving down the aisle. "Let's assume the OTs phished for my password, stole it, and then erased it. That would explain resetting the server and my losing the data connection. That would mean they can now access the server remotely, same way as I did. But," he said pulling, out his phone, "if I try to access it one more time remotely and I fail, *any* remote access will be blocked for twenty-four hours, including theirs. That'll leave the only access from here—this keyboard. But the OTs are not the only ones who can access this server."

"The Imagineers," Finn said. "Engineering."

"Yes. SOP," he said, meaning standard operating procedure, "for an attempted raid on a server would be to send Security first and someone from Base, second. The Security guy makes sure the room's clear. The guy from Base checks the server, runs virus-scanning software, studies and prints the log."

"So?" Finn said.

Philby was already unplugging and collecting wires from the backs of other computer servers. Finn followed along like a lost dog.

"So we need the guy from Base to access the server," Philby continued.

"I think we established that."

"He has to *enter a password*," Philby said. "The system's *master password* is the only thing that can override a lockout. Look for a camera."

"What?"

"A webcam. Usually little round balls about the size of a golf ball."

"I know what a webcam looks like," said Finn.

"So find one."

"Where?"

"This is a giant room devoted to computers, and only computers. Somewhere in here are Security webcams as well as personal webcams. Just find one!"

"You're telling me Security can see us?"

"Probably. Could be. But there are hundreds, probably thousands of cameras around the Parks. They're not going to focus on here unless we give them reason to. *Until* we give them reason to. That's why I haven't tried the password for the third time. First, we need a camera."

The boys split up to search.

"Is that one in the ceiling?" Finn called out.

"Yeah, probably. But it's too hard to deal with."

Finn kept looking, ducking down another long aisle of stacks of electronic gear.

"Somewhere here," Philby said, "There has to be. . . aha! I've got it!"

He'd found a freestanding webcam alongside a keyboard at one of the desks. He traced the USB cord and unplugged it.

When Philby got on a roll, there was no stopping him. His actions became frantic as he hurried with the webcam back to the DHI server. He dragged a chair into place, climbed up onto it, and placed the webcam on the top shelf, wedging it between a pair of speakers.

"Run the wire down the back there," Philby directed Finn.

Finn did as he was told. Together, they worked furiously, running wires, changing the position of the camera. Finn still didn't know what Philby was up to.

Philby double checked his phone and said, "No cell service, but it's a good Wi-Fi signal down here."

Philby handed his to phone Finn. "Can you see my hands?" he said, placing them on the keyboard.

Finn viewed the phone's screen. It was the video

image from the webcam Philby had installed. It showed the keyboard and Philby's hands.

"Unreal," Finn said. "Yeah, your hands and the keyboard."

He took his phone back. "Check the cold room for hiding places," he said, referring to a second server room with which the boys were familiar. "Room for both of us. It has to be good. We can't be found."

Finn entered a small room crowded with big, lumbering machines. The bigger and more sensitive electronics ran more efficiently when kept extremely cool. He found space behind a computer the size of vending machine.

"I've got something," he called out.

"Stand by!" Philby called back. He used his phone to make a remote connection. He then tried his password for the third time. The computer bumped the access page and warned that access would now be denied for twenty-four hours.

He glanced at his watch. Given the past history of the DHIs and this server, he gave Base five minutes to respond.

* * *

It took only three minutes. A Security woman named Joyce Brighton, who'd worked Security for eleven years, the past three in the Utilidor, entered the server room with a cup of coffee in hand.

She glanced around, well aware that false alarms outnumbered real ones 20 to 1.

She surveyed the empty room, and reached for her radio. Then she stopped.

What on Earth was that foul odor?

It smelled like a Dumpster.

* * *

Philby and Finn remained hidden behind the towering rack of servers when the door to the supercooled room opened. Over the steady sound of the air conditioning and the computer fans could be heard a nose sniffing. Philby looked down at the brown muck and pieces of food and litter adhered to his clothing. Unfortunately, he'd already grown accustomed to the foul odor. Clearly the guard had picked up on it.

The nose worked the air in short little sniffs. The sound moved toward the two boys.

"What in heaven's name is that smell?" said a woman softly to herself.

The guard reached the towering enclosure they hid behind.

"Ah-ha!" the guard said.

She tried to squeeze herself between the two

enclosures. Finn and Philby had slipped through; judging by the sounds she was making, she was not a perfect fit.

"Joyce, what's your twenty?" a male voice said over her radio. "Fresh coffee when you're ready."

The woman guard stood there, basically stuck between the two metal enclosures. She was maybe two feet from Philby. Her hand shot out from the gap, and nearly touched him as she tried to get to her radio. After a second try, she backed out into the main part of the room.

"Pour me a cup. I'm on my way. Tell Base that Data Operations is clear. They can send their guy over."

* * *

The "guy" was not a guy at all, but a woman from Maintenance who arrived from the Studios in less than fifteen minutes. Philby had Finn hold the phone while he watched the image from the webcam. A pair of delicate hands appeared in frame and typed in a sixteen-digit string alphanumeric password. Philby knew what to watch for: he had Finn study the first eight finger motions, while he took the second set. Philby had sketched out a keyboard on a piece of notepaper; he marked the finger movements with Xs and numbered them.

The technician spent another twenty minutes putting the server through its paces—a full virus scan and a reboot. Apparently satisfied that there'd been no breach, she slid the keyboard back in its tray and left the server room.

"What now?" Finn asked.

"Now," Philby answered, waving the piece of note-paper, "I do my magic and you and Maybeck get to sleep. We're back in business."

* * *

Maybeck sneaked out from under the cardboard boxes. The two guys had been told Base was "good." They finally left.

His hand hovered over the STOP button.

Then he thought to send Philby a text.

want me to stop it?

Tucked in behind the plywood wall, he waited. And waited. When no text came back, he decided the reception was bad. He had to make a decision. Too much time had passed since the system had been restarted. By now, Finn and Philby had either been blown out of the system or were safe.

But his job was to keep the trash system down. He

could stop it again, hide amid the boxes, and see what happened.

He hit STOP.

* * *

As Philby and Finn left Data Operations, Philby noticed that the overhead rumble stopped.

"Maybeck," he said.

"About time!" Finn said.

The two boys hurried back and reentered the trash system. They moved incredibly quickly this time, knowing exactly where they were going. Reaching the vertical pipe through which they'd entered, Philby knocked three times. The lid opened and Maybeck reached down a hand.

"Hurry!" he said into the dark.

He helped Philby up, then Finn.

"Oh, man!" Maybeck said. "You guys *reek* like diaper poo."

"Nice to see you, too," Finn said.

Minutes later, they were attracting unwanted attention on their way out. But thankfully, the state of their smell kept the curious at bay. They cut a wide swath as they walked out of the employee gate at the front of the Park.

Finn caught sight of the time and called his mother.

The arrangement had been for them to be picked up in Downtown Disney, but they were already late. He was going to have to risk the truth, or something close to it.

"Good grief!" she said as they piled into the car, Maybeck riding shotgun, Finn and Philby relegated to the back. "You two look disgusting."

"We went Dumpster diving," Finn said.

"You what?!"

"I threw my wallet away by accident," Philby said. "It was on this food tray, and I just dumped it in there by mistake, and by the time I realized it they'd already emptied the trash—"

"So they went Dumpster diving," Maybeck said.

"And we found it," Finn said.

"In the Magic Kingdom," she said. "What happened to Downtown Disney?"

"Our plans changed."

"You aren't allowed in the Magic Kingdom without permission." His mom didn't miss much.

"Something came up," Finn said.

An ominous silence overcame the car's interior. His mother was clearly considering how far to push her son with the other boys in the car. "Well, at least it has a happy ending," she said, letting Finn off the hook. For now.

She rolled down the window. "Can I just say, you

stink?" She burst out laughing, as did the boys, though their laughter was faked.

Then she went through the typical mom stuff: "Did you have a good time?" "Did you see any friends?" "How much money did you spend?" It was like she was reading from the same script anytime Finn did anything with his friends.

"Willa's mother called." She dropped it like a bomb and checked the rearview mirror for impact. The thing about his mother: she could lay little traps that he would fall into before he knew it.

"She said you knew what it was about," his mother continued.

"Yeah. Okay, thanks," Finn said.

"So," she said, addressing Maybeck, "now you can tell me the real reason you were in the Magic Kingdom. And if you lie, I'll know it. And I won't be happy."

She met eyes—mother eyes—with Finn in the rearview mirror.

"It's probably nothing you want to hear about," Maybeck said.

"Try me."

Maybeck hesitated.

"Mom," Finn said.

"We had an understanding, correct?" his mother said.

Philby knew that of all the parents, Mrs. Whitman had a love of all things Disney, and was maybe the only parent to support their efforts. He said, "The Overtakers crossed over Willa and she's stuck in the Syndrome."

"That's why her mom called," Finn said, joining in on the explanation. It wouldn't look good if Philby was the only one telling the truth.

"They tricked us and phished for my password—a back door to the DHI server—and they got it. They blocked us out and I couldn't Return Willa."

"Oh, my . . . And tonight?" she asked. There she was, staring down Finn in the rearview mirror again.

"The Utilidor," Finn said.

"The server room," Philby said. "We had to gain access to the server. We set up a trap and the maintenance people fell into it. I trapped the master password, which allowed me to create a new back door. I can control the server remotely again now."

"How do you know it wasn't the Imagineers or Maintenance who locked you out in the first place?" she said.

"Attenuating circumstances," Finn said.

"*Extenuating*," his mother corrected, then added, "Which were . . . ?"

Finn answered. "If someone from Disney had locked us out, it would have meant we were in big trouble. They'd have called you and Dad, right? The parents? But that didn't happen."

Mrs. Whitman nodded. She pulled off the highway and into a gas station. She parked the car and faced the three boys. "I realize I don't get all of this, but if you're back in the server, why not just bring Willa back now?"

"I tried when we were down there," Philby said. "A manual Return is different than using the fob. When we use the fob, our DHIs and the signal are in the same location—the same projection coordinates. A manual Return only works for sure at the landing—the hub in MK, the fountain in Epcot. If her DHI is not on the plaza, there's no guarantee it will link up."

"So we've got to get her to the plaza," Finn said. "We're doing everything we can for Willa. What we need now is to get home and get to sleep."

"To cross over," she said. She didn't sound pleased.

"Willa's mom," Maybeck said, "knows she can't take her to the hospital because of what happened to Philby when his parents took him."

"It's up to us to get her back," Philby said. "Tonight."

Mrs. Whitman put her hands to her temples like she had a headache. "But to get her back you have to use that button, right? It's in one of the Parks somewhere, isn't it?" She was basically talking to herself. "Which Park?"

"Epcot," both Finn and Maybeck answered at once.

"You have to find her first."

"Yes," Finn said.

"And then use the button to bring her back."

"The fob. Yes," Philby said. "It's the best way. But as a backup, I can bring them back remotely."

"Why would you need a backup?" she asked.

Philby responded, though tentatively. "Because . . . for some reason she hasn't used the fob to Return. We don't exactly understand that. The first thing is to find her."

"So, shouldn't I be taking you to Epcot?" she asked.

Finn looked dumbstruck.

"We'd never get in," Philby said. "And even if we could, it would be too—"

"Dangerous," Finn said.

"Risky," Maybeck said.

"Dangerous, or risky?" she asked.

"Both," all three boys answered, simultaneously.

Finn said, "We need to be DHIs. It's way safer."

"These are just Disney villains," she said, as if trying to convince herself. "They are *fictional* characters."

The boys said nothing. Unless you'd met Maleficent face-to-face, there was no explaining it.

"I thought they locked them up," she said.

Philby said, "There's no real way to know, but, yeah, we're pretty sure they're locked up."

"Then who's doing this?" she asked.

"You wouldn't believe us if we told you," Finn said.

"Try me."

"The two we've seen so far are Cruella and the Evil Queen. There are probably more."

"Oh, I *hate* the Evil Queen," she said. Then she started laughing, and the boys joined in. She cleared tears from her eyes as they stopped. "What are you going to do? How can I help?"

"Seriously?" Finn said, wondering if the Overtakers had gotten control of his mom. This was his mom, right? "For one thing, you could call Jelly and Philby's parents and tell them they're spending the night."

"I can do that. What else?" she asked.

Philby explained: "We have to get Finn and Maybeck to cross over and find her. As long as they can get her to the fob, we're good. If something's wrong with the fob—which seems possible—they need to get her to what we call 'the landing'—the center of the Park, the fountain. Then I can bring them back manually, without the fob."

"We could use a parent on our side," Finn said. "If the parents gang up on us . . . it will not be good."

"Meaning, you could use a parent in case something goes wrong?" she asked Philby.

"Uhh . . ."

"What could go wrong?" she asked. "You're saying Finn and Maybeck might not Return? Like Willa?"

"I suppose."

Finn held his breath. *Think of Willa*, he was chanting to himself. "Her mother's really freaked out," he reminded. "We know we can get her back."

Mrs. Whitman put the car in gear and peeled out, throwing the boys back in their seats.

"I hope you know what you're doing," she said.

* * *

Philby's mother wouldn't let him spend the night. Having lost her son once to the Syndrome she didn't approve of his spending time with his Keeper friends. Despite the newspaper stories spreading rumors that the Keepers had defended Disney World from its villains, she had a limited view of their purpose. She didn't give two cents about Disney World keeping its magic. Not if it put her son at risk. It wasn't like he was saving the world or something. It was an entertainment company. Some theme parks. She wasn't about to sacrifice her son for the sake of larger profits. Her resistance to anything Kingdom Keepers was tempered by an appreciation for the money Disney continued to contribute for Philby's future college expenses; she wasn't going to look a gift horse in the mouth, but she had limits.

So Mrs. Whitman had dropped Philby home, taking Maybeck and Finn with her.

Philby had placed a towel at the bottom of his door to block the light from reaching the hallway, so when his mom checked it would look like the lights in his room were out. He sat at his computer.

ready? he texted Finn over Skype.

yes, Finn texted back.

its working. i'm in. good 2 go

Finn texted:

k, 9

Philby returned:

cm

Finn leaned back in his chair, his mother sitting on one side, Maybeck on the other, Finn's father snoring from the other room.

"This worries me," his mother said.

"It's good news."

"Not that," she said. "But that I don't understand half of what you're texting."

"It's like a code."

"I know that, Finn. Don't get smart with me."

His mother got irritable if she stayed up late. This was going to be a long night.

"Once Maybeck and me get to sleep, Philby'll cross us over."

"Maybeck and I," she corrected. He ignored her: way too tired. "What about you getting back?"

"We'll find the fob. No sweat. If it's not working, we've already set up a time and Philby can manually Return us."

"The manual override he talked about," she said.

"Yeah, exactly," he said.

"What time?"

"One."

She sat back. "You all have thought it through, haven't you?"

"It's what we do, Mom."

"Yes, but . . . You're fifteen."

"Almost sixteen," he said.

"It's a lot to deal with."

"Not really," he said. He could hear her rethinking her decision to allow him and Maybeck to cross over.

"It's dangerous. Risky," she said. "You both said so."

"Exaggerating," Maybeck said. "You know Philby. Remember, Mrs. W., when we cross over we're holograms. Stuff passes through us."

"What kind of stuff, Terry? Are you saying they try to hurt you?"

"It's Disney World. Nothing bad happens," Maybeck said.

Finn wondered if they'd used this excuse one too many times.

To Finn's relief, she nodded. She was definitely tired.

"We've got to get to sleep," he said.

Maybeck climbed onto an inflatable mattress on the floor.

"With your shoes on?" Mrs. Whitman said to Maybeck.

"Mom," Finn said, "we know what we're doing. Go to sleep. We'll see you in the morning."

"As if," she said. She was even beginning to talk like him.

* * *

The 9 Finn had texted had let Philby know his mother was in the room. The *cm* that came back from him meant "Call Me."

Now, with her gone, Finn climbed out of bed and let Maybeck know what was going on. He double-checked that his door was fully closed and returned to his computer. He called Philby, and spoke at a whisper.

"What's up?" Finn said.

"There's something weird going on," Philby said. "Willa's projection coordinates are for Epcot, but the current default for the Return is in MK."

"How could that be? The fob's in Epcot."

"It was when we last saw it."

"Why would the Imagineers reset the default?"

"It doesn't make sense. Not for the Imagineers. The point is, we've lost the Return somehow. I'll definitely have to cross you back manually from here."

He made it sound so simple. One of Philby's greatest qualities was his confidence. He wasn't arrogant or a bragger; he just happened to be right most of the time—a know-it-all who didn't get all up in your face with it. To hear him even slightly uncertain was alarming. Finn didn't say anything about it. Philby lived with more pressure than most of them, stuck with the Professor role.

"So, we're good to go," Finn said. "One o'clock."

"Yeah, sure. I just wanted you to know where we're at. I can Return you manually. All I'll need is a signal."

"I'll bring my phone."

"Yeah," Philby said, "but they don't always work, so we go with one o'clock or a signal if you find her earlier."

Philby had a plan for everything. He provided Finn with a way to signal him that Philby couldn't miss.

"Okay."

"But no matter what, if you can't send a signal, you and Maybeck should be at the plaza by one—an hour and a half from now."

"It isn't much time. It's a big place."

"I realize that."

"Philby," Finn said, "if this doesn't go right, it's not your fault. Okay? Forget about that. Just, whatever you do, don't let anyone else cross over. Three of us in the Syndrome is enough."

"Do not go there."

"I'm serious."

"So am I," said Philby. "Don't even go there."

"If that happens, get to Jess. Maybe she'll have dreamed something that will help us. But don't freak out. Come into the Park as your real selves. We'll find you. We'll figure it out together."

"Okay, now you're definitely freaking me out," Philby said.

"Just promise."

"Yeah, okay. I won't panic."

"Someone's got to keep it together."

"I thought that's your job," Philby said.

Maybeck placed a hand on Finn's shoulder, over-hearing the conversation. It was not what he expected from Maybeck.

Finn hung up, and a few minutes later the boys went back to bed. It was not easy for either of them to fall asleep. Finn didn't know how much time passed, but he woke up lying on the concrete at the edge of the Epcot fountain plaza. He'd crossed over.

"Took you long enough," came the familiar voice of Maybeck.

Finn got up off the concrete, checked his hands for the shimmering blue outline, and grinned. It felt good to be back.

He sat with his back pressed against the concrete retaining wall that formed the fountain.

"So? How do we find her?" Maybeck said.

Finn looked around. Epcot began at the golf ball–shaped Spaceship Earth; two huge areas ran off to both sides, with a half dozen attraction pavilions in both directions. The plaza fountain gave way to the lake surrounded by replica World Showcase countries, with Big Ben, the Eiffel Tower, and other world land-marks.

"Mexico," Finn said. "We start with Philby's plan."

* * *

For close to an hour, Willa had huddled behind a rock in the Primitive Man display inside Spaceship Earth. Earlier, she'd heard two men speaking French—cathedral guards—as they'd passed on the ride. She'd made herself as small as possible, and held her breath to make no noise. One of the guards had apparently jumped out of the car he was riding, but by doing so he tripped a sensor and shut down the ride, at which point there had been a flurry of discussion.

Realizing his mistake, he and the other guards had left quickly. One of the advantages of being a hologram—Willa had not tripped the system.

Assuming Disney maintenance men, and possibly Security personnel, would follow up on the ride's emergency shutdown, Willa had relocated to a display that included a Roman guard.

Things had been quiet for some time now, and so she ventured out, determined to search for the Return. Determined to get home.

She would start with Lost and Found. If a Cast Member discovered what looked like a garage door opener, he or she would turn it in. Because the Keepers had lost the fob once before, Willa knew exactly where to look.

She took her time, careful to advance and pause,

advance and pause. After determining an area was clear, she would move a little bit farther. Thankfully, the Lost and Found wasn't far: in the back office of a small building tucked away near the entrance gate turnstiles.

She reached the building, concentrating on her thin blue outline to make sure her hologram was *all clear*, and then walked through the back door.

She arrived into a tiny office with event posters covering the walls. There were two desks, one cluttered, one neat. Two computer terminals. Two phones.

The phones presented her with an opportunity she had not, until now, considered. She could call Finn or Philby and . . . except, she didn't know their numbers. They were on her phone as speed dials, but her phone was back home. She knew Charlene's number by heart; Charlene could relay a message. She would need to lose her DHI state at least slightly in order to be material enough to pick up and handle a telephone, but at this point being afraid wouldn't take any effort.

First, she checked the metal cabinet marked Lost and Found. Unlike when Finn had to go into the cabinet months earlier, it wasn't locked now. Inside, she found over a dozen cell phones, clothing, wallets, jewelry, driver's licenses, credit cards, and four sets of car keys—all with black fobs. But not the Return.

Her conclusion was that the OTs had stolen it, as she'd suspected. She eyed the phones and the computers. Did she dare start down the road of fear in order to become material enough to work the devices? Once begun it was hard to turn back. Fear fed on fear.

But what choice was there? She thought of her mother trying to wake her while in the Syndrome. Her fingers, knees, and toes tingled. She picked up the phone and dialed.

Charlene answered.

"It's me!"

"Willa?"

"I'm in the Syndrome."

"We *know* that. But how—"

"I'm in Epcot. I'm pretty sure the OTs have the Return. You have to tell the boys not to come after me. It's obviously a trap!"

"I . . . ah . . . I think it's too late. The plan's for Finn and Maybeck to cross tonight."

"But they can't. They . . . *we* . . . can't Return."

"Philby got back into the server. It's going to be all right."

"No, it's not. Not anywhere close."

"Finn and Maybeck should be there by now."

"I need Philby's number," Willa said. "I keep it on speed dial, but—"

"Yeah. Okay. Hang on."

As Willa waited, she looked down at the phone to see a line light lit. By using the phone, she'd given herself away. She hung up immediately. She had to get out of there!

She tried walking through the door, but bounced against it. Her fear had gotten the better of her. It was a sickening, downward spiral. She tentatively opened the door and slipped outside, pulling it shut quietly behind her.

When she turned around, a shape appeared around the corner of a building and quickly ducked back.

"Finn?" She spoke his name aloud, though only in a whisper. She glanced around haltingly, ensuring she was alone.

"*Pssst!*"

He reappeared.

She waved, so happy to see him! Finn stepped out into the open, and she realized he'd come in disguise— he was wearing the same stupid costume, shorts and a T-shirt, that his DHI wore in the Magic Kingdom. She hurried toward him, a combination of relief and anxiety overcoming her: relief they'd found each other; anxiety over the thought of telling him there was no way to Return.

"Oh, my gosh, Finn! It is so good to—"

He evaporated into a wisp of smoke that reformed into something darker and larger . . . until she found herself facing the Evil Queen.

She screamed. Her hologram outline dimmed.

"You . . . witch!" she uttered angrily.

"You are correct. *This small girl, impossible to lose; she now finds no way to move.*" The Evil Queen waved her index finger in a tight circle.

Willa tried to run. She could hardly lift her legs. She was quickly surrounded by cathedral guards. Behind them, on the points of the compass, four crash-test dummies on Segways.

Cruella De Vil stepped out from behind the Queen.

"Well, well. I have to compliment you, dearest," she said to the Evil Queen. "You're quite the little Venus flytrap."

The Queen ignored her. "The judge asked you a question, little girl," the Queen said to Willa, her eyes squinting. "I fear you were rude to him. Let me explain that being rude to me will have far more . . . devastating results. Hmmm? Do I make myself clear?" The Evil Queen stepped forward. Willa found her beauty bewitching and powerful.

She nodded against her will. The sensation in her limbs slowly returned. Her legs no longer felt like they weighed a ton.

"Then out with it," the Queen ordered. "Or suffer!" Another flick of her hand and Willa bent over in a convulsion, like she had been punched in the stomach. This despite her being in her state of partial DHI. She hated to think how that would hurt when flesh and blood.

The Queen waved her hands again and her lips trembled as she chanted some kind of incantation.

Spiders appeared out of cracks in the pavement. Hundreds, thousands of them. Small ones. Red ones. Black ones. HUGE ones. They swarmed at Willa's feet, leaving her in the center of an oozing circle of hairy spiders. If she moved even slightly . . .

She was terrified, which dampened her DHI, making her more vulnerable. She was outmatched. The Queen got what the Queen wanted.

"WHAT DID JEZEBEL DRAW?"

"A face! A man," Willa volunteered, still bent over, her stomach in a knot. The spiders encroached.

The witch cackled with laughter that sounded like breaking ice. "Who? What man? And be careful you don't lie, little thing." She began to sing. "'The Itsy Bitsy Spider . . .'"

The ring of spiders tightened at Willa's feet.

"A man . . . in uniform."

\* \* \*

Finn's DHI climbed the stone steps running up the center of the Mexico pavilion, a Mayan temple with balconies of flowers on either side of the center staircase. He'd taken this same route with Philby; he knew what he was doing. Maybeck's DHI had already reached the top, climbing as effortlessly as a cat.

"Wait up!" hissed a humiliated Finn.

"Move it!" Maybeck said. He watched Finn climb. "It's only a set of stairs."

*Tiny stairs, steep stairs*, Finn felt like saying, but he kept his mouth shut.

"Memo to Whitman: I don't think you're going to be able to see Willa from up here. So what, in the name of cream cheese, are we doing here?"

"Doing what Philby told us to do," Finn whispered back. "Into the booth."

"The IllumiNations booth? How's that supposed to help Willa?"

"Remember in *The Wizard of Oz*, the man behind the curtain?"

"Sure. The old guy. What about him?"

"That's you. You're the man behind the curtain. You're the one controlling things."

"I'm liking this plan more and more, Whitman."

*I knew you would*, Finn nearly said. "Okay, so pay attention."

The longer he sat there staring at his computer monitor, the more concerned Philby grew. The webcam view was of the Park as a whole. He could see a few black specks move from time to time, but they looked about the size of ants. He couldn't tell who or what they were, or what they were up to. *If Finn is going to send me a signal*, he thought, *it had better be something good. Otherwise, I might miss it.* So he focused intently on the most recent development: a thick group of ants had congregated between Spaceship Earth and the office building near the entrance. That couldn't be good. It might be a meeting of Security, or a cleaning or maintenance team getting ready to deploy around the Park, or it could easily be Overtakers.

When Philby heard rustling in the bushes outside his window, he looked away from his computer.

The window was unlocked. Not good. What if there was a serial killer creeping around their house?

When he heard more brushing of sticks against the side of the house, goose bumps raced up his arms— something was out there, and it was too big to be a dog.

More like a person.

* * *

Willa was not scared of spiders; she was *terrified* of them. They moved as a mass around her bare feet within

235

inches of touching her. Her DHI was anything but pure, making her physically vulnerable.

"What kind of uniform?" the Queen asked.

She'd said too much already. She hated herself for having said anything. "A security officer," she lied. "Like at the airport."

There were two huge vultures following behind her. Cruella steered clear of the birds as she walked around Willa, studying her.

Willa's eyes followed Cruella.

"I don't think so," the Evil Queen said. She waved her hand. The spiders swarmed over Willa's feet and started up her ankles. She cried out and kicked with both legs, like running in place, but the spiders kept coming. Screaming, she brushed them away, but there were thousands of them, and each time her bare feet landed she felt them squish beneath her while a hundred more climbed onto her.

"Get them off!"

Willa jumped out of the oozing black circle, but a vulture came at her, flapping its large wings, and stuck its grotesque bald head and curved beak into her face, driving her back. She leaped to her left, and the second vulture blocked her there as well. She fled back into the swarm of spiders. Some had reached her knees. As fast as she could brush them off, they gained on her.

"STOP IT!"

"What kind of uniform, dear?" the Queen said in a perfectly calm voice.

"Military, I think. Those things on his shoulders." She jumped and hopped and swatted at the spiders.

The Queen waved the spiders down and off her. They formed the doughnut again, with Willa at the center.

"That's better, my little ugly duckling," the Queen said. "More details, and I'll keep them off you."

Willa collected herself and looked up, intent to meet eyes with the Queen. But what she saw just beyond the Queen nearly stopped her heart: Finn. Her friend Finn, not the Queen's copy of him. He wore all black and was carrying the shimmering blue line that said he'd crossed over. Finn, who'd come to rescue her.

The Evil Queen caught Willa's eye movement and, without looking behind her, made a sweeping, surprisingly graceful motion toward Finn, her lips moving, but making no sound. Whatever she had expected to happen to him did not. The blue line around Finn's DHI shimmered, though only slightly—he was only part hologram. He rushed Willa, lowered his shoulder, and hit her like a football tackle, throwing her onto his shoulder. He took off at a run.

Spiders raced up his back, Willa brushing them off furiously. She looked down: the stream of spiders had stretched into long black line like a . . .

Snake.

Gigabyte, the twenty-foot python, was a matter of yards behind Finn. The vultures flew on either side of him.

Back at Gigabyte's tail, the remaining spiders turned into rattlesnakes.

"Finn . . ." Willa gasped, laying atop his shoulder. "Snakes."

The rattlesnakes moved faster than the giant python.

"Finn?" she said.

He could feel himself slowing down—the more frightened she became, the heavier she was to carry.

"Don't . . . look!" he said. He followed the path past Innoventions West and aimed for the fountain plaza, now in sight. Maybeck's timing was going to have to be perfect, or between the snakes and vultures they would lose their chance to Return.

The fountain was now only a matter of twenty yards away. A figure appeared on the far side, toward the lake: Maybeck, running at a full sprint, two CTDs on foot chasing him.

\* \* \*

Maybeck counted down in his head: thirty-nine . . . thirty-eight . . . thirty-seven . . .

He had a pair of robots on his tail, pursuing his DHI at lightning speed. One of them had gotten close enough to fire some kind of Taser, but because of his DHI state, its electrodes and wires had passed right through him.

Up ahead he saw Whitman carrying Willa on his shoulder, and some kind of broken shadow slithering behind him. Behind the shadow came the Evil Queen and Cruella. If this had been Philby's plan, he was out of his skull. They'd walked right into a nest of Overtakers.

"Uncool!" he shouted as he skidded to a stop, seeing the snakes—not shadows but snakes!—braiding themselves around the feet of Finn's DHI.

"Do NOT look down!" Maybeck added.

Finn looked down. His blue hologram line faded and the tangle of snakes locked around his partially mortal ankles, and Finn fell, dumping Willa, whom Maybeck caught in his arms.

Maybeck had lost count. Eighteen? Twelve? Whitman had told him he had to keep count.

*Oops . . .*

Finn rose to his elbows, but surrounded by hissing rattlesnakes, he froze.

"Welcome, boys," said the Evil Queen, finally catching up.

Maybeck helped Willa keep her balance as he put

her down. It was a clever move—it put her within an arm's length of Finn. If she dared to reach across the snakes, they could hold hands.

* * *

Philby stared out his window. It was not a serial killer; it was Hugo Montcliff, and more important, he had Elvis in his arms. Elvis, an inside cat, had disappeared earlier that afternoon and Philby's mom had been distraught. Hugo would be a family hero for years to come.

Philby threw open the window. "You found him! My mother's going to saint you."

"He was wandering around the Evans' house."

"Need the couch tonight?" Philby knew Hugo couldn't suffer his parents screaming fights all night.

"You mind?"

"Climb on in," Philby said, making a gesture like a hotel doorman. Hugo passed him Elvis and followed through the window.

Philby felt a shiver, but blamed it on the night air.

"Sorry, I've got to be rude," Philby said, shutting and locking the window, "but I'm jamming." He pointed to his desk. "It's late, so be as quiet as you can. Wouldn't want to wake up my mom. Towel's in the closet. I'll catch you in the morning."

"Maybe I shouldn't stay." Hugo's voice had dropped an octave. He spoke softly, sounding hurt.

Philby, who was now a step closer to his desk, looked back at his friend, feeling sorry for him. "No, I didn't mean that. I'll be done in a couple minutes."

"Is that Epcot?" Hugo said, stepping closer.

"That's amazing you could recognize it," Philby said. His screen was nothing but some lights, the shimmering water of the lake, and . . . the little ants had moved to the fountain plaza.

*That has to be Finn and Maybeck.* But there were way too many ants on the screen—if it was Finn, he and Maybeck weren't alone.

"Can I play?" Hugo asked.

"Ah . . . it's not exactly a game, and, ah . . . You know, if you don't mind, I'm a little busy right now."

"Oh, but I do mind," Hugo said. "Don't touch that keyboard."

Philby spun around. With Hugo having been outside in the dark, he hadn't gotten a good look at him, especially given that he'd been holding Elvis. The cat had won Philby's attention—*by design*, Philby thought. Because Hugo's eyes were a vivid green.

Hugo had brown eyes.

Philby couldn't believe it! Hugo? Of all people! After all Philby's family had given to the boy! He felt overcome with anger and disbelief.

He saw his terry cloth bathrobe and belt lying on his bed. The belt would work to tie Hugo up.

Philby charged.

Hugo knocked him out of the way and onto the bed. Where had that kind of strength come from? Philby did a somersault and sprang from his haunches, launching himself at the boy.

To his right, a burst of color erupted across his computer screen.

The signal.

* * *

The lake burst into flames, flooding the night sky and illuminating every pavilion in a wash of golden light. It reflected off the face of the Evil Queen. It danced in Cruella's eyes.

Finn hopped to his knees and stood, leaning to reach across the tangle of rattlesnakes and touch Willa's outstretched hand.

It was not only the water burning. A dozen towering torches surrounding the lake had also burst into flames. But the water effect, part of the IllumiNations show, was a spectacular sight: giant balls of orange flames boiling off the water's surface and rising into the dark, looking like the surface of the sun.

The timing of the effect had been Maybeck's job: to schedule the pyrotechnics that Professor Philby had discovered on the control booth's computer when he and Finn had visited two nights earlier. More than a thousand different pieces of ordnance on water barges, and a half-dozen laser projectors mounted on top of pavilions, were all synchronized by the IllumiNations computer. Following their spotting Willa and the Queen on the Security video, Maybeck had scheduled the fire events, giving himself five minutes to leave the control room, climb down the Mayan Temple, and catch up to Finn. With it nearing one AM and the scheduled manual Return, maybe the pyrotechnics would offer a needed distraction.

Given that it looked like all of Epcot was on fire, there was no way Philby could miss the signal.

Now all he had to do was remotely tell the DHI server to Return them.

* * *

Philby witnessed the wash of flames engulfing Epcot's lake and stretched for the computer's Return/Enter key.

But Hugo held him by the shoulders, struggling to get his arms around Philby's chest and squeeze the wind out of him. Philby stumbled back, his fingers hitting the spacebar instead of the Return key.

He threw an elbow into Hugo's stomach, and groaning, Hugo let go. Philby regained his balance . . . took a step toward his desk . . . and was tackled to the floor.

He went down hard, face-first. Philby rolled over and kicked out, catching Hugo in the face. But Hugo scrambled on top of Philby, pinning his shoulders and winding up with a balled fist. As Hugo drove the fist toward his face, Philby jerked his head. Hugo punched the floor. Philby's hand found the wicker trash can; he raked it across Hugo's face and the boy went off him.

Philby rolled and shoved his hand into Hugo's face—the fake green eyes staring back, unflinching and terrifying. Philby couldn't look at those eyes. He turned away.

Hugo grabbed both of Philby's wrists, pushing up, trying to get Philby off; Philby pushed back, trying to hold Hugo down. Their arms began to tremble, then to shake.

Light flashed from the computer, the lake alive with fire.

Philby managed to pin Hugo's left arm with his knee and reach for the computer with his right hand. Hugo rocked side to side attempting to free his arm, and making it impossible for Philby to properly aim his fingers. He missed the Return key three times in a row.

Hugo kneed Philby in the back, freeing his hand, which he used to palm Philby below the chin and propel him back toward the bed.

Hugo jumped up and reached for the Escape key, which would close the current window—Philby's link with the DHI server.

Philby had bit his lip; he tasted the salty tang of blood in his mouth. He was *mad*.

Elvis was just standing there on the bed like a spectator. Philby grabbed him and held him just behind the front legs and lunged for Hugo using the same technique his family members used to train Elvis to use his scratching pole. It forced Elvis to extend his front claws—claws that now tore through Hugo's shirt, leaving eight narrow tracks of blood behind as Philby dragged him down the boy's back, and then tossed Elvis back onto the bed as Hugo let out a gut-wrenching scream.

Philby spun Hugo around, tripped him, and dumped him to the floor. He stabbed for the Return key.

THIS ACTION CANNOT BE UNDONE
DO YOU WISH PROCEED? Y/N

He hit *Y*.

The bedroom door burst open. A wrinkly-faced woman with no makeup, an adhesive strip across the bridge of her nose stretching her cheeks, and wearing a pair of pajamas covered with cartoons of Marge Simpson, shouted: "BOYS!"

Both Hugo and Philby stopped cold.

"What in the devil is going on, young man?" Philby's mom said to him. The next thing she said was, "Elvis?" in a loving and kind voice of pure affection.

Hugo stood up, unlocked the window, threw it open, and dove outside.

Philby watched the bandwidth meter spike in the bottom right corner of the computer screen. The DHI properties of the holograms were being saved back to the DHI server. The Return. The whole process could take anywhere from ten to sixty seconds.

Precious seconds.

"Dell?" his mother said.

"Please, Mom, no!" Philby said, seeing his mother march toward his desk. "Remember what happened to me?" he said in a begging tone. "If you shut my computer, it'll happen to all three of them—Finn, Willa, and Maybeck. Mom! You don't want that to happen."

Shutting the computer, putting it into sleep mode,

would send his friends to sleep along with it. Stuck in the Syndrome.

* * *

Finn couldn't take his eyes off the trembling hands of the Evil Queen held high above her head. She reminded him of a major league pitcher in his windup. She was about to deliver some kind of spitball, sinker spell, that would make the spiders and rattlesnakes look like kids' stuff. Something nasty.

The flames licked off the lake.

Tears ran down Willa's face as she mouthed, "Thank you," to Finn.

The Evil Queen threw her hands at them with a witch's fury, her lips spouting an incantation.

*"Children in peril*
*Children in fright—"*

But she stopped before completing it.

Willa had disappeared.

Finn watched as Maybeck sparkled, became transparent, and vanished.

Finn sat bolt upright in bed. His own bed, at home. Maybeck blinked furiously from his air mattress.

Finn felt something on his leg and threw back the covers.

A rattlesnake.

He screamed a bad word loud enough to be heard two blocks away.

He shook his leg like a maniac. The snake flew up and was caught, dangling from one of the paddles on his ceiling fan.

His father threw open his bedroom door and switched on the light, his mother craning over her husband's shoulder.

When Finn's ceiling light switched on, so did the fan.

The snake began circling overhead. The fan gained speed.

"FINN WHITMAN!" his father thundered, glaring at him. His father had run out of patience for the Kingdom Keepers after their earliest adventure. Wanting his son to focus on academics first and sports second, he had little tolerance for Finn's claims of saving Disney from its villains. Although he appreciated the college money that resulted from his son's participation in the program, and even secretly enjoyed some of the attention and fame that rubbed off on him for being Finn's father, this kind of nighttime interruption to his family was exactly what he objected to and found so offensive.

He didn't need a manual to understand why his son and Maybeck were fully clothed in black, wearing shoes, and sweating profusely while in air conditioning.

"I had a nightmare," Finn said.

"Lying will only make it worse for you."

The rattlesnake was currently rotating at warp speed, wrapped around the fan blade.

"Mom? Please?" he said, flicking his eyes to the ceiling fan.

His mother spotted the snake and went ashen white.

"Sweetie," she said to her husband, "come on back to bed. Let's deal with this in the morning. Nothing to be done now."

Mr. Whitman seemed unmovable. "Terry," he said, "do I have your word you two will go back to sleep? No shenanigans?"

The rattlesnake was losing its hold. Six inches of the snake was now sticking off the end of the fan's paddle.

"Yes, sir."

Mr. Whitman trusted Finn's friends more than he did his own son.

Mr. Whitman made a grunting sound of disapproval, allowing his wife to pull him out of the doorway. She stepped forward, made a face of pure horror, and reached for the light switch. As she shut off the light, she closed the door.

Finn heard a thump, but couldn't see in the darkness.

His father opened the door again and peered inside. "What was that?" he said. "Are you testing me, son?"

"No, sir!" Finn answered.

The rattlesnake had hit the door. It was hanging in a coil from the pair of hooks on the back of the door, its tongue flicking in the direction of his father's head.

Finn sprang out of bed. "Sorry, Dad. Won't happen again. Good night." He toed the door and shut it in his father's face.

His father called softly through the door: "We'll discuss this in the morning, young man!"

The snake turned toward Finn.

"Whitman!" Maybeck hissed, having backed up to the wall.

Finn dove into his closet and grabbed his laundry bag and a hanger. He'd seen this on the Discovery Channel.

"You gotta help me!" Finn whispered.

"Oh, yeah, as if that's going to happen."

"I need you to hold the bag open."

"Pass."

"I can't do both at once."

"No way!"

"Maybeck!"

Maybeck approached cautiously and held the bag. "This feels like the losing end of this deal."

"You want to handle the snake? Be my guest."

The snake's rattle was going strongly, raising every hair on Finn's body. If his father heard it, he might as well let the snake just bite him now.

Maybeck held open the laundry bag, his arms extended supernaturally. He was basically a ZIP code away. Finn hooked the snake with the hanger and lifted it carefully from the door's twin clothes hooks. The snake hung heavily from the U of the hanger.

Finn lowered it slowly and Maybeck caught the snake in the bag.

"Window!" Finn hissed.

Maybeck moved that direction. Finn opened the window and Maybeck extended the bag outside.

"Okay," Finn said, "let go."

"I can't," Maybeck said. "My fingers are frozen."

"Let . . . go . . ." Finn said, uncurling Maybeck's fingers one by one.

The bag crashed down in the plants.

Shutting the window, Finn heaved a sigh of relief. Maybeck hadn't moved. He looked like a statue.

"It's out," Finn said.

Maybeck shook his head and finally managed to step away from the window.

"We'll have to check the bag in the morning and make sure the snake is gone," Finn said.

"You can if you want," Maybeck said.

Finn texted Willa and Philby.

Willa texted back immediately, thanking all three boys. Philby texted a few minutes later:

trouble here. group skype b4 skool @ 7:45

Reading the text over Finn's shoulder, Maybeck whispered, "He thinks he had troubles. I gotta hear this."

# 8

THE KEEPERS MET ON VIDEO conference fifteen minutes before buses and parental rides departed for school.

Finn: "We had a tricky situation last night."

Willa: "As in, Maybeck and Finn saved me."

Finn: "And Philby."

Maybeck, looking over Finn's shoulder, said, "It was the Evil Queen and Cruella."

Charlene: "Same as Downtown Disney."

Charlene was using her own video image as a mirror while applying mascara.

Willa: "The fob was missing."

Charlene: "Did you check—"

Willa: "The Lost and Found? Yes. Not there. Gone. It's got to be why they crossed you, Charlene. Finn and Philby come into the Park and the three of you lead them to the fob. You Returned and they stole it. None of us saw that coming."

Maybeck: "Whoa."

Charlene: "They stole it, because . . . ?"

Maybeck: "We become stuck in the Syndrome, for one thing."

Philby: "First the server, then the fob. If we hadn't managed to hack back into the server last night, Willa would still be stuck there."

Finn: "I guess I can see how that helps them break out Maleficent—I mean, it takes us out of the picture—but it's sure a lot of planning, a lot of work, if you ask me."

Philby: "Which means we're missing something. The bigger picture."

He then described his fight with Hugo.

Philby: "Obviously, they knew I would try to Return you three. They sent Hugo to stop me. Hugo must be the one we can't see in the photo. I still can't believe he'd do this to me."

Maybeck: "To us."

Charlene: "This just gets creepier and creepier."

She applied one last stroke of mascara and twisted the tube shut.

Willa: "But the real reason they wanted me was for me to describe Jess's sketch. The one she showed me at school."

Finn: "We need to see that up close."

Philby: "Question—how did the Evil Queen know you'd seen the sketch?"

A general silence.

Finn: "A green-eyes. One of the spies saw Jess show Willa."

In light of Hugo and Luowski, this seemed like the best explanation.

Charlene: "So we're not safe at school and we're not safe crossed over. Anyone feel like a vacation?"

She won some laughter—but not much.

Charlene: "Seriously, any ideas? I've got to get downstairs. The bus'll be here any minute."

Philby: "Stay here a second longer."

He waited for everyone's attention on-screen, especially Charlene's.

Philby: "What if we missed a major clue? Finn saw Cruella on the telephone at Downtown Disney."

Maybeck: "We all agreed that was bizarre."

Philby: "But what if she and the Queen were DHIs at the time?"

Silence.

Philby: "What if the phone call was to request a manual Return? It's possible DisneyQuest serves as Downtown's centerpiece. We don't know."

Maybeck cursed.

Finn: "Using the phone as the signal to send them back."

Philby: "Exactly."

Willa: "That's why they want the fob so badly. To make it easier *for them* to Return."

Philby: "I think so, yes."

Maybeck shouted, and Finn cupped his ear.

Maybeck: "Hold on! Wait a second."

Philby: "We know they took control of the server. It was them who locked me out, not the Imagineers. I was never buying that. We got all hung up on it being about us, about controlling us. Locking us in the Syndrome. And sure, that's probably part of it, but it also may be what they want us to think."

Finn: "It explains them stealing the fob. But how could they have done it? How could they have turned themselves into DHIs?"

Philby: "The same way we turned Amanda and Jess into DHIs."

Another long silence.

Willa: "But think about it. If they need the Return, if they can cross over as DHIs, then when that's happening they're asleep, right?"

For a moment it seemed as if the connection had failed—no one moved in their respective video windows. Charlene was no longer concerned with catching her bus.

Philby: "Makes sense."

Finn: "I'll tell you one thing; the Queen wasn't any DHI last night. She was throwing spells all over the place."

Charlene: "So last night she was real. But if they stole the fob for themselves, then they must be planning to cross over into one of the Parks, and a manual Return is just too hard for them to pull off."

Willa: "They're afraid of Jess knowing something about this. They've always tried to control her, from clear back at the start. If we can see the future, then maybe we can stop them. That's got to be what they're worried about."

Charlene: "And you're right, Willa; if they're DHIs, then they're asleep somewhere. We know that much."

Maybeck: "I see where this is going and I'm liking it."

Philby: "If we trap their DHIs, they'll be stuck in SBS. They won't be able to wake up and we'll have defeated them. But before you freak, remember we don't have their powers. We can't throw up laser jails and probably can't put fear into them the way they can with us. It's not the same."

Maybeck: "Back up, Philbo. Forget trapping their DHIs. What we want to do is distract their DHIs. We want to find where they're sleeping. Long as they're sleeping, they are totally vulnerable. Totally. We can slap on the cuffs, blindfold and gag them so they can't throw spells or do anything to anyone. We turn them over to Wanda or the Imagineers, and that's two more behind bars."

Philby considered the words "behind bars" and thought of Wanda and his first contact from Wayne. His thoughts moved past Wanda to Maleficent and Chernabog and their being locked up somewhere. As so often happened with him, it just struck him like a lightning bolt. The answers to math equations came this same way; science assignments, too. A spark of understanding in his brain.

Philby: "Prison! The reason they need to be DHIs has to do with Maleficent and Chernabog—"

Finn: "So they can break them out."

Philby: "I think so, yes. It's their end game. It's everything they're about."

Charlene: "How could that possibly work?"

Philby: "Who knows? But that's their plan. It adds up."

The mention of Wanda had Finn wondering about

her. They'd gotten her out of jail, but she hadn't been back in contact with them. Did she fear police surveillance? Or someone worse? She had a hearing scheduled for Monday morning.

Willa: "If they're asleep, it's somewhere in the Parks."

Maybeck: "Out of the way. Someplace no one's going to bother them."

Finn: "Or find them."

Charlene: "Hello? The Parks are ginormous."

Maybeck: "There can't be that many places. Cast Members are all over the place all the time. We can figure this out."

Maybeck didn't often play cheerleader. None of the others knew quite what to say.

Philby: "Don't forget, we surprised them last night by having access to the server. They thought they'd locked us out. But if they go DHI, I should be able to detect it. I won't know exactly where they are, but the ISP, submask, and router data will help narrow it down. That would allow us to have two teams: one, like Maybeck said, to challenge their DHIs and keep them busy, while the second team tries to find where they're sleeping."

Maybeck: "Thing is, they've got the fob. The minute they figure any of this out, they Return, and then we're in the deep woods."

Finn: "We can't rely on sending signals anymore. That was close last night. I think we should hide one of our cell phones in each of the Parks. We'd all know where to find them. If we need out, we call Philby and he takes us out manually."

Philby: "Makes total sense."

Charlene: "You expect me to give up my cell phone? Seriously?"

Willa: "Finn, we need to check with Jess about that drawing."

Finn: "No problem. And I want to talk to Wanda. We can't ask her to risk anything since she was arrested. But who knows how she might help us?"

Philby: "If we're dividing up teams, I vote for Maybeck, Finn, and Charlene to go after the sleepers. Amanda, Willa, and Jess can play cat-and-mouse with the Evil Queen and Cruella. DHI against DHI."

Willa: "I don't mean to be a buzzkill, but I am so grounded. It's like my mother's got me on suicide watch or something—she wakes me up every couple hours. I mean, I *want* so badly to be part of whatever we're doing, but . . . I just don't know."

All the Keepers spoke at once. No one expected anything from Willa. She'd been through enough. She apologized profusely; it was clear she wanted to be included if they crossed over, but if caught by her mother it could threaten them all.

Finn: "Well, the rest of us should dress for action each night. Philby will cross us over when he knows the Overtakers have crossed. The first thing we do when we enter a Park is to find the hidden cell phone in whatever Park we're in. Got that? That's our way out of the Park: we call Philby for a Return."

Philby: "One small problem. When I hit the Return you'll all Return as long as you're somewhere near the landing point in whatever Park you're in. So that makes the girls' job more complicated. We need to get the fob back. Whichever side has the fob has freedom."

Maybeck: "Easier said than done."

Charlene: "Are we forgetting anything?"

Willa: "Probably."

Finn: "So, we start tonight."

Willa: "Be careful in school. The green-eyes are out there."

Moments later, Finn disconnected from the conference call, a pit in his stomach about probably forgetting something.

\* \* \*

Finn arrived at school feeling like an idiot: he'd forgotten it was a "free dress" day. That should have meant professional sports team jerseys for boys and short-shorts for girls—since neither was allowed at Finn's school—but living in Orlando, it turned into a Disney costume contest for half of the fifteen hundred kids. Worse, a few students came as one or more of the Kingdom Keepers, and Finn didn't know whether to feel honored or mocked.

But he looked tragically normal in a pair of shorts and a striped T-shirt. Even Amanda had gotten into it, showing up in a pressed white shirt and plaid skirt, which he assumed was connected to Harry Potter. At least a third of the remaining girls and more guys than he'd expected came as vampires. But it was Disney and Marvel Comics that won by a long shot. *Iron Man* characters. *Alice in Wonderland. Toy Story.* Every witch, dwarf, princess, and mermaid in numbers that staggered the imagination. Added into the mix were girls who dressed as princes and boys dressed as witches, so that the bathroom ended up a confusing mix, which was exactly where Finn found himself as he heard the familiar voice.

"What are you looking at, Whitless?"

Luowski's voice, but the body of the Russian madman in *Iron Man 2*, complete with the scars and bad teeth and something coming off the ends of his hands, which were supposed to be bolts of electricity but looked more like Christmas-tree tinsel. Finn felt sorry for the guy: the costume got close, but in the end didn't work.

Finn realized that he was looking at himself in the mirror—like the last time he'd run into Luowski in there. The situation was doubly strange because he didn't remember coming into the bathroom. Nor did he remember turning on the faucet, which was currently running.

"Hey, Greg."

In addition to the Mickey Rourke look, Luowski was wearing the green contacts. Something Finn took note of with added apprehension.

Finn chanced a glance at his watch: eight minutes had passed since the end-of-school buzzer. For a moment he couldn't remember having been in school at all that day. He could force himself to imagine, if not actually remember, having entered the boys' room, but he had absolutely no recollection of the past eight minutes.

The Evil Queen? Had someone dressed up like her been behind him in the mirror just a few seconds before Luowski? Was that a memory, or his imagination?

He cleared his throat. "The more important question, Greg, is why are you hanging around the boys' room staring at other guys staring at themselves in the mirror?"

"I . . . ah . . . Who said I was?"

"Picture's worth a thousand words." Finn pulled his phone out of his pocket.

Luowski said, "Your girlfriend's waiting outside."

"I don't have a girlfriend."

"Not what I hear."

"Well, you hear wrong."

Finn turned around and faced the taller Luowski, standing about chin height to him. But Luowski might as well have been six-feet-five and 280 pounds for the way Finn felt. He didn't want anyone—including Greg Luowski—messing with Amanda.

"Take a look yourself, Romeo." Luowski motioned to the door.

Finn had something to say to Luowski, but knew it would earn him a punch in the face, so he bit back his words.

He was back in the hall heading for the front doors, not feeling quite right. It bothered him that he'd lost eight minutes of his life. Nothing like that had ever happened to him before. He and the other Keepers had often discussed "side effects" of being a DHI: the extreme fatigue mixed with the occasional insomnia. He wondered if the side effects included memory lapse. Eight minutes. Gone.

He swung open the school doors.

Amanda stood at the bottom of the steps, turning her head toward him just as Finn arrived through the doors. *His girlfriend* . . . Was he supposed to get used to that? He felt happy to see her—almost too happy.

Light-headed. Weightless. He seemed to float down the steps toward her.

She stood among a group of girls. A few covered their mouths, hiding their smiles as they saw Finn. He had no idea how stupid he looked. But his vision blurred to where there was only Amanda. The others girls looked almost Photoshopped in, blurry and unidentifiable.

He didn't know why, but he looked behind him—Luowski-the-Russian-madman stood at the top of the stairs, grinning. Finn was halfway down when Amanda approached him.

"Walk me home?" Amanda said. That was a first. He'd walked his bike with her plenty of times, but he couldn't remember her asking for him to.

"I like that shirt," he said, having retrieved his bike.

"It's Jess's."

"You look good in it." What a stupid thing to say. It fit her pretty tightly and she was going to think him a creep.

"Thanks."

They walked a block. Two. Five.

"You're awfully quiet," she said.

"Luowski was bugging me in the bathroom," he said, wondering where that kind of honesty came from. "He's one of them."

"Are you sure?"

Finn caught her up on the recent street confrontation and Luowski's comment about not believing in magic.

"That's fairly direct," she said.

"It is. And there's more." He told her about Hugo and Philby.

"Ohmigod, they actually fought? Like with fists?"

"Like with."

"Well, I can see why he's creeping you out."

"Yeah."

"So, you gave me that message," she said.

Finn had forgotten completely about that. It felt like a week ago. It had been the same morning in U.S. Government class. "Oh, yeah."

"You really are distracted."

"Sorry."

"The note said you wanted to talk to me."

This explained why she was waiting for him outside school. He felt like an even bigger idiot. This was one of those days to wipe off the calendar.

"I . . . we . . . the Keepers, need you and Jess. To cross over, or be ready to cross over." He went on to explain the morning conference call.

She hesitated. "I told you about Mrs. Nash threatening to send us back to the Fairlies."

"Why would she do that, anyway? I mean, besides you two messing up? If they wanted you in the Fairlies they would have sent you there when they found you two."

"The one thing I learned when I was there," she said, "is that you never can trust anything to do with that place. They told us one thing, but it was so far from the truth it wasn't funny."

"But if they wanted to observe you, or whatever—"

"How do we know they aren't observing us now? How can Jess and I be sure Mrs. Nash isn't being paid to spy on us and report back?" Amanda said.

"That's a little paranoid."

"You wouldn't think so if you'd been through what we've been through."

"No, I'm sure not."

"I didn't mean to sound so . . . bossy," she said.

"I didn't take it that way," said Finn.

She reached over and found his hand, and for another block she held it, and he liked it.

They stopped in front of the familiar blue house with yellow trim. The twenty-minute walk had felt more like five. Time was all messed up for him. Many of the other houses on the block were Spanish influenced and one story tall. Mrs. Nash's house looked older, and it was two stories.

Finn slapped the kickstand down and faced Amanda. He knew exactly what he wanted to do—he'd just never done it exactly like he was about to do it.

Jess stepped out the front door, looking panicked.

Finn stepped up to Amanda and grabbed her by the shoulders. It was almost as if he was compelled to do this, as if he'd been told step-by-step what to do.

Much to his surprise, Amanda made no effort to pull away from him. He'd expected maybe a slap in the face.

"My shirt!" Jess hollered, making it sound like a crime.

Something was wrong. Finn knew it. He knew Jess was running to stop them from kissing, but he didn't want to be stopped. He saw Luowski in the lavatory mirror and it just as quickly slipped out of his thought, like a wet bar of soap in the shower.

Jess's shouting about her shirt turned Amanda's head in her direction. A conspiracy to stop him from doing what he *had* to do.

He reached out, took Amanda's chin in his fingers, and turned her toward him.

He brought his lips to hers and, as their lips met, it wasn't just any kiss, but a ringing-in-your-ears, blinded-by-the-light kind of kiss that went on much longer than he'd expected. Amanda's eyes opened and there was a world in there. A place he'd never been.

He drew back. He saw Amanda standing there looking stunned and all dreamy as well, but he suddenly couldn't remember what he was doing there. Couldn't remember how he'd gotten there. He felt startled, dizzy. Then he spotted his bike and wondered if he'd ridden here. Or had he walked the bike?

Why am I here? he thought.

Jess skidded to a stop.

"No!" she roared.

Amanda's knees went out from under her. She'd fainted. For a moment, Finn remembered the kiss and he felt . . . proud—the kiss that knocks them off their feet. But there was something about Jess's panic that pulled him out of it. Something about the way Amanda collapsed so suddenly.

*What have I done?*

Jess's face went ashen. She said, "That's *my* shirt!" as if that explained anything.

"What's going on?" He felt as if he had been shoved out onto a stage and didn't know his lines, didn't know the role. It was some kind a nightmare he'd walked into. He tried to wake himself up.

"*She's* wearing *my* shirt! Not me."

"I . . . don't . . . understand." Finn shook Amanda,

praying it was a practical joke, but sensing there was nothing funny about it.

Then Jess shook Amanda's shoulders and it was clear this wasn't a joke. Her body was slack, like she was asleep. She was definitely not moving. Her breathing was incredibly slow and lethargic. All of Jess's shouting and crying wasn't going to change things.

"Wake up!" Finn said desperately, not knowing if he meant it for himself or for her. He went woozy; could barely keep his balance.

Amanda was unresponsive.

Jess looked up at Finn and said, "What have you done?"

\* \* \*

Finn blinked and looked around, terrified. He remembered Luowski in the lavatory, the kiss, but not how it all connected. Why had he come here in the first place?

Jess looked up with tears in her eyes, kneeling by Amanda.

"I . . ." Finn said, "don't know what happened . . . I didn't mean . . ."

"Help me," she said, pulling Amanda's arms toward her. "Mrs. Nash will be back at four. We need to get her inside, upstairs, onto her bunk."

"Wake up . . ." he muttered.

273

"Finn! I need you *now!*"

Finn's senses were dulled, his head thick. "I didn't mean it," he said.

"WE HAVE TO GET HER INSIDE," Jess said, tears running down her face. "RIGHT NOW!"

Finn took Amanda's legs, Jess her arms, but Jess was crying too hard so Finn scooped Amanda up in his arms and carried her.

"I've got her."

He staggered toward the front steps, still trying to grasp what had happened.

The door opened as several girls hurried out to help. They got Amanda upstairs and onto the lower bunk.

He had so much he wanted to say, but the horrified expression on Jess's face said it all.

"We'll tell Nash," Jess instructed the other girls, "that Amanda's sick and is sleeping off a headache. That'll cover her at least for tonight."

"What's up?" one of the girls asked. "So she fainted. So what's the big deal?"

Jess and Finn met eyes. Jess said, "She bumped her head when she fell. She'll be all right, but she might sleep through the night."

Finn's heart stopped: The surprise hologram of the Evil Queen; Luowski's sudden change in attitude. He'd been so certain he'd escaped the Queen's spell, but now her words returned to haunt him:

*As soft as a whisper*
*No one will tell*
*The curse, reversed*
*Seen by the sister*
*When kissing Jezebel*

"You . . ." he muttered, looking at Jess. It felt like a bomb going off. The pieces of a puzzle forming in your mind and finally fitting. "It was supposed to be you!"

Jess paled considerably.

She knows, Finn thought.

"It's Nash!" came a voice from the hall.

"Back door!" Jess to Finn. "Hurry!"

Finn hesitated, looking down at Amanda, feeling horribly responsible.

"You can't stay! GO!" Jess said. She pushed a folded piece of paper into his hand. He stuffed it into his pocket. "Take this. I thought it was *me,* too."

Finn moved for the stairs, but a girl waved him back. Finn stopped, teetering on the top step.

"*Pssst!*" Behind him, another of the girls had opened a window leading onto the roof. She motioned out the window.

Finn had the sneaking suspicion he wasn't the first boy to be hurried out of Mrs. Nash's house.

The girl at the window pressed her finger to her lips. He was to go quietly. She pointed to the far right of the roof.

Finn looked back. Jess had dried her tears, but her color had failed to return. She hurried to him and handed him a folded napkin. He pocketed this as well.

*She knows it was supposed to be her*, he thought.

He ducked out and was gone.

* * *

They met at five PM in the back room of Crazy Glaze. Maybeck's aunt left them alone, wearing a worried face; she knew better than to ask what was going on.

Philby's time was limited. His mother was waiting in the car outside; she expected him out no later than six. Charlene had Willa on speakerphone, which sat on the table next to a dozen glazed, but unfired, coffee mugs.

The collective mood was anxious. Maybeck was not tossing out his usual jokes.

Finn started off by confessing to them about the video chat where Wayne had transfigured into the Evil Queen, his going *all clear*, and her attempt to put him under a spell, which he recited word for word. He told them about the second encounter with Luowski in the boys' room, and about his kissing Amanda, and her collapse.

No one openly criticized him, but their disappointment in him was obvious. The Keepers were a team, and by not telling them earlier, he'd effectively gone solo. He didn't need to be reminded where that had now gotten them.

"First Charlene, then Willa. Now Amanda," he said. "But it was supposed to be Jess."

"So the Evil Queen got you with the spell," Willa said. "And then the mirror in the bathroom. The Evil Queen is all about 'mirror, mirror.' Maybe Luowski reinforced the spell or something."

"The question is," Philby said, ever the practical one, "how do we break this particular spell? If a kiss started it, a kiss is not going to end it." He glanced over at Charlene, remembering their kiss.

"'Reverse the curse,'" Maybeck said. "Maybe she told us without meaning to. In Amanda's case, the kiss made her into Sleeping Beauty instead of waking her up from a nap. Right? So, someone remind me how Sleeping Beauty got cursed in the first place?"

"She pricks her finger on a spindle that Maleficent creates," Willa said over the speakerphone.

"Maleficent? Seriously? Now there's a surprise! So

we find a spindle—a Disney spindle, a Park spindle—and we give Amanda a splinter from it, and we see what we see," Maybeck said. "What?" he said, when he found himself facing skeptical looks. "Does someone have a better idea? She reversed the curse, so why shouldn't we?"

"It does make sense in a weird, Maybeck kind of way," Charlene said. "There have got to be spindles in the Parks. We could at least *try* it, right? It's better than doing nothing!"

"Can we come back to it?" Philby said. He pushed his laptop to Charlene, asking her to Google "Disney spindle." "I don't have much time, and there's stuff about the log I absolutely have to tell you about."

Charlene went to work, typing furiously.

"Go ahead," Finn said. "But make it quick." Philby could be a talker, and Finn had no patience for that. He wanted Amanda back, *right now*! He couldn't remember ever feeling this on-edge, this . . . guilty.

"Finn and I hacked the MK server last night, as you guys know, and I downloaded the activity log. I'll skip the details, since getting Amanda back is way more important, but still, this could affect everything. Basically, the OTs have made themselves into DHIs. I have the proof. Empirical data. They first appeared on the Animal Kingdom server, a week ago. But get this:

four ID numbers. So the Evil Queen and Cruella have company—and we don't know who. Other OTs? If so, they're probably ones we haven't met yet, which is kind of freaky. Let's hope it's not Luowski or Sally Ringwald, or some other kids—but that's my first guess. Sally warned Amanda and Charlene that there were more of them than we could imagine. Maybe she meant DHIs. That's what I'd do if I were looking to defeat us: create other DHIs to take on ours. Level the playing field. Make it equal ground."

"Good Godfrey," said Maybeck.

"What's more important—*much* more important—is that after a lot of crossing over and Returning in AK, their data tags make a handshake with a router at DisneyQuest on the night of the school thing."

"The night we saw them," Willa said over the phone.

"Yeah," Philby said.

"But that's not possible," Willa said. Only she and Philby understood the technical side and therefore spoke the same language. "The firewalls—"

"Had to have been breached," he said.

"They jumped?"

"They jumped," he confirmed. "Further evidenced by data cloning onto the DHI servers in MK, the Studios, and Epcot."

Finn raised his hand like a student in class. But Philby was focused on the phone and Willa.

"So they can go anywhere we can go," Willa said. "And places we can't go," she added.

"English is spoken here," Maybeck said.

Philby said, "Here's the four-one-one: Disney's careful—super careful—about protecting their data. Each Park has only two data pipes leading in and out. One is for backup. The other is the one typically used. They have major—and when I say major, I mean *major*—firewalls to keep data in and hackers out. That's part of what DHI shadow is all about—it's not just projectors. When we physically walk outside of the Parks and outside of those firewalls, we're lost by the system. When we reenter another Park, our IDs are picked back up and we project."

Maybeck said, "Keep it moving."

"Anyway, there's a DHI server for each Park for a reason: our data can't flow through those firewalls."

"But theirs can?" Willa asked.

"The OTs have pulled it off somehow," Philby said. "It's called jumping. They jumped from Animal Kingdom to DisneyQuest and back. They then propagated—spread," he said, directing the translation to Maybeck, who made a cruel face back at him, "their data packs to each of the Park servers. The only way to do that was to breach the firewalls. It's radical stuff. Big-time stuff. And I'm sorry, but I don't see them pulling it off without the help of an Imagineer, and not just any Imagineer, but someone high up—someone with detailed knowledge of the firewalls."

"Wayne's warning," Finn said. "It had to do with the servers, and about a friend turning his back."

"That was me," Charlene said.

"Maybe not just you," Finn said. "Maybe the Queen's got an Imagineer under a spell, or there's an all-out traitor among them."

"And not to get too *Conspiracy Theory*, or anything," Philby said, "but what if that's how Wanda got caught? What if an insider sold her out to the cops? You want to know why we haven't heard from her since your mother bailed her out?" he asked Finn. "It's because she's convinced it will only put us in danger—that her every move is being monitored, that she's contagious, and doesn't want us catching her cold."

You could have heard a pin drop.

Finn said, "Jess's sketches." He passed them around the table counterclockwise, starting with Maybeck. Both were photocopies. Finn described them for Willa. One of a military guy; the other, the kiss in front a massive building.

"They don't do anything for me," Maybeck said, passing them on.

"But it's what the Queen wanted from me," Willa said. "The most recent one: the military guy."

"So just to clarify," Charlene said, "you were supposed to kiss Jess so she couldn't draw any more of these? Couldn't see the future? Do I have that right?"

"I wish we knew," Finn said. "But, yeah. I think so."

"I thought you said you kissed Amanda at Mrs. Nash's," Philby said. "So what's with the multiplex behind you two?"

"No clue," said Finn. "You know how her 'visions' mix stuff up. I thought it might be school. But you're right—it could be a movie theater or an outlet mall or something."

"So," Willa said over the phone, "we have two sketches that don't necessarily help us, but are apparently of huge importance and interest to the Queen. Amanda's in a coma because of them. We think there's a possible jailbreak attempt but we don't know where or when, and the woman who might be able to help us is probably under police surveillance. What am I missing?"

"You make it sound so ugly," Charlene said.

"What about the spindle theory?" Finn asked. "I mean, seriously, is that all we've got?"

"Reverse the curse," Maybeck said.

"As much as I'd like to say we might find a Disney character capable of countering a spell by the Evil Queen, I can't think of any," Philby said. "Anyone?"

No one piped up.

"No," Philby said. "It's logical that if a kiss put her into this, I suppose a prick from a spindle might get her out."

Maybeck said, "It's got to be worth a try. Maleficent and the Queen are playing for the same team. The Queen throws a spell onto Finn about reversing the curse. I mean, how can we ignore that?"

"We've got to try something," Finn said. "We can't just abandon Amanda. Mrs. Nash will hospitalize her. She's already threatened to send the girls back to the Fairlies. This will seal the deal."

Charlene said, "Do I have to be the one to say what we're all thinking but no one wants to say?" She was internally fuming over the kiss, but she held her tongue about that.

"This I've got to hear," Maybeck said.

"This is exactly what they want: us focusing on Amanda instead of them."

Finn said, "I know. I know." He nodded reluctantly. "But that's where I am. Until Amanda's awake, I don't care what the OTs are up to."

"How did it feel when you were crossed over

without your consent?" Maybeck said, attacking Charlene. "'Cause I can tell you, I didn't like it. Not one bit."

"I'm just saying: we can't ignore everything else that's happening. That's all."

"Agreed," Philby said.

Finn said, "You all know where I'm at."

Maybeck said. "Here's another idea: We lay a trap, capture the Evil Queen, and waterboard her until she tells us how to get Amanda back. Spindles? Seriously, what was I thinking?"

"There are weaver spindles in Epcot's Morocco," Charlene reported, reading from Philby's computer. "And in China the acrobats spin plates on spindles. Those are the only ones I can find."

Finn said, "I vote we get both of those and try them on Amanda. We do it right now, tonight, before Mrs. Nash freaks out and does something random."

"But what if they want us focused on Amanda? When Amanda and I questioned Sally Ringwald, she mentioned Saturday morning. That's *tomorrow* morning. What if tonight's the start of the future? What if tonight is the jailbreak?"

Finn fingered the page torn from Jess's diary. The boy and the girl kissing. The building in the background that looked like steps, or maybe a multiplex. Something was bothering him about it, but he couldn't make sense of it. He looked up. Everyone was staring at him. They seemed to be waiting for him to say something.

He looked around the table at his friends. He thought about Amanda collapsing to the ground—that look in Jess's eyes. He felt worse than he'd ever felt.

"We'd better get started," he said.

# 9

THAT NIGHT, FOUR OF THE KEEPERS entered Epcot prior to closing, while Philby monitored the DHI server traffic from home, prepared to warn them if bandwidth usage indicated the presence of OT holograms. Finn entrusted Dillard Cole to Park hop and hide three of their four phones in the Magic Kingdom, Animal Kingdom, and the Studios in the event they later crossed over.

Finn's mother dropped him, Maybeck, and Charlene off in the Epcot parking lot. She planned to stay in the car, prepared to help them make a hasty retreat if needed. After much begging and promises made by Finn that both mother and son knew would never be kept, she had visited Wanda Alcott in her apartment on his behalf. If the OTs were watching Wanda— his reasoning went—the arrival of a grown-up at the apartment was unlikely to stir much interest. The visit was short, but significant. Finn's mother, working from a note card and passing along Jess's two sketches, briefed Wanda on the events of the past week, culminating in the Keeper theory that they had all been betrayed by someone within the Imagineers—who was either under the spell of, or cooperating freely with, the Overtakers. From what his mother later told Finn, this news had apparently come as no great surprise to Wanda; she had been avoiding contact with the Keepers because she harbored the same suspicions. However, now, given the immediacy of their need, she'd agreed to help.

Finn, once again in baseball cap and sunglasses, hid his phone—the fourth and last—outside Mouse Gear in a wall-mounted metal fixture near the Epcot plaza. Leaving the phone behind made him painfully aware of the isolation that resulted. But should they fail in their efforts and the need arose to cross over later that same night, they gave themselves a chance to Return, and that overruled all other considerations.

The three Keepers—Finn, Maybeck, and Charlene—used the employee passes Wayne had provided a year earlier to enter Epcot by an employee entrance shortly after eight PM.

Within minutes of their arrival into the Park, Maybeck said, "Do you see who I see?"

No Park visitor would have recognized her with her dark hair up in a bun and a Rays baseball cap worn backward. She looked tomboyish in a loose-fitting, man-tailored shirt, and dark green Capri pants. But for those who knew her well, there was no mistaking Willa.

They caught up to her, showering her with smiles.

"But I thought—" Charlene said.

"Yeah, well . . . my mother has a library board meeting tonight, and my father took a sleeping pill because he's flying to Europe tomorrow, and they can ground me for eternity for all I care, but there's no way I'm leaving Amanda under some stupid spell."

Her act of courage elevated the spirits of the entire group. She would team up with Maybeck in Morocco, while Finn and Charlene took China, as already planned. Philby was home monitoring server activity. Willa had "borrowed" her father's BlackBerry and called Philby to give him a way to reach them. Charlene had brought a pair of walkie-talkies that had a short range; her family used them on ski trips. It wasn't a perfect setup, but Finn felt confident they could at least communicate one pair to the other.

They split up.

He and Charlene caught up to Dillard at an outside merchandise stall in front of Mexico. Like two spies, Finn accepted the pass of a folded sheet of paper from his friend, and Dillard was gone, off to scout China and Morocco. Dillard had written down detailed descriptions of the locations for the phones he'd hidden in the other Parks. For Finn, desperate to free Amanda, it felt like the hastily assembled plan was actually coming together. He radioed the locations to Maybeck so that all four of them now knew how to execute a Return if later needed.

On Dillard's part, playing even a small role in a Kingdom Keepers mission was the thrill of a lifetime. He'd often begged Finn to turn him into a DHI and make him part of the group. Finn had told him that was impossible, though he was now reconsidering, beginning to wonder if expanding the Keepers might be necessary. The Overtakers were outnumbering them. Something had to be done.

Willa and Maybeck headed around the east side of the lake; Finn and Charlene, the west. Remaining alert for crash-test dummies, Security patrols, jesters, trolls, spiders, vultures, and a twenty-foot snake, they kept to the crowds.

They acted as if they were in no hurry, just kids out for a fun time in Epcot. The World Showcase pavilions slipped past: Canada and the United Kingdom's Big Ben on one side; Mexico's Mayan Temple and Norway's Stave Church on the other.

They worked to blend in, keeping their heads down. Many kids would know what they looked like. Finn felt like his face had been displayed on a "wanted" poster. Their DHI host characters were known from the Parks, from an Internet game, and merchandise. Despite them all wearing sunglasses—at night—they had to protect themselves from being recognized and mobbed by fans.

Near France, Maybeck spotted a Segway ridden by a Security guard. Forbidden from visiting the Parks without permission, he and Willa hid inside the London tea shop and let it pass. They then continued past America, Italy, and Germany, finally facing the brown stucco buildings of Morocco, halfway across the lake from where they'd started.

"This is my favorite country in all the World Showcase," Willa said in a hush. Not that Maybeck had asked. "I used to get henna drawings on my hands or ankles, these beautiful designs that didn't wash off for weeks."

"I haven't spent a lot of time here," Maybeck said. They remained just outside the entrance to the country's courtyard, across the main path that encircled the lake. "I have this thing about robes. Priests. Witches. Doesn't much matter to me. I hate them all."

"Robes? Seriously?"

"I don't know where it came from or why it bugs me so much. For some kids it's clowns. Or sharks. I don't love snakes or spiders, either. But guys in robes—girls, not so much—give me the creeps."

"And they wear robes in Morocco? I've never noticed," Willa said.

"Sometimes they do. Yes, sometimes they do," he said defensively.

"Well, if I see a robe I'll warn you," she said.

"Besides," he said, "I like hanging with you better." He looked away as if watching for Overtakers. "Charlene's way too happy and cheerleader for me most of the time."

"And I'm not happy?"

"I didn't say that. But you and me, we've got similar energy levels. I'm not talking about smarts, I'm talking about . . . energy."

"You . . . you know I kinda like Philby, right?"

"Kinda?" Maybeck said.

Willa blushed.

"Everyone knows you like Philby except Philby."

"Yeah, well, that's Philby. Maybe that's what makes him so easy to like."

"Are you saying I'm not easy to like?" Maybeck said.

"I did not say that. You're very easy to like."

"You've got that right," he said.

Willa bit back a smile. "So tell me something: Do you like to be called Donnie or Terry better?"

"I couldn't care less," he said.

"You must have a preference."

"Sadly, no. Call me whatever you like, just don't call me—"

"—late to dinner," she said, interrupting. "That's a very old joke, Donnie."

He shrugged. "I'm an old soul."

People were already positioning themselves around the lake, reserving prime spots for the upcoming fireworks display. The Keepers planned to use IllumiNations to their advantage.

"Do you think we're wasting our time with this spindle thing?" Maybeck asked, since it had been largely his idea.

"I . . . ah . . . You and I have both been trapped in the Syndrome, so I don't have to explain to you why I'd do anything to break the spell on Amanda."

"That doesn't exactly answer my question."

"I can see how it makes sense."

"You think we're wasting our time."

"I have no other plan," she said. "No one had any other plan. 'Reverse the curse,' Donnie. It makes sense. It really does."

"I just don't want to be the one wasting our time." He sounded younger all of a sudden, apologetic.

"Finn and Philby make a lot of the tough decisions," she said. "Especially Finn."

"You're holding out on me, girl," Maybeck said, catching an expression passing across her face.

"I . . . it's something someone told me when I was in SBS. If you're nice to me, maybe I'll share it. Or maybe I'll just share it with the girls."

"I can be very nice."

"That's for me to judge."

"Weaver spindles," Maybeck reminded, the crowd inside Morocco thinning as the fireworks neared.

"The gift shop. Yeah."

"There's a gift shop in the World Showcase? Now there's a surprise," he said sarcastically.

"They sell small rugs. There's a rug loom on display. Spindles. I'll create a diversion. You grab one of the spindles. Simple," she said.

"Why does the black kid have to be the thief?"

"That's awful. That's *not it at all*, and you know it. First of all, you're just Maybeck to me, 'kay? Second, you're not a thief, but you are a boy. You're better at this stuff."

"Boys are better at stealing?"

"If you're chicken, I'll do it," she said.

"Okay, good. You do it. I'll create the diversion."

"You're serious?"

"Absolutely."

"Okay," Willa said reluctantly, clearly unhappy with the arrangement.

As the Disney voice announced the start of Reflections of Earth, Park guests rushed the lake in droves, forming a human ring fifty people deep around the entire lake.

Maybeck said, "If we get separated, we meet outside the bathrooms by the train display at Germany. It's just around the—"

"I know where it is."

"You're mad at me."

"Am not," she said, clearly lying. "It's just I've never stolen anything in my life, and that was a record I was hoping to keep."

"And I have?"

"I didn't say that!"

"We can flip a coin if you like."

"I like."

"You got a coin?" he asked, checking his pockets.

"I'll do it," she said. "Just don't say I never did anything for you."

"You won't get caught because my job's to make sure you don't get caught."

"You never quit, do you?"

"Hey, if you don't believe in yourself, then who will?"

* * *

Finn hip-checked Charlene, turning her down the wide, curving jungle path between Mexico and Norway. It dead-ended into a wide wooden gate, a Cast Members-only entrance to the right. In the soft shadow of darkness appeared the shape of a woman, and Charlene startled.

"It's okay," Finn said, encouraging Charlene forward. "It's Wanda. She's expecting us."

Wanda Alcott greeted them both with hugs, holding on to Finn like she might a nephew. Her gratitude for his bailing her out of jail was written all over her face.

"It's all arranged," Wanda said. "They added the extra show. It starts any minute. Better from here on if it's just us girls."

Finn nodded.

Charlene knew the plan, but not Wanda's involvement.

"Should anything go wrong, and Lord knows it can," Wanda said, "I've arranged a way out for you; and for the other two, for that matter. The characters are all on your side," Wanda said.

"The Cast Members," Charlene clarified.

"Some of them, too," Wanda said. "But no, Charlene, I mean the characters. They have been supportive of all of you from the beginning."

"But, that means . . . From the *beginning*?" She felt

overwhelmed. Their support could change everything.

"My father was reluctant to organize them—quite honestly, not knowing whom to trust. But the dust has settled. Hmm? And there's every indication now that they've come together as a group. It's tremendous progress, and it's in large part because of the example you've set. For so many years—decades—they've been individuals; they've enjoyed the flattery of daily attention. Like with movie stars, that creates some interesting personalities—just read the tabloids. But so many of them want the magic to remain in the Parks. Their very existence is at stake. If the Overtakers have their way, they'll all be wiped out. Gone. Hard to imagine a world like that."

"I don't want to imagine a world like that," Charlene said.

"It's not just the Overtakers we have to worry about," Finn said. "There are Security guys who've come after us before. It's not like we can trust just any Disney employee."

"No. There are definite pockets within various groups to watch out for. The poison has spread."

"To the Imagineers?" Finn said.

"I spoke with your mother. In any war there is the threat of double agents."

"And we're at war?" Charlene said.

"We will be soon. Darkness descends," Wanda said, looking up into the night sky.

She grabbed Charlene by the hand, nodded to Finn, and led the girl through the Cast Member doorway.

Charlene looked back at Finn through the gloom, her face a mask of worry and concern.

Finn suddenly felt horribly alone.

* * *

Fireworks exploded over the lake.

When Maybeck created a diversion, he did it Maybeck-style: big time. He knocked over a tall urn containing tiki torches. The resulting cacophony was like a stampede of wild horses, the chaos compounded by Maybeck's intentional fumbling as he tried to rectify the situation. He kicked the torches around in a storm of rattling bamboo, and set the urn rolling toward the checkout desk. The two Cast Members remaining in the store hurried over to help.

Willa, standing alongside a straw basket containing a very real-looking cobra that flicked its tongue at her, grabbed the weaving spindle from the loom on display and pulled hard to break the yarn. But the display was deceptive. The yarn was not really yarn but some kind of unbreakable nylon string. It wasn't going to break no matter how hard she pulled. So, with the Cast Members laboring to help Maybeck with the spilled tiki torches, Willa began unwrapping the string from the spindle as fast as she could.

Maybeck glanced in Willa's direction several times, clearly annoyed and frustrated by her taking so much time. Finally, she reached the end of the string and the spindle came loose. She stuffed it into her pocket and nodded slightly when she caught Maybeck looking.

Together with the Cast Members, Maybeck collected the torches and stood them back up in the urn and the urn was moved back into place. Maybeck apologized profusely and slipped out one side of the store as Willa left opposite him. She turned left, toward the brightly exploding sky and the mobs of people watching the spectacle.

A Security guard on a Segway was headed right for her. Then she spotted a second Segway on Maybeck's side. Willa turned around and walked in the other direction, deeper into Morocco. The stolen spindle felt like it weighed a hundred pounds in her pocket. She thought about tossing it. But if the Security guy was watching her, he'd see.

She glanced over her shoulder. The Security guy had stopped at the store.

She faced forward and found herself looking into the eyes of an old man—a street beggar. There was at once something sad about this poor man, and yet something else vaguely familiar. She stopped abruptly, both afraid and intrigued. Maybeck appeared behind the old man, coming around the far corner. Perhaps the old guy caught the shift in her vision, or maybe he had eyes in the back of his head, but he knew someone was there. He backed up, forming a triangle with them.

"Should I call the authorities?" he asked in a creaky old voice. "Do you think they might be interested in a missing spindle?"

"But how—?" Willa's breath caught.

Maybeck stopped. He and Willa exchanged a look of despair.

"Go on your way, old man," Maybeck said.

"Old man? Do you think so?" As he laughed, the silk veil that hung across his chin billowed like a sail. He paused a moment, looking between them, making sure he had their attention. "I . . . want . . . your . . . magic. I will spare your lives if you give it to me now."

Willa felt a shortness of breath. There was something about the way he'd said "magic" that cut to her core. She'd never considered herself as possessing any magic, and yet here was this weird old man not only claiming that, but wanting her to hand it over. It was like someone trying to rob you of something you didn't know you possessed.

"Wait a second! Who are you?" Maybeck stepped back and indicated for Willa to do the same.

"Think you can outrun me, do you? That would be a terrible mistake to make."

"I can outrun you on one leg, old man," said Maybeck.

The silk veil dropped, revealing a pointed jaw. The old man's body stretched and grew taller.

Willa understood why his jaundiced eyes had seemed so familiar. The person who stood before them was not an old man at all. It was Jafar.

Willa's gasp echoed off the walls.

"Lest you forget what I'm capable of . . ." Jafar said, and immediately transformed into a cobra—the clothes falling in a pile on the cobblestone street at his feet. The cobra lifted its head and its neck flared.

Maybeck muttered, "Willa, I don't do snakes."

No wonder the cobra in the store had looked so real, she realized. "Don't . . . move!"

"Not planning on it," Maybeck said.

The cobra aimed first at Willa, then at Maybeck.

"One leg, huh?" she said.

"Very funny. What now?"

Willa addressed the cobra. "We are willing to listen to your proposal."

The snake moved with insane swiftness into the leg

of the fallen pants, and suddenly Jafar stood before them once more.

"Good decision," he said.

Each time the fireworks boomed, Willa flinched. Colors flashed on the walls surrounding them, turning their faces blue, red, green, and white in rhythmic pulses.

"Exactly what magic are we talking about?" Maybeck asked.

"The window magic."

"Windows? Like the software?" Maybeck said.

"I don't think we're talking software," Willa said. "What kind of windows?" she asked Jafar.

"Window magic," he said. "I wish this also. What the evil one has, I must possess as well."

"Windows," Maybeck said, still confused and trying to wrap his head around their situation. For him, Jafar was one of the worst Disney villains out there. He killed people, or tried to; he placed no value on human life. Maybeck assumed he'd just as soon turn into a cobra and bite them dead as let them walk away. So, it came down to convincing him he could get what he wanted without knowing exactly what he wanted.

Beside Maybeck, Willa backed up a step. Jafar seemed in opposition to, or ignorant of, Maleficent's Overtakers. Both possibilities fascinated her. Was there division in the ranks? Did Jafar command a splinter cell?

Speculation fled as she caught sight of a display carousel in the open doorway to the gift shop immediately behind her.

"What's up?" Maybeck said softly in her direction.

Jafar seemed to understand he was outnumbered. He looked between them like a fan at a tennis match.

"Hang in there with me," she said.

"Hanging," Maybeck said.

Jafar raised his thin, hideous hand and said, "Don't make me do something I'd rather not."

But Willa kept moving ever so slowly toward the display carousel and the merchandise it contained: necklaces, fans, hand mirrors, Aladdin turbans, scarves, and more.

Jafar said, "You *will* give me magic. Only then will I let you leave alive."

"You are one generous dude," Maybeck said. "And right now I'm thinking there's no one we'd rather give our magic to than you. Trouble is, right now, we can't be giving our magic out in the open. You know? We bring the magic, and next thing you know all those people out there are going to want it. And that's no good for any of us. You with me?"

Jafar trained his yellow eyes onto Maybeck, stopping him in his tracks.

"You don't have it, do you?" Jafar sounded crushed and angry. Extremely angry. "I misjudged you. Magic is not something you can leave behind. One either has it or not. And if you don't have it, you are of no use to me."

Willa had to hope not only that her current line of thinking was correct, but that she had perfect pitch. She also had to remember back to second grade—which for her had been an unpleasant time, when her two front teeth had been roughly the size of her thumbnails, and her classmates had teased her for being so ugly.

She grabbed hold of a snake-charmer's flute from the display carousel. In second grade, it had been a recorder flute for the Christmas show. She drew it to her mouth, and played a haunting melody from a faraway land that she'd just heard inside the store.

Within the first few notes of the snake-charming melody, Jafar slapped his ugly hands over his large ears and backed away from her, already beginning to sink to the ground, shrinking away like a snake inside a wicker basket.

Maybeck looked on in amazement. "How did you—?"

"Shut up! Get ready to run."

"I do not need to get ready. I am so out of here."

"Come over behind me."

Maybeck slid over behind Willa and, with her continuing to play the melody, the two backed away from the recoiling Jafar.

She dropped the flute.

They turned and ran.

* * *

Finn stood in the front row of the crowd of the hundred or so people surrounding a roped-off area designated for the Chinese acrobats. Fireworks tore holes in the sky, as a coach and a group of twelve girls and eight boys appeared in gymnastics uniforms. The crowd broke into applause.

The girls were mostly all tiny and young, wearing light blue leotards, all with basically the same bob-and-straight-bangs haircut. The somewhat older Chinese boys formed a line behind, hands clasped behind their backs, flexing their arm muscles, and awaiting their turn. It took a moment for Finn to recognize the third-to-last girl in line as Charlene. She wore a wig that matched the other girls'. With the addition of some eye makeup and blush, she blended in surprisingly well. But just seeing her there made Finn think how stupid a plan this was. There had to have been a better way than this to get the spindle. But there was no turning back now.

The coach—a strong looking older guy with a bald

head—clapped his hands twice and the show began. Finn looked away, not wanting to see what a fool Charlene was about to make of herself. Despite her claim that she'd seen the routine "enough times to know it by heart," Finn knew that seeing it and being able to *do* it were two different things. With his eyes averted and squeezed shut, he cowered from what he expected was going to be a collective gasp as Charlene missed a move and crashed. The show opened with tumbling acts that defied belief: diving through hoops, two girls at a time. Somersaults. Human pyramids.

No collective gasp. Finn squinted one eye open, surprised to see Charlene flying through a hoop and landing in a somersault. The crowd cheered.

Not only did she know the routines, but she executed them flawlessly. Flying bodies, camera flashes, and a cheering crowd occupied the next several minutes.

A roar erupted celebrating a standing pyramid— four girls across on the bottom row, Charlene one of them.

All at once, Finn felt a hand on his right shoulder— a very hard hand. Then another on his left shoulder. He was in the grasp of two mean-looking warriors— Huns—with severe brows and narrow eyes. They wore ancient, decorative armor and were incredibly intimidating to look at.

The spectators around Finn stepped back and took pictures.

Finn glanced toward Charlene, who was no longer in the pyramid. The girls had stood to the side: it was the boys' turn. More applause.

The two guards hauled Finn out of the crowd, as video and digital cameras captured it all.

There was no messing with these guys; their grip unrelenting as they marched him toward a circular building that looked like a giant hat.

Finn said, "I'm actually more interested in the acrobats than a private tour."

They said nothing. He wasn't even sure they spoke English. They tossed him through an open door and then turned their backs, blocking him from leaving.

He was standing in a vast, circular room, the air still. Chinese lute music played. A haze filled the air, streaked by flickering light from projectors. Film footage of Chinese landscapes played on the 360-degree screen. Finn looked for any marked exit signs, and saw only the one being guarded by the two men behind him.

He heard footsteps in spite of the loud music. A cold shiver passed through him as Shan-Yu from *Mulan* stepped out of the haze.

Leader of the Huns, a barbarian warlord, Shan-Yu's shoulders were wide, his head large, and his expression fierce. He wore a thin, wispy mustache on an otherwise brutal face.

"You are leader?" he asked, his voice heavily accented.

"Me?" Finn said, putting the sunglasses up onto the cap. "I'm just a Park visitor."

"The Invisible Ones. You are leader?"

Invisible Ones, Finn thought. That was new.

"Yes. That would be me."

"Tell your emperor to send his strongest armies. I'm ready," the warrior said.

"I have no emperor," Finn said. "We have no army."

"Only emperor have no emperor. You do not look like emperor."

"I am *not* an emperor."

"Then tell your emperor to send his strongest army."

"Why would he do that?" Finn asked.

"Leader of Invisible Ones, I am not afraid."

"Of me? I mean you no harm. What exactly do you want?"

"What does every man want?" Shan-Yu asked.

An Xbox? A PS3? Finn thought. "Immortality," he answered.

Shan-Yu appeared impressed.

"How is immortality achieved?" he asked.

"By doing greatness. Or," Finn added, "great evil."

"By winning wars. By commanding empires. The gods approve of those who do their bidding."

Finn had studied China in fifth grade. He understood there had been child emperors younger than he was, so he couldn't play the kid card. Instead, he thought the better idea was to impress Shan-Yu. Or try to.

"But is not the man who builds the bridge for the army more important than the army?" he asked. "The man who makes the bows more important than the archer? The man who trains the horse more important than the rider?"

Shan-Yu answered, "The man who commands the army is more important than all of them, for the army does his bidding."

"His bidding, or the gods' bidding?"

Shan-Yu took a step closer. "You are indeed a wise leader. I see that clearly in you."

"I am a humble servant serving the lord . . . Disney. My lord is great and powerful. His reach is wide, his army vast."

"You and the other one enter my kingdom without invitation. This makes you both spies. In my kingdom, spies are put to death."

"I . . ." *DEATH?* he was thinking. And why was Shan-Yu speaking only of his own kingdom? There was no mention of the Overtakers as a group. "If you put me to death, how will I tell my emperor you are ready for him?"

"So you have emperor. This clearly makes you spy."

"No . . . no . . . no! Metaphorically!" Finn tried again. "My army is but five strong."

"Five battalions? Five legions?"

"Five *warriors*," Finn said. "We present no threat to you, great lord! Our fight is with the Green One."

Shan-Yu stepped back at the mention of Maleficent. It didn't give Finn the impression the two were the best of friends.

"When two leaders share a common enemy," Finn said, "does that not make them brothers? Allies?"

"You are a sorcerer, Invisible One. A confessed spy. Spies are killed, not negotiated with. If you cannot deliver your army . . ."

He withdrew a curved, gleaming sword from its scabbard, the ring of steel echoing like a bell.

Five of Shan-Yu's warriors appeared seemingly out of nowhere. They had him surrounded, all five with their hands on their sword hilts. Finn could picture his head lying on the floor.

"Shouldn't we talk about this?" he asked Shan-Yu.

"Kill the girl," Shan-Yu called out loudly. "I will take care of this one myself."

Finn glanced to the door and the backs of the two guards. He had to reach Charlene before the warriors did. She wouldn't see them coming. Like him, she would think they were part of the show.

With each step Shan-Yu took toward him, Finn took a step back, glad to see that with all the armor he wore, the man was not terribly light on his feet. The film moved ahead from ancient times to the present. A high-speed train zoomed around the circular wall.

Shan-Yu knew of Finn's "magic." The Invisible Ones. He'd probably seen their Epcot DHIs and marveled at the holograms. If Finn could impress him, perhaps he could intimidate him.

He closed his eyes and relaxed toward a state of *all clear*, knowing it would only last for a matter of seconds.

Light played across his eyelids—a glint from Shan-Yu's sword, or the bullet train's headlight?

His limbs tingled. A slight smile played across his lips.

He heard the blade slice the air and fought not to open his eyes. He wouldn't be able to hold *all clear* if he saw a blade aimed for his neck.

*Swish.* The sound moved left to right.

He opened his eyes.

An off-balance Shan-Yu glared at him, staring in

disbelief. Clearly, he'd cut through Finn's neck and had expected his head to fall. The General looked over at the sword's blade and back at Finn.

Finn stepped forward and walked through him.

Shan-Yu cried out and spun around, swinging his sword.

Finn turned immediately and walked through the man for a second time, his limbs tingling as his *all clear* timed out.

For Shan-Yu, Finn had vanished. Each time the General had spun around, the boy had stepped toward him and disappeared.

Real magic.

Now he spotted Finn and studied him more closely. "Most impressive," he muttered.

"We share the same enemy," Finn said. "Join us." He held out his hand.

Shan-Yu studied Finn's hand, then looked him up and down. "Allies share their resources. Will you share this power of yours?"

"I . . . ah . . . It isn't mine to share."

"GUARDS!" Shan-Yu thundered. "KILL HIM!"

Finn sprinted for the door, splitting the warriors as they were turning around. He ran hard.

"CHARLENE!" he hollered, approaching the audience huddled around the acrobats.

He spotted a stick flying end-over-end from the center of the show. *The spindle.* He jumped up and caught it in midair.

He spotted her. Charlene ran across the acrobats' mat, flew through the air, and hit a mini-trampoline. She flipped over the heads in the crowd, landing neatly in stride with Finn as the spectators roared.

"You took long enough," she said, the two running full speed.

"Had an appointment with royalty," he said. "Shan-Yu."

"What now?"

"Finn!"

It was Dillard. He'd turned over a plastic barrel. Soda cans and ice belched from its open end as Dillard sent it rolling toward the oncoming guards like a bowling ball heading for the pins.

Finn spotted a girl waving at them from a dugout canoe beneath a sky thundering with fireworks.

The guards were forced to dive out of the way of Dillard's barrel.

"Coming through!" shouted Dillard, clearing the crowd for Finn and Charlene by running through angry guests. Dillard was not fat, but he wasn't small. When he wanted a crowd to part, it parted. Having cut a path for his friend, he held open a space at the railing. Finn and Charlene jumped the railing and hurried down into the canoe.

Waiting there was Mulan. She raised her bow and arrow.

"Don't shoot!" Dillard said, clambering over the railing.

"HURRY!" Finn said, reaching to help Dillard aboard.

Mulan fired an arrow.

*Thwack!* It struck something hard.

Finn looked up to see it had landed in a shield carried by one of Shan-Yu's warriors. Mulan's two warriors, two boys older than him whom Finn hadn't seen until that moment, pulled on paddles. The canoe moved swiftly away from shore and out into the flashing lake. Color rained from the sky.

"You are safe now," Mulan said. "We will pick up your friends at the bridge and we will carry you however far you need to go. The river, it is long."

Charlene looked down at the spindle in Finn's hand.

"We got it," she said.

"We got it," Finn echoed.

# 10

Mrs. Whitman picked up Finn, Maybeck, Willa, Dillard, and Charlene from Downtown Disney, where Mulan had dropped them. The conversation in the canoe had gone something like this:

"So," Finn said, "are you really Mulan, or a Cast Member playing Mulan?"

"Let me ask you something," the beautiful warrior woman responded. "Who were you running from just now? Cast Members?"

"Ah . . . yeah . . . okay. I get it," Finn said.

Dillard looked confused, but impressed. Maybeck and Willa remained silent, kneeling near the second thwart from the stern. They looked back toward the shore, bewilderment on their faces.

Maybeck said, "No matter how much I think I'm used to what goes on here, it still freaks me out."

The Chinese warriors navigated the lake, weaving the canoe between the exploding barges of fireworks, the air heavy with the tangy smell of gunpowder.

"By now, the Reflections of Earth team, led by Sam, has seen us," Mulan explained. "Sam is the Crew

Chief. His men have powerboats, and we are forbidden from being out here, so, unless you would like to explain yourself to Park Security, which I have no intention of doing, I would suggest you pick up a paddle and help out."

That put all conversation on hold. Charlene, Dillard, Finn, Maybeck, and Willa grabbed paddles and began digging into the water with all their strength. The canoe raced silently across the black surface of the lake.

The gigantic globe of the Earth was spreading color across the water.

"If we can make it to the bridge at France before Sam catches us," Mulan called out, "we can play a trick on him."

Everyone put their backs into it. The canoe moved smoothly and silently. They left the fiery barges behind.

"We'll be harder to see over there," Maybeck said.

Mulan explained, "The light from the barges will blind them. It'll buy us some time."

Finn saw a powerboat zooming toward them.

"That would be Sam," Mulan said.

"Faster!" Finn cried out.

Less than five minutes later, Sam's Security boat motored beneath the bridge leading to France. On the walkway that was meant to imitate the quay along the river Seine in Paris, there were some boxes, a bicycle, a chest, and an upside-down canoe.

Hiding beneath the inverted canoe, tucked into balls and holding their shins, were two warriors, Mulan, and five kids, with barely an inch of space left over. The motorboat turned, heading back into the lake.

Now, riding in the Whitmans' car, Finn needed yet another favor from his mom.

"We need to make a stop."

"Finn . . ."

"Please."

"Am I not supposed to ask why?"

"If you ask, I'm going to have to lie, and since I don't lie to you, it might be better if you don't ask."

She huffed. "Dillard, what, if anything, do you have to do with all this?"

"I'm an innocent bystander."

That cracked up everyone in the car.

"My sense is, Dillard," Mrs. Whitman said, "that no one in this car, including me, is entirely innocent." That quieted them down. She said, "Where to?"

Finn gave her the address by intersection. He added, "It might be good if you stopped, like, a half block away."

"Finn?" she scolded.

"I'm just saying. . . ."

"What have I gotten myself into?" Mrs. Whitman complained.

"We're trying to save someone, Mrs. Whitman," Charlene said.

"Someone important to us," Maybeck said, in a rare moment of genuine concern.

"Someone who needs us," Willa added.

Mrs. Whitman nodded thoughtfully. "If I were a kid again," she said, "I would want you all as my friends." From then on, she didn't ask any more questions.

Finn and Willa met Jess in back of Mrs. Nash's house. Maybeck and Dillard staked out the street in case green-eyes were secretly watching the foster home. Charlene stayed by the car, having borrowed Mrs. Whitman's phone to call Philby to catch him up.

Jess looked tired and unwell as they huddled in the shadow alongside a freestanding garden shed behind Mrs. Nash's house.

"How is she?" Finn asked.

"Nothing," she answered in a whisper. "She hasn't moved. Hasn't changed one bit."

"These should help," Finn said producing the acrobat's spindle. Willa passed her the weaver's spindle. "You'll need to carve off a splinter and prick her finger."

"I really do not want to do this," said Jess.

Willa said, "Think of it as giving her a shot. She's going to wake up. This is all going to be over."

Jess's sad eyes said it all: she didn't believe Willa. She may have wanted to, but she didn't.

"We're going to wait here," Finn said, "for the good news."

"You can't stay," Jess said. "Mrs. Nash is inside. Supposedly I'm putting out the trash," she said, indicating the bulging plastic bag at her feet. "I can't do this until later. I'll e-mail you," she said to Finn, "depending what works out."

"You'll let us know right away?" he asked.

"As soon as I can."

"We'll be waiting," Finn said.

"Yes. I know that." She thanked them both.

"Are you sure you're okay?" Willa asked, deeply concerned.

"She's so still, so . . ."

Dead-looking, Finn thought. He'd carried her. He knew.

"It'll be over soon," Finn said. "She's going to be fine. Reverse the curse."

"I hope you're right."

Jess disposed of the sack of garbage, slipped the two spindles down her pants to hide them, and returned inside.

"She's bad off," Willa said.

"Yes. I noticed."

With everyone back in the car and Mrs. Whitman driving, she dropped Maybeck off first. Once outside the car, he leaned back in and gave Willa a hug.

"You were great tonight."

"You, too."

He ran down the driveway and was gone.

Willa was next. She sneaked around the house to slip inside. There was no car in the drive; thankfully, she'd beaten her mother home. Then came Charlene, whose mother waved to Mrs. Whitman from the front door.

"Dillard Cole," Mrs. Whitman said, "does your mother know where you've been?"

"Ah . . ."

"He's been over at our house," Finn said. "Kinda."

"That's what I thought," said Mrs. Whitman.

Finn stopped his friend with a hand on the shoulder. "Dude, you were awesome tonight." Finn smiled. "Just don't ever do it again."

"It was way cool."

Dillard said good night and headed inside.

"It's nice you two are connecting again."

"Mom, don't get all mushy on me."

"It's Amanda," his mother said to Finn. "You contacted Jess, so it must be Amanda."

"It is," Finn said. Long ago, he'd promised never to lie to his parents, and he worked daily to keep that promise. He could, and did, stretch the truth when needed, but he never outright lied.

"You needed something from the Park to help her."

"Yes."

"Did you get it?"

"We think so, yes."

"So you stole something from Epcot."

"Borrowed."

"Finn?"

"Borrowed. We will return them. I promise."

"Them," his mother said.

She was way too smart. He couldn't give her this kind of data to work with.

"You wouldn't believe me if I told you, Mom. We should leave it at that."

"I believe a lot more than your father believes."

"I know that."

"Speaking of which, you let me handle your father when we get home. Go along with whatever I say."

"Aye, aye," Finn said.

"And don't try anything without telling me first. We're in this together now, Finn, like it or not."

*Not*, Finn thought, but didn't say. "Okay," he answered.

His mother tried too hard with her explanation. She would never make a spy. Finn's father gave him the corner-of-the-eye look that typically made Finn feel like running straight to the bathroom. Instead, he shrank off to his room feeling troubled, the sound of the blade coming for his neck still fresh in his ears. What if he'd misjudged his sense of *all clear*? What if the *all clear* had expired more quickly?

* * *

The simplicity of Jess's e-mail message compounded Finn's pain.

It didn't work. Thanks for trying.

He stared at the computer screen as if by just looking it might change the message.

Neither spindle had worked. What a stupid idea it had been! Finn had been so convinced that reversing the curse would do it.

He convened an emergency video conference. Philby, Willa, and Maybeck were able to attend. Charlene's mother had turned off the family Wi-Fi for the night, so she followed along on the family's landline telephone, with random updates from Willa.

Philby said, "I thought one of the spindles would

work. I have to tell you, the more I thought about it, the more it made sense."

Charlene said, "They were the only two Google hits that make any sense. But remember, in the movie it's a spindle from a spinning wheel."

"She's right," Philby said. "I've been doing some research . . ."

Surprise, Finn thought.

". . . and in the original fairy tale, after the curse is put on the princess, the king forbids anyone from owning a distaff or spindle. The distaff holds the raw fiber; the spindle collects the spun thread. Spinning *wheel*," he emphasized. "And when you Google Disney World plus 'wooden wheel' you get a single decent lead: the waterwheel on—"

"Tom Sawyer Island," Finn said.

"You got it. A wooden wheel."

"I'm not liking this," Maybeck blurted out. He and Finn had once been attacked on Tom Sawyer Island by Stitch and had been made to swim among alligators.

"The spindle thing was your idea!" Philby protested.

"But this is so totally OT," Maybeck said. "They put a spell on Amanda and the only solution leads us into a trap. I mean, come on!"

"Relax. We can't steal a waterwheel," Finn said.

"No," Philby said, agreeing. His voice held that know-it-all tone that Finn had come to resent. "But what if we could bring Amanda to it?"

"She's down for the count," Maybeck said.

"That's right," Philby said. "She's *asleep*."

Maybeck broke the resulting silence. "Are we done?"

Finn answered, "Philby's saying that if Amanda is asleep then technically he could cross her over."

"WHAT?" Maybeck exclaimed.

"Why not?" Philby asked. "When we're asleep we cross over."

"Is that possible?" Charlene asked. "You're saying she'd awake as her DHI?"

Philby answered, "It's possible. I think it's worth a try. We cross her over, prick her finger with a piece of the waterwheel, and when I Return you all, the Amanda at Mrs. Nash's wakes up."

"Let me spell this out for you," Maybeck groaned. "T-R-A-P."

Charlene objected. "The OTs couldn't possibly think we'd cross her over, Terry. Whatever they may have planned, it can't be this."

"And remember," Finn said, "they wanted Jess in that spell, not Amanda. Depending on the green-eyes, they may not even know it's Amanda who's down."

"It doesn't change it from being a trap," Maybeck said.

"We owe it to Amanda to try anything we can think of," Finn proposed.

"But what about the bigger picture?" Maybeck said. "The jailbreak? It's going down tonight, right? Sally Ringwald basically told us so."

"So you and Charlene will go to sleep dressed to cross over in case Philby detects network traffic. Does that satisfy you?"

"I don't like it," Maybeck said.

"By tomorrow morning," Finn said, "Mrs. Nash is going to drag Amanda off to the hospital. Maybe even sometime tonight. We know how dangerous that is for her. Philby knows."

"It only makes things worse, Maybeck," Philby said. "Much worse."

"We can't just sit around talking," Finn said. "We tried and failed. So what? We've got to try everything. A wooden wheel. Who knows? That could be it. I can let Wanda know our plans. She might help."

"Or she could be the traitor," Maybeck said. "We'd never suspect someone who'd been arrested, would we?"

"So noted," Finn said, experiencing a chill. "And if it is a trap, or she's a traitor, then it's going to be up to you and Charlene to get us off the island." He would send Jess an e-mail keeping her in the loop, keeping her hopes up.

"That's what I'm talking about," Maybeck said.

* * *

Finn arrived in front of Cinderella Castle alone, sitting a few feet from the Walt Disney–Mickey Mouse statue at the center of the hub. He waited, and waited, knowing Philby's next attempt would be to cross over Amanda.

He caught himself holding his breath as a shimmering image of Amanda lying down appeared, and then fizzled and faded as he watched.

"Come on. . . ." he muttered.

The same image reappeared. It grew stronger and more solid, and the blue line formed around it.

Amanda blinked and opened her eyes.

Finn swallowed away a knot in his throat.

"Can you hear me?" he said.

She blinked, but did not look in his direction. The spell seemed to still be holding her.

"It's me," he said. "We crossed you over into the Magic Kingdom. I think we can help you."

Her eyes popped open again.

Finn scouted the area for signs of OTs. He felt vulnerable with her apparent inability to move.

"Can you sit up?" he asked, moving over to her and helping to raise her back.

He spotted motion in some shrubs by the ramp up to the castle.

"Don't move," he whispered in Amanda's ear.

He froze. A dog came out of the shrubs. A big dog.

"It's . . . Pluto," he told Amanda. Pluto was no villain. If he'd come to help, it had to be Wanda's or Wayne's doing.

Amanda still hadn't fully come around. Her eyes moved more freely, but she wasn't speaking.

"Here, boy," Finn hissed, holding out his hand. Pluto was big, and stronger-looking than Finn would have expected. The dog faced him, sniffing the air. He wagged his tail and sat down.

"We are here to help," Finn said.

Pluto turned toward the bushes, wagging his tail violently.

"What is it, boy?"

Pluto barked. Just once. But loudly, causing Finn to again jump back. Pluto was trying to warn him of something or someone in the bushes.

"Amanda?" he said softly, without taking his eyes off the bushes.

"I'm here."

He turned to look. She looked tired, but she was working on smiling.

"I feel a little zoned."

"I can explain it all at some point. But for now: can you move? We should get away from here."

Pluto darted over to the bushes, his tail still wagging. Finn tentatively followed, crossing the street and edging closer to the bushes. Pluto's tail was going like a windshield wiper.

Finn sneaked up and parted the bushes. He couldn't believe his eyes. "Minnie?" he said in a whisper.

She gave him a sweet, humble look, lowering her head while looking out the tops of her big eyes.

"I'm Finn," he said. "Over there, that's Amanda."

Minnie nodded.

Finn looked around the area. "Mickey?" he asked her.

She lifted her arms and shrugged. She looked crestfallen.

"He's not here," Finn said, making it a statement.

She shook her head.

"Not here with you?" he said, thinking aloud, "Or not here in the Magic Kingdom?"

She shrugged for a second time.

"I . . ." He couldn't think what to say. He was awestruck. Mickey and Minnie were rock stars. He recalled what Wanda had told him. "Are there more of you?"

Minnie hesitated. Pluto nudged him from behind. He looked back to see Amanda trying to get to her feet.

"Thanks!"

He hurried back to her. Minnie and Pluto followed.

He helped Amanda stand up and held her by the arm. "My friend's in trouble," he told the other two. "I, *we*, need to get onto Tom Sawyer Island."

Minnie smiled and nodded. She lifted a finger as if to say, "Just a minute!"

Pluto came around and heeled at Finn's side.

"You're staying with me," Finn said. The dog nodded.

Minnie saluted Finn and took off running in the direction of Frontierland.

"I'm guessing," he said, "you're staying to protect us." The dog yipped. "And she's gone ahead for some reason." He barked again.

"Are you talking to Pluto?" Amanda asked with a dry voice.

"Are you all right?" he asked.

"I've been better. My head weighs a thousand pounds."

"We need to go," he said.

"I can manage. Are you going to tell me how I got here?"

"I kissed you," he said.

"I don't think so," she said. "That's not something I would forget."

"I promise. I kissed you. It was a spell, intended for Jess." He walked her off the hub and toward Frontierland, condensing and summarizing her story into as brief an explanation as possible.

Pluto nudged between them and leaned into Amanda.

"I think," Finn said, "he wants you to hold onto his collar."

Pluto's tail went wild with excitement.

Amanda reached down and took hold. Pluto lifted his head proudly. His tail shot up like a flagpole.

"This is definitely strange," Finn said.

\* \* \*

Jess was not a mother. She had never even owned a pet. Like the other Fairlies, she had never met her mother, had no idea if she had living relatives. The closest thing she had to a family member was Amanda, whom she thought of as her sister. In fact, she and Amanda often introduced themselves as sisters. So, as the Kingdom Keepers carried out their plan to cross Amanda over into the Magic Kingdom in hopes of reversing the curse, Jess sat by her sister's bedside.

A few minutes earlier, she thought she'd witnessed the cross over: Amanda had twitched and shuddered and, more encouragingly, her eyes had begun moving rapidly beneath her closed eyelids.

The other girls in Mrs. Nash's house were supportive of her effort to keep Amanda's condition secret. This included their roommate, Jeannie Pucket, who until now had often been a real knucklehead. But Jeannie had come through for Jess, not once but a number of times—holding off the curious Mrs. Nash and buying her unconscious roommate precious time.

It wasn't going to last much longer, Jess thought. It seemed inevitable that Mrs. Nash would find out. That, in turn, would mean doctors, and a long downward spiral for poor Amanda.

With her diary open to the kiss, a page she had photocopied for Finn, her eyelids drooped and she briefly nodded off. Her diary slipped from her hands, landed on the bed, and fell to the floor. The sound of the book landing shocked her awake, and she looked around the room as if she'd been asleep for hours.

"It's nothing," Jeannie said. "You dropped your diary, is all."

Jeannie leaned down to retrieve it. About to hand it to Jess, she hesitated.

"If you don't mind," Jess said, "that's private."

Jeannie knew it was private—it was her diary—a source of ongoing tension between the two. Jeannie could allow her curiosity to get the better of her.

"I know. I know." Still, Jeannie was reluctant to hand it over, her attention fixed on the sketch. Finally, she passed the diary back to Jess. "Have you been there?" she asked. "What's it like?"

"School?" Jess asked.

"What are you talking about?"

"Winter Park. Where Finn and Amanda go."

"That's not Winter Park High," Jeannie said. "That's the Lake Buena Vista power plant. I just wrote a paper on it for science class."

"Science class? Lake what?" Jess said.

Jeannie traced the stair-step profile of the structure in the background of the kiss.

"It's called the Lake Buena Vista Cogeneration Facility. Hang on. I'll show you." Jeannie dug through some papers on her desk, including a bunch of printouts from various Web sites. She singled out three of these and passed them to Jess.

"So?"

Jeannie leaned over Jess's shoulder, selected the

second of the three printouts—a photograph taken at a great distance from the power plant—and traced the stair-stepped roofline of the facility. She then pointed to Jess's diary and traced the same pattern.

Jess went silent, her eyes dancing between the two images. She knew her dreams often combined locations or activities.

"What exactly does it do?" Jess asked.

"Electricity. It powers Disney World and local businesses."

"Disney World." Jess felt light-headed. This was *not* coincidence.

"Water and sewage treatment, too. Natural gas. Everything. I got an A on my paper," she announced proudly.

"As in electricity for the Parks?"

"Exactly! Yeah. That's the Disney part. They wanted to own their own electricity and stuff. You know, so it was more reliable and everything."

Jess traced the two rooflines again—from the Web site and from her drawing. They weren't simply similar; they were identical.

"Where exactly is this place?"

"It's way out on Disney property. As in, the boonies."

"Disney property? You sure about that?"

"Hello? An A? Did you know that at one point Walt Disney had planned for Epcot to be this futuristic city, with homes all around it? How cool would that have been?"

Jess barely heard her. Her brain was stuck back on Disney generating its own power. She'd drawn a Disney power plant in her diary without knowing it. It had to be hugely significant.

She had to contact Philby. Now!

\* \* \*

Philby had his hands full. He kept one eye on the clock in his computer's toolbar. The other eye jumped between the dozen webcam views from the Magic Kingdom's Security server as he tracked Finn through the Park. His cell phone rested on his lap in vibrate mode, the laptop bridging his thighs. He sat on the toilet—lid closed—of what his mother called the "powder room," a small, windowless bathroom with a corner sink near the front door of the house. He had the bathroom's door locked: there would be no unexpected intrusions by Hugo or anyone else tonight. He could not afford to leave the Keepers stranded.

The e-mail from Jess caused him to perspire. He Googled "Lake Buena Vista Cogeneration Facility." He had a fine memory, so when a photograph of the power plant popped up, he immediately matched the similarities with Jess's diary sketch. From what he read, the power plant supplied all of Walt Disney World with power. If something happened to the Florida electric grid, Disney's facility promised an uninterrupted flow of electricity to all of its Parks and hotels.

And computer servers, he thought.

Jess had foreseen its importance in one of her dreams. That the kiss used the power plant as a background did not necessarily connect the two: Jess's diary pages often mixed images and time lines. But it established its importance—Jess's track record was well proven.

With the power plant's direct connection to the Parks, and its location *outside* the Parks but still on Disney property, the OTs jumping the Disney firewalls suddenly took on tremendous significance.

Control of the power plant meant control of the Parks—the Overtakers' ultimate goal.

He had no way to reach Finn to update him. But he did have Maybeck and Charlene asleep and on standby to be crossed over.

He brought up his rendering of the router traffic he'd mapped from the DHI server's log, already chastising himself. There had been several pings to a router out in the middle of nowhere. On Google Maps it just came up as an area of swampland—but now he saw his error: for security reasons, power plant locations were blocked from Internet maps. He'd been looking at the power plant all along, because those pings represented OT DHI traffic.

The OTs had been to the Lake Buena Vista Cogeneration Plant several times in the past week.

At that moment, his DHI traffic alarm sounded and a red message flashed on his screen: +70% BANDWIDTH USAGE.

Philby tried to focus, his breathing rapid, his heartbeat out of rhythm.

*They're there right now!*

\* \* \*

Pluto was waiting for them.

"This way!" Finn said, gently steering Amanda while trying to move her more quickly.

"Why are we running?" she asked.

"Visitors," Finn said, glancing back.

Pluto's hackles had been up for the past several minutes, and he kept looking behind them, his eyes a knot of concern.

Finn had tried to see whatever it was back there that was bothering Pluto, but only caught a shadow crossing the empty Park path in Frontierland.

"You see that?" he asked Amanda.

There it was again: the flash of translucent eyes from the shadows, like a deer on the side of a highway.

Amanda skidded to a stop, for she'd seen them, too, but for the first time.

"Another dog?" Finn asked.

Amanda's blue hologram line faded as she lost a considerable percentage of her DHI to fear. "Not a dog," she said. "Did you see how high off the ground that was?"

They were walking backward now, still moving in the direction of the Tom's Landing raft dock, but refusing to take their eyes off the shadows by Country Bear Jamboree, where they'd both seen the pair of eyes.

An animal's rapid breathing could be heard drawing closer.

Finn whispered, "That has to be a dog! Listen to it."

"It's tall. Very tall. Pluto is a Great Dane," Amanda reminded him. "And there's another in the movie *The Ugly Dachshund*."

"Never seen it."

"The dog or the movie?" she asked.

They walked faster now, keeping their eyes on the moving shadows while trying not to fall. They heard a wet slurp from what had to be an extremely large tongue. Another flash of eyes.

"Ehh!" Amanda reached for Finn and clutched his arm tightly. He actually appreciated the contact, though not the reason for it.

A sliver of light from one of the few lighted streetlamps played like a knife's edge across the path, severing the darkness. Through the shaft of light strode a long, hairy creature, rail thin, malnourished and mangy, only a few inches visible at a time, like it was being painted by a tiny flashlight. It had enormous paws and four stick legs, but it was absurdly oversized, had pointed teeth, and a stream of drool that turned their stomachs.

Finn said harshly, "That's no dog."

"A wolf," Amanda said, her voice quavering. "That's the Big Bad Wolf."

The thing was as tall as a bicycle, and looked to be about as fast.

"What now?" she asked.

The wolf lumbered out into the light, its back haunches moving fluidly, its ribs showing through the tangle of filthy hair.

A bone-chilling growl from behind them. Pluto, who'd been leading the way, had stopped and was turned toward the challenger.

"No, boy," Finn said. It was no match.

But Pluto stood his ground as Amanda and Finn backed up past him, putting himself between them and the wolf.

"Come, Pluto!" Amanda whispered harshly.

The dog did not budge, but lowered himself onto his front paws and tucked his tail between his legs. Pluto looked back at Finn with noble eyes.

"He wants us to run," Finn said.

"You speak dog, do you?"

"Are you strong enough?"

"Are you kidding? Believe me, I'm wide awake."

"On three," he said.

"Are you sure about this?"

"No," Finn said.

* * *

Pluto had lived long enough to be the age of an Egyptian mummy in dog years. In that time, he'd learned a few tricks. Not the kind of tricks like roll over or shake hands, but the kind of tricks to play on other animals pursuing you. Over the years these tricks had been refined to the point that they approached actual skills—pie in the face, tongue in the mousetrap, peanut butter in the dog bowl. They'd been well-documented in all the cartoons.

338

When faced with the Big Bad Wolf—emphasis on Big and Bad—Pluto had the luxury of seeing it play out as a cartoon. Where others would've panicked, he saw an opportunity for entertainment and amusement. In a cartoon, no matter how hard the punishment, the dog always got up to play another day.

It never crossed his small mind that the wolf would actually eat him. In Pluto's world, a dog could fall out of a tree, or get hit by a bus, and come out of it with nothing more than stars floating around his head and his eyes rolling in their sockets. One quick shake and everything was better.

So it wasn't a question of fear, it was a question of how to make this really funny, and the more inventive the solution the better.

He spotted it easily: one of those plastic grid fences meant to keep people off sidewalks or out of gardens or away from construction. They used them all the time in the Park. It was currently wrapped around an island of flowers with a sign hanging from it saying a bunch of words he couldn't read but he was pretty sure ended in "Thank You." Pluto was no Rhodes scholar.

With the wolf's confident stride picking up pace, Pluto knew the trick was to get him running. That was when he gave the boy the signal.

For a second, the boy and girl just continued walking backward, which put a glitch in his plan. Humans could be so boneheaded. So he barked.

And that got the kids moving. They took off toward Minnie and the dock like he'd fired a starting gun. That prompted *el lobo* to spring into action. It bared its teeth, squinted its eyes and charged. That was when Pluto realized this might not be so much fun. He'd never seen an animal move so fast. It was as if the creature had been shot from a catapult. Pluto had badly misjudged the time necessary to pull of his stunt. Wolf seconds were different than dog seconds.

With nothing but four-legged teeth coming at him, Pluto found the end of the mesh fence with his own mouth and bit down hard. He wrestled a stake from the soft dirt and then backed up as fast as he could drag it, dislodging one stake after another. The fence stretched across the path—halfway, three quarters.

The wolf's confidence or hunger had him running much too fast to come to any kind of graceful stop. Instead, as Pluto stretched the fence and wrapped it around a small tree, the wolf's paws scratched and clawed at the concrete path but found no traction. He lost his footing, tucked, and rolled, colliding with the fence, which aimed him on an angle toward the water across from Pecos Bill Café. The wolf backpedaled but failed to stop his momentum. He tumbled head over heels into the water.

Pluto turned and ran, seeing clearly there was only one thing scarier than the Big Bad Wolf, and that was a big, MAD wolf.

* * *

Minnie waved Finn toward the raft that serviced Tom Sawyer Island. He and Amanda had just heard a violent splash, turning in time to see a violently angry wolf swimming violently for shore. Pluto bounded toward them at full speed, the panicked look in his eyes needing no translation.

The two kids wound through the empty waiting line for the raft ride. Amanda shrieked and slid to an abrupt stop; Finn crashed into her from behind.

An unconscious pirate lay at his feet. He was gnarly looking, with a scrub beard, a pockmarked face, and bent nose. A bandana worn as a skullcap hid most of a particularly nasty bump. Finn looked between the fallen pirate and Minnie, who stood on the edge of the raft, a shore line in one hand, the other tucked behind her back.

"Minnie?" Finn said.

She hung her head and pulled her hand from behind her back, revealing a large wooden pin, part of the raft.

"She did this?" Amanda asked Finn.

"I'd say she charmed him."

"Thank you, Minnie," Amanda said.

Minnie blushed, and slowly a smile overtook her. She looked devilish as she waved them onto the raft invitingly.

Finn reached to catch Amanda by the arm. "Wait!"

Amanda turned.

"The question that needs to be asked," Finn said rushing his words, one eye on the wolf swimming for shore perhaps fifty yards away, "is why is a pirate guarding the raft to Tom Sawyer Island? He's a long way from home, over in Adventureland, and what's so important about this raft?"

Minnie waved at them more frantically—the Big Bad Wolf was climbing up the shore. Now shaking the water off.

"Overtakers?" Amanda said.

"We know the pirates belong. There's no question about that. So why guard the island? The same island where Stitch attacked Maybeck and me. It doesn't make sense. This island's of no importance. It isn't even that popular an attraction."

"Because the Queen knew you might figure out the waterwheel's importance?" she said.

Finn nodded. "Makes sense to me. He's here to stop

us, or to catch us, or both. And the only problem with that is—"

"He won't be the only one."

"Bingo," he said.

Minnie was jumping up and down and pointing to the wolf, who was now back on the path in the distance, lumbering toward them, his pink tongue swaying from his teeth.

"So we'll need to be careful," Amanda said.

Pluto jumped onto the raft as they climbed aboard. Minnie tossed the line to shore, stepped behind the wheel, and skippered the raft across the small waterway. The wolf reached the loading dock, but too late, stretching toward the raft now just out of reach. Minnie, behind the wheel, reminded Finn of Mickey in a very old black-and-white cartoon he couldn't remember the name of. It might have been the first animated cartoon Walt Disney had ever drawn.

"Where *is* Mickey, I wonder," he said to Amanda.

"I don't think she wants to hear it," Amanda said.

"No. But it's troubling."

"Everything about this place is troubling."

She reached down and placed her faintly outlined DHI hand atop his, and he felt it, his own outline dulled somewhat by the sense of excitement and terror her reaching out to him represented.

"I like you a lot, Finn."

"Same here."

"You like you a lot, too?" she said. And they both laughed. "Thank you for everything you're doing for me."

"I got you into this in the first place," he said, guiltily.

"I'm a big girl," she said. "No complaints." She rubbed the back of his hand with her fingers.

The raft bumped to shore. Pluto jumped off. Minnie hopped onto the dock and expertly secured the raft to it with a line. She extended a hand and helped Amanda off the raft. Finn jumped down.

"We shouldn't be long," he said, eyeing the water-wheel that was only a matter of yards away.

Minnie saluted.

"We might need a quick escape, so maybe you could wait for us here?" he proposed. He didn't want to get Minnie in any more trouble.

Her big black eyes tracked across the water to the Big Bad Wolf, still lurching from the dock and looking to be considering the swim.

"One thing at a time," Finn said.

Minnie nodded.

Finn, Amanda, and Pluto headed up the path, turning toward the waterwheel at Harper's Mill.

"This feels too easy," Finn said, fearing a trap.

Amanda squeezed his hand, and he looked down to realize he was not pure DHI. But he was not about to let go to fix it.

# 11

MAYBECK WOKE UP in an office with gray carpeting, three gray desks, chairs on wheels and trash baskets lined with clear plastic bags. He caught sight of a pair of running shoes with gold-and-silver sparkles thrown into the covering like sequins and knew it could only be one person.

"Charlene?" he whispered dryly.

She crept around to him on hands and knees. For once, she was not wearing her nightgown but instead a black leotard top and black jeans. And those cheerleader shoes.

"Where are we?" She'd dressed and gone to sleep, as Philby had requested. Maybeck, on the other hand, had heard from Philby.

"It's an electrical power plant on Disney property. We're about ten miles from the Parks. Philby tracked the OTs' DHIs here. We're supposed to observe and report."

"Observe what?" she asked.

"We'll know when we see it."

They came to their feet and approached the office

door. Maybeck opened it a crack. The facility emanated a constant low-level hum, a rumbling that came up through the floor. The two were looking down a bland corridor, office doors on either side. At the end of the corridor in both directions were lighted exit signs.

"If you're wondering which way to go," Charlene said in a whisper, "check out the wear of the carpet. I'd say, right."

The hallway carpet was discolored and worn to the right; it grew progressively lighter and less-used to their left.

"Good catch," he said.

"The thing is," she said, "if something should go wrong, we don't want to both get caught, and to be honest, I'd rather you try to rescue me than me try to rescue you. So why don't you let me go first? You keep watch, but hang back."

"I don't know about that."

"Why? Because you're a guy? Who's the more athletic?"

"Who's the tougher?" he countered.

"I'll go to the end of the hall and stop to listen. I'll signal you," Charlene said.

"Since when are you the leader?" he asked.

"Have you got a better plan?"

"Just be careful," he said. "If it's them, if it's the

Evil Queen and Cruella, and who knows who else as DHIs . . . well . . ."

"I get it."

Charlene moved down the hall door by door, pausing to listen, giving him a thumbs-up at each. She displayed the grace of a gymnast, raised on tiptoe, almost dancing. At last she reached the door beneath the exit sign.

Maybeck followed. The droning hum bothered him. It was like a bad sound track to a scary movie. It made it hard to hear anything, harder still to think. Power plants were huge facilities. How were they supposed to find a couple of holograms in a place this size? And what would happen to them if they were found first? More importantly, a power plant ran 24/7, so there had to be employees on the job.

He glanced back down the hall, his toes and fingers tingling as he saw something bolted to the wall near the ceiling. The Lake Buena Vista Cogeneration Facility had security cameras. He and Charlene had likely already been spotted as intruders.

* * *

The fifteen-foot diameter wooden waterwheel spun lazily at the side of Harper's Mill. When Finn looked back across the water the wolf was gone. It might have made him feel better, but it did not. It made him realize that none of the Parks were magical for him anymore—not at night. They were mysterious, often dangerous, and always surprising. He kept his senses on full alert, worried for Amanda and grateful to have Pluto by his side.

"We need a splinter from the wheel," Finn said. "Then we hope for some magic."

"Yes."

"We'll have to break a piece off or something. I'm not sure how we'll do that."

"I don't love it here," she said.

"No. I was just thinking how my opinion of the Parks has changed."

"No doubt," she said.

"Pluto!" Finn called, winning the dog's attention. "Defend!"

Pluto licked Finn's hand, looking dog-dumb.

"Patrol!" he tried. The dog sat and offered moon eyes.

"Guard!" Amanda said harshly.

Pluto barked once sharply and went rigid.

"Good boy," Amanda said. She ruffled his ears and Pluto pawed at her.

Pluto put his nose to the ground and headed off.

"You charm all the boys," he said.

"Shut up."

Finn led her over to the moving waterwheel. It was fed from the top by a waterspout. Water cascaded down its paddles, turning it.

"If I had a knife, or razor blade, or something . . ."

"How 'bout a rock?" Amanda said, bending down to pick one up.

He felt like a moron. "Yes. Like a rock. That might work," he conceded. He smashed the inside edge of the huge wheel but the wood was old and hard, and pressure-treated against the water. It was like hitting rock against rock.

She said, "It should be one of the spindles, one of the spokes, right?"

"Yeah." Again, she made him feel stupid.

The spokes were constantly moving.

"I can climb on," Amanda said. "You know, like Johnny Depp and Orlando Bloom in *Pirates*."

"I'm pretty sure that was special effects," Finn said.

"I can do this," Amanda said, judging the wheel's rotation. She jumped between the outside slats to inside the moving wheel and ran like a hamster, adjusting her stride to match the wheel's revolutions. As she got the hang of it, she turned to Finn and said, "No problem! It's kind of like a treadmill."

Every few steps, she would have the speed wrong

and start climbing with the moving wheel, then have to adjust.

"It's not like I can stay on here forever," she said. "Say something."

"Run your hand on the slats," Finn said. "Try to catch a splinter."

"Eww!" Amanda said. "It feels like dog snot. Disgusting!" She yanked her hand away, jogging to keep pace. "Bad idea."

Finn knew what had to be done, just not how to do it. He studied the moving mechanism, trying to think how Philby would see it.

"I need you off of there," he told Amanda. "Please. Jump off."

Amanda timed her dismount, but slipping between the moving slats was harder getting off than on. Stuck between slats, she got carried up and around, and Finn pulled her off before she went around again. The two tumbled to the ground.

"The only way to do this," Finn said, "is to break it."

\* \* \*

At the same moment, Philby was comparing himself to a sponge left too long under the kitchen faucet; there came a point where the sponge could absorb no more water. He was currently monitoring a dozen Security webcams inside the Magic Kingdom, the DHI bandwidth, and was attempting to determine the direction of the unexpected data traffic to see if he could pinpoint where the Evil Queen and Cruella were sleeping during their DHI activity. It was too much. His brain was ready to burst.

The closet-sized bathroom was getting warm and the air stale. The laptop's battery was burning up his thighs. If his parents caught him in here he and the Keepers were doomed.

Juggling all the open windows on his computer and computing hundredths-of-a-second differences in transmission times on the log, his finger stopped on a particular line of data. He reviewed the times again, his finger sliding down the TRANSMISSION column. Using the router data, he could trace the source of the original transmission to a location, and the location to a Google map. It was like a juggler trying to handle seven items at once.

His finger crossed from the router data to the map, and back again just to make sure.

"Oh, no," he said aloud, quickly double-checking his findings.

* * *

"The cotter," Finn said. "It's a pin that holds a wheel's axle in place."

Amanda was listening to him, but with her back turned. She was focused instead on the change in Pluto's stance, and a *crunching* coming from the bushes.

"I think something's out there," Amanda whispered.

"Apparently, so does Pluto," Finn said, equally softly.

"If you have plans for the wheel, I suggest you get to it," she said.

Finn hurried around the mill house and found the door. The inside was small and dark, the air stale and moldy smelling. His hologram glowed slightly, casting a pale light in front of him. The wheel axle sat in a closed yoke resting atop a shoulder-high post. It did not connect to any kind of millstone; it was all for show. A curved band of steel wrapped over the spinning axle, securing it in the yoke, with a wooden pin bisecting the axle to keep it from slipping out. Finn could feel his fingers and toes, knew his DHI was far from pure given the events of the past several minutes. He used a section of pipe from the floor to pound the wooden cotter from the axle, which began to creep slowly out of the yoke, like a screw unscrewing.

He hurried back outside and, rounding the corner of the mill house, stopped dead in his tracks.

Alligators.

Three of them. The biggest looked a lot like Louis

in *Princess and the Frog*—but a *mean* Louis. Standing between the alligators and Amanda was a very nervous-looking Pluto, low on his haunches, growling.

"Finn?" Amanda called out, not taking her eyes off the beasts.

"Yeah, I see them."

"Help?"

"Yeah," he said.

The waterwheel's loose axle caused it to spin off-center; the wheel and its external post vibrated and shook. It seemed like the whole mill house might come down.

Finn sped up the process. He raised the pipe high over his head and smashed it full-force down onto the outside post and yoke.

The alligators slithered back, away from the sound. Pluto crept forward, expanding his protection of Amanda.

Finn struck the post again. The wood split. He struck yet again.

It broke.

The waterwheel rocked violently side-to-side, causing the water to spray.

"Get . . . away!" Finn hollered.

He grabbed Amanda.

"Slowly!" he said.

With each step backward, Louis and the two other alligators ventured forward, forcing Pluto back as well.

"Pluto! Come!" Finn commanded.

But the dog held his ground. He barked once, sharply.

With a thunderous explosion, the waterwheel broke loose of the mill house. It hit the ground spinning, throwing water out in front of it as it rolled straight for the alligators. The closest of the giant lizards lost a section of its tail as all three turned and fled into the woods. The huge wheel smashed into some trees, teetered, and fell, crashing down onto a section of stone wall along the path, wood flying.

"That's it!" Finn said. He reached for Amanda and took hold of her arm, snagging a large splintered piece from one of the struts.

Amanda turned her head, knowing what had to be done.

Finn stabbed the tip of her index finger, drawing blood.

"Oww!" she cried out, immediately sucking on her bleeding finger. "Nowww whawt?" she asked, her words difficult to understand with a finger in her mouth.

Finn considered this a moment. "I don't think we'll know until you Return. Although they might know on the other end—at Mrs. Nash's." He glanced around, believing there was at least an hour to go before the manual Return.

Pluto moved to the bushes and was barking.

Finn and Amanda sat down on the stone wall, out of breath.

"So where'd those alligators come from?" she asked.

He looked over at her gravely. "That's the question, isn't it?"

"It was *my* question," she said.

"And the pirate that Minnie took out, and Stitch, back when Maybeck and I were here last year. I mean: it just doesn't add up. All that for Tom Sawyer Island? Why?"

Amanda sucked her finger, and shrugged. "That's what I'm saying."

"If all this security was for Cinderella Castle or Space Mountain or Splash Mountain, I think we would think that the OTs were protecting something valuable to them. I don't know what. But this island? Off by itself. Hard to get to. Nothing here once you do get here . . ."

"Isolated," she said. "And with a fort on one end." Her eyes met Finn's relaying a fierce intensity. "You told me that you guys talked about the OTs needing somewhere to sleep while they're DHIs—the way we all sleep in our beds. What better place than someplace like this?"

"We have at least an hour to get back to the hub," Finn said. "We might as well . . . try."

"We might want to speed it up," she said, pointing. Pluto had pulled back. The alligators had returned.

* * *

"This place is very big," Maybeck said to Charlene.

They had made their way down the facility's main floor, passing more offices, conference rooms, and a coffee lounge. They'd also passed a half-dozen security cameras. The underlying roar of the place grew progressively louder.

"You think Security has spotted us by now?" she asked.

"Honestly? I'm wondering why no one's come after us. In a weird way, I don't think that's the best sign."

"The OTs got them?"

"It might explain why no one has bothered with us."

"That's depressing."

Maybeck stopped at the end of the hall.

"You do realize," Charlene said, studying her DHI's somewhat shaky blue outline, "that our best defense is being one-hundred-percent hologram?"

"As if that's going to happen."

"So you're scared, too?"

"I don't get scared," he claimed. "I get . . . aware. But I'm *very aware* at the moment. Yes." He paused, his hand on the door. "Here we go."

He opened the door and waved her through. They stepped out onto a steel catwalk that surrounded a central space. Three stories below two huge turbines whined. From the turbines ran a tangle of pipes and wires. The walls were decorated with signs warning of HIGH VOLTAGE! DEATH ON CONTACT! Nice calming stuff.

Just barely audible was a woman's complaining voice.

The Queen? they both wondered.

Maybeck raised his voice just loud enough to be heard. "Check it out!"

A blue uniform hung from the railing. Perched alongside of it was a blue jay frantically flapping its wings. Charlene looked first to the uniform, then to the blue jay, then back to the uniform.

Maybeck said, "I think we know what happened to the security guards." He indicated the blue jay. "I'd say someone spelled them."

"The Evil Queen did that?" Charlene said.

"Well, it wasn't Bambi."

"Whose side are they on?" she asked.

"If someone did that to me, I know whose side I'd be on. But with a twisted sister like her, who knows?"

"So, what now?" she said.

"We split up, and we head down toward those voices. If one of us is caught, maybe the other can do something about it."

"And?"

"We listen to whatever's being said." He studied their surroundings. "I'm taking the stairs on this side," he declared.

Charlene took in the interconnected pipes, the railing, and the catwalks on each level.

"I can climb down there," she said.

"FYI: There are stairs on the other side. Might be easier."

"And more obvious. They could be watching them. I'm going to climb it," she declared.

"Whatever," Maybeck said. "Just don't make me have to rescue you."

"Other way around," she said.

"Not likely."

"We'll see."

The blue jay cawed loudly, startling them both.

The faint voices below paused with the cry of the bird.

Maybeck whispered: "See you down there." He tiptoed off toward an exit sign.

Charlene stayed well clear of the blue jay and climbed over the metal rail, one foot placed carefully after the other. She possessed a climber's eye, able to look up at a climbing wall and quickly plot and remember an exact route. Descending was altogether different; it was much more difficult to climb down than up. For her, plotting a descending route was twice the challenge.

She hesitated a moment, seeing a possible route play out in her mind's eye—each toehold, hand and finger grip she would take. One pipe to the next; one clamp at a time.

She drew in a deep breath and made her first move.

\* \* \*

Philby heard Elvis meowing on the other side of the bathroom door.

"*Tssst!*" He tried to discourage him using the family tongue-between-the-teeth sound.

"MEEEEOWWWW!" Elvis wailed, sounding like a police siren.

"*Tssssssssst!*"

*Bang! Bang!*

He was jolted back against the well of the toilet.

"Dell?" His mother.

"Busy," he said.

"You open this door this minute!"

Philby said, "Be right out," while looking for somewhere in this shoe box room to hide his gear.

"OPEN THIS DOOR!"

When his mother shouted like that, he lacked resistance. He obeyed, turning the knob.

Seen from his mother's perspective, her son, fully dressed, was sitting on the closed toilet, his computer open in his lap, a phone, also on, resting on his thigh. Her face burning a new shade of crimson, she said nothing; she simply extended her hands expecting delivery of the goods.

"Mom, I can't."

"I don't want to hear it, young man."

Her hands, now shaking with rage, remained extended.

"Mom."

"It's nearly one o'clock. We'll discuss it in the morning."

He glanced at the time. How had the time passed so quickly? One AM? Finn would be expecting the Return.

"Mom! Please! Just listen."

"I'll listen in the morning." She added, "Maybe."

Philby had never seen her in this particular state

before—like a teakettle boiling over. Wayne had said that a friend would turn his back and betray them. He hadn't mentioned mothers.

He closed the laptop and handed it to her, feeling like a traitor. Maybe that was it, he thought: Maybe *I* am the traitor Wayne warned us about.

\* \* \*

"Guard!" Finn hated to put Pluto at risk, but the dog seemed their best chance to get out of this with all their limbs intact.

"Higher ground," Amanda said. "It's the best defensive position."

"Move slowly," Finn said.

They backed up, taking small steps, never taking their eyes off the alligators. Pluto saw them, but held his ground.

"Good dog!" Finn called out.

They slowly worked up the hill, reaching a path.

Amanda said, "Did you know that alligators can run thirty-five miles per hour?"

"TMI," Finn said.

"If we turn and run—" Amanda proposed.

"—they'll have us for breakfast," Finn said, completing her sentence for her. "I'm thinking: Scratch's Mine."

"You can't be serious!"

"It will force them into single file. They'll have to switch directions, which slows them down. If we hurry, we get out the other end of the tunnel ahead of them, at which point we head *uphill*, which is not what they'll instinctively think. By the time they figure it out—*if* they figure it out—we're gone."

"What if we just made a run for it? For Minnie? The raft?"

"Yeah, okay. I'll put you onto the raft. That works," Finn said.

"Me? What about you?" she said.

"I . . . The thing is, after everything we've figured out . . . Philby, me, the others. You and Jess. I need to check this place out," he said. "The pirate, Stitch, the alligators. It just doesn't add up."

"Then I'm not going."

"You should."

"Well, I'm not."

"I can do this alone," he said.

"Keepers work in pairs," she said.

Technically, she was not a Keeper. But it seemed like the wrong time to remind her. He thought maybe that was her point.

She said, "What if I, you know, used my . . . What if I pushed?"

"You're mostly DHI at the moment."

"Actually, I'm barely DHI. Trust me, I feel much more human than hologram. What if, once we're inside the mine, I could push the gators, and we could run for Minnie? Being inside the mine will concentrate the push. I wouldn't need much for it to work. We could tell Minnie to leave without us. The gators might be fooled, and think we'd left."

"We'd be trapped here," he reminded.

"So we'd tell her to hang on the other side and wait for our signal."

It seemed like the best way to get the gators off their trail, but a plan not without risk. If Minnie had to abandon the raft . . .

He said, "I guess if the push works, we go for it. If not, we'll rethink."

"On three?"

"No. Let's just keep backing up. When they reach the path, we make our move," he said.

"What about Pluto?" she asked.

"He's a dog. He'll figure it out."

The two backed up slowly. The alligators slithered forward. Pluto retreated. Step by step, they all moved in a choreographed manner.

"Ready . . ." Finn whispered.

"Set . . ." she said.

The first alligator—Louis—placed his paw on the path.

Finn and Amanda turned and ran.

* * *

With her arms and legs wrapped around the pipe like a koala bear hugging a tree, Charlene slid down another three feet, finally stopped by a junction clamp. The temperature in the main building was warm, as were some of the pipes she touched. The turbines screamed in a high-pitched whine. Half-deaf, she didn't hear the sound of flapping wings, didn't sense the attack until it was upon her: a shadow sweeping across her face.

Charlene ducked, and swung out with her left arm, catching a bird's wing. It struck a pipe and fell, feathers fluttering.

A second jay dive-bombed and sank its small talons into her scalp, tearing loose two large clumps of hair. Charlene cried out. Her scalp was bleeding. She sought a toehold but missed, catching herself at the last second. Now a third jay, wings tucked, came at her like a missile. She swung her arm like a baseball bat and sent it into the outfield. The bird struck the wall and was knocked unconscious.

It tumbled and landed atop one of the turbines with a *thunk*.

The voices stopped. Only the whine of the turbines persisted. The jay that had torn her hair out cawed and dove once more. Charlene deftly switched pipes, dropped lower, and switched back, using the elbow in the bigger pipe to shield her.

A glowing image appeared on the floor below. Maybeck? she wondered. Fearing it might not be, she adjusted to the far side of the pipe, putting an intersection of steel and PVC between her and the glow.

Charlene was looking down on a head of dark hair surrounded by a crown. The Evil Queen. Charlene reared back as the Queen looked up. A diving blue jay suddenly altered course and flew past Charlene—the Queen had redirected it. It landed on an electrical conduit below. The wounded jay atop the turbine managed to fly off.

The jays cawed furiously.

Over the roar of the turbines, a woman's low voice shouted, "Hurry up! There's no time to waste!"

Charlene moved quickly lower, down the pipes, using clamps and valves as toeholds. With speed and agility she descended, desperate to overhear more of what was being said.

How she regretted having separated from Maybeck. They could be working together; worse, Maybeck was something of a wild horse without a bit or bridle when left on his own.

She slid down the final few feet of pipe, arriving onto the facility floor—concrete with a thick layer of gray epoxy paint. She settled herself and dared to look past the pipe she hid behind.

Directly in front of her were more pipes and machinery. Just past these was a walkway designated by wide lines of bright yellow paint, one side of which was a concrete wall with windows looking in on a control room, the door to which was propped open, its center glass pane broken; cubes of safety glass littered the floor. Inside, she saw a bald guy in a chair, who looked either asleep or dead. There was a redheaded woman in a similar condition next to him. Cruella De Vil, the Evil Queen. And a . . . *kid!* Charlene could only see the back of his head—he was hunched over a computer—but there was no mistaking him for anything but a teenager. She couldn't see his face.

Charlene was distracted by movement to her right— the jays flying like jets in formation. They banked right and disappeared behind the machinery. Something moved in the shadows, escaping.

Maybeck.

The Evil Queen sensed Maybeck and abruptly turned around. She and Maybeck were on opposite sides of a cinder block wall.

Charlene ducked behind the pipe, her back to its

warmth. She had no way to warn Maybeck, no way to monitor what was happening. Then, overhead, a blue flash—the jays diving for Maybeck again.

She heard a series of caws. Maybeck shouting.

Then, the Evil Queen growling, "Bring him to me!"

* * *

It took Philby time to settle down. He'd never seen his mother quite like that. She'd stayed a few feet behind him and had marched him to his room like he was a convict. He'd wanted to ask her for the computer back but thought she'd have probably hit him with it—definitely not worth the risk.

His bedside clock read 12:51.

He couldn't leave his friends stuck in Epcot and the Cogeneration Facility as DHIs. He needed Web access—and he needed it now. He possessed a dirty secret: a fifth DHI had been added to the Queen's growing team. He'd spotted the addition in the log—it was still rocking him with aftershocks.

Mind racing, he thought of his father's desktop Mac in his study. The trouble was, his study was an extra bedroom, and to get to it Philby would have to pass his parents' bedroom. He doubted his mother would actually kill him, but he knew that to be caught was not an option.

368

Philby paced his room, frustrated and guilt-ridden. He stopped and looked at the lowered shade and thought about Hugo attacking him. His world was upside down: friends were enemies; family members were enemies. His only friends were asleep in their beds and would never wake up until and unless he Returned them. The success or failure of their attempt to free Amanda fell onto him. Their survival fell onto him.

Was he really supposed to just climb into bed and go to sleep?

*As if!*

He sneaked down the hall on tiptoe, a shaft of yellow light playing from his parents' bedroom. His mother would be propped up in bed reading. He knew how difficult it was for her to get back to sleep. If he moved too quickly, she'd spot him. The trick was to slip by incredibly slowly, back to the wall so he could watch *her*. If she moved even a tweak, he'd jump across and she wouldn't know if she'd seen him or not.

Step by step, his back to the opposite wall of the hallway, Philby edged into and through the patch of yellow light. He was right out where his mother could have seen him, but she never raised her head. At last—it seemed like several minutes—he was back into shadow and out of her sight.

He made it to the study door, and turned the handle incredibly gently to avoid her hearing.

Locked!

He didn't know the door could be locked. He stared at it in disbelief.

"Not a chance," she said.

He startled and nearly screamed. Didn't dare turn around, but finally gathered the courage. She was in her pajamas, her reading glasses perched on the bridge of her nose.

"That you would even try this is such a disappointment. What are you thinking?"

"I'm thinking of my friends. I'm thinking of that time I was caught in the Syndrome and how awful it was on you and Dad. The hospital. Nothing working. They are *counting* on me." He was a grown boy, he reminded himself, fighting back the tears. Embarrassed by them. "Do you know what that feels like?"

"I think I might have a slight idea. Do you have any idea what it's like to be a mother? To love another so, so much that you can't breathe?"

"I cannot let them down. I *will not* let them down. I don't care what the consequences are. It has nothing to do with Disney. Nothing to do with magic or entertainment. It's about friendship, Mom. It's about being reliable and responsible and all the stuff you and Dad preach but never let me live."

He watched her nostrils flare, which was not a good sign. Most times, that was the signal the time bomb was ticking. But her eyes glassed over and her lips trembled and she moved toward him.

"You're such a good boy," she said, her arms outstretched. "I am so proud of you."

"You . . . what?"

She embraced him in a way he'd never felt before. More than a hug. It felt like she might never let go.

"You're so grown-up."

"Mom?"

"I'm so sorry," she said. "I was only thinking of myself. It makes me . . . I get so scared for you and the others. I never want to lose you. I'd never, ever, forgive myself."

"But that's exactly—"

"Yes," she said. "I know. I understand."

"You do? Seriously?"

"I want to help. I want to know everything. *Everything*, you understand?"

He nodded.

"Go on. Do whatever it is you need to do. I'll be along in a minute. I want to turn off the light so we don't wake your father."

\* \* \*

"How's it going?"

Jeannie Puckett's grating voice. Jess had nodded off while sitting with her back to the wall next to the bunk bed. She blinked repeatedly while orienting herself. She immediately realized the impact of the dream she'd just been *living*. She reached for her diary.

"Give me a few minutes," she said, her pen already at work.

She drew the picture in her head, allowing it to flow out of her hand rather than force it onto the page. It was almost as if the pen were alive and she was there only to keep it upright. Something miraculous transpired between her hand and the paper, a power far beyond anything she would lay claim to.

Lines appeared, like a gate or maybe the teeth of a comb. Shadows. Behind the teeth of the comb were bookshelves, or perhaps a bench. The pen kept moving. Jess looked for what was there, what was coming. A box—no, a window—in the center of the wall between the bookshelves. Or were the bookshelves church pews? Was the window really a frame hanging on the wall? Not bookshelves at all, but a cot or a bunk. A priest laying on the bunk. No, a woman. A bench on the floor between the bunks. They *were* bunks. Not a comb, but prison bars.

Her pen stopped. The woman sat up from the bunk

and stood and crossed the far corner of the jail cell standing in the corner.

Jess tried to quickly sketch the woman in four postures—sitting, standing, crossing the room, standing in the far corner.

A woman in robes.

*Maleficent*. Smirking, but quickly losing it so that her emotions were unreadable.

The smirk lingered in Jess's mind. She tried to sketch it. Couldn't get it right.

Something else . . . something bothering her. Something about the way Maleficent had crossed the cell. What was it?

"Look at that!" It was Jeannie again.

It broke the moment. The images on the diary page were static again. Fixed. Unmoving. Jess worked to finish what little she could envision. She would have to get it to Philby by e-mail—and e-mail was a risk in Mrs. Nash's house, like everything else that could possibly be fun.

Jeannie rushed to Amanda's side. "LOOK AT THAT! What's it mean?"

Jess collected herself and looked up.

Amanda's arms were still by her side but her hands had moved, palms toward the foot of the bed. They were jerking ever so slightly like a crossing guard signaling a stop on the corner.

"She hasn't done anything like this. Right? This is like totally new. Right? So what's it mean?" Jeannie asked.

Jess shook her head.

"I have no idea," she said. But in fact, she had a pretty good idea. She'd seen Amanda do that before. She'd even worked with Amanda so she could learn how to control it.

\* \* \*

Standing twenty feet down in the mine, palms outstretched, Amanda scooped the air as if cupping water, and then threw her arms forward and pushed the water out in front of her as the alligators entered.

They lifted off the ground, their feet paddling the air. She pushed again, and the already levitated alligators sailed out of the mine tunnel.

"Come, boy!" she heard Finn cry out.

Pluto had been caught in the push as well. He'd traveled about ten feet and had fallen, sprawled on all fours.

"Run!" Finn cried.

The mine shaft angled sharply left. The alligators had recovered quickly, now only a few feet behind Pluto, who trailed Amanda.

"Go! Go! Go!" Finn shouted.

The tunnel straightened out but the floor tipped left, off level.

Amanda tripped. Finn stopped and turned to help her up.

*SNAP!* An alligator's jaw nearly caught his foot.

Amanda spun and pushed.

The alligator lifted and flew like it had been caught by a hurricane. It collided with the others. Three white bellies flashed in the dark, rocketing away from the two kids.

With one final turn, they reached the mouth of the mine shaft and popped outside.

"You go uphill," Finn said. "Hide up there. I'll meet you." He turned and ran. Looking back, seeing her hesitate, he said, "Up!"

Amanda turned around and started climbing up a rocky incline.

Finn, with Pluto briefly by his side, hurried along the path, only a matter of yards from Huck's Landing. Pluto, seeming to understand their role, held back, waiting for the alligators.

Finn reached Minnie and the raft, already pushing her off as he explained, "Head across to the other side and wait for our signal. We need to trick the alligators!"

Minnie nodded and threw a lever forward. The raft began to pull away.

Finn ducked back up the path past Potter's Mill, looking down in time to see Pluto flying through the air and just catching the raft with his front paws. Minnie lunged and pulled him on board.

The three alligators didn't hesitate for a second. With the raft motoring away, they slithered into the dark waters and were gone, lost in swirling flashes of green, scaly tails.

\* \* \*

The boy in the chair of the power plant control room spun around, and Charlene nearly shrieked with what she saw. This was no Disney villain. It was just a boy. A regular teenage boy, if you discounted the shimmering green outline that contained him. By the look of him, based on Philby's description, she already knew his name: Hugo Montcliff.

The scope and ramifications of what she saw so overwhelmed her that she intentionally avoided thinking about it. On the one hand, this felt like the end of the world; on the other, Maybeck had been captured and there was no time to contemplate what it all meant for the Keepers.

Hugo was in the control room, throwing switches

and spinning dials. He barked out an order, sounding like a grown-up.

"Not yet, sonny! Hold off a minute!" With a sweep of her hand, the Evil Queen, outside the control room, transfigured the three blue jays into gorillas. They stood well over five feet tall and were pure muscle and teeth. They obeyed her command—"Bring him to me!"—springing into action and surrounding Maybeck.

Charlene searched for something—anything—resembling a weapon: a hose; a steam valve? There had to be some way to help Maybeck.

Hugo called out again. The sound generated by the machinery altered pitch, groaning lower. Charlene felt it in her teeth.

The holograms, including her own, sputtered and dimmed. Red lights flashed on the wall like those from a police car.

Charlene moved closer, now near enough to see through the Queen, almost like an X-ray. In the Queen's translucent right hand, she held the fob—the Return. The device appeared solid, seemingly unaffected by the loss of electric power.

"I said not yet!" The Queen appeared ready to throw a spell at Hugo, if he wasn't already under the effect of one.

Hugo made adjustments, and the pitch in the room

climbed higher. The red lights stopped flashing. The holograms and their outlines returned.

But by the time the DHIs strengthened, two things occurred: first, Maybeck used the moment of his faded image to slip past the gorillas, who no longer had hold of him; second, Charlene stepped out from behind the pipe and picked up a shining stainless steel sheet, part of a metal box connected to the turbines. She held it behind her like a surprise gift and moved bravely toward the Queen, who turned in her direction at the last second.

Maybeck vanished into the machinery. The gorillas appeared dumbfounded; to them it was like he was suddenly invisible.

Just as the Queen raised her hand to throw a spell while saying, "Well, what do we have here?" Charlene pulled the stainless steel panel from behind her back and held it up like a mirror in front of the Queen's face.

"Oh . . . my . . . what a beautiful, beautiful face that is." The Queen reached out to vainly take the mirror and, as she did, loosened her hold on the fob.

Like a magician or pickpocket, Charlene swept the fob out of the Queen's hand, replacing it with the edge of the mirror, and pocketed the fob.

Maybeck appeared from behind her, grabbed her

arm, dragging her into the control room. He closed and locked the door.

"We can't allow them to kill the power," he said. "I just realized what they're trying to do."

* * *

Just as Finn caught up to Amanda, he lost her: she shimmered, sputtered, and disappeared. As quickly as she'd vanished, she reappeared.

"That was so weird," she said. "You just kind of broke up and disappeared."

"You, too," he said, holding his hands in front of his face. "They look okay now."

"Very strange." She reached out and pulled him down hard, behind a rock. "Careful," she said, pointing. "Another pirate. This side of Superstition Bridge."

"What was that about?" Finn said. "What just happened?"

"The projectors?" Amanda said.

"I guess. Or maybe Philby tried to Return us, but we're too far from the hub so it didn't work."

"Might be."

"Never seen anything like it."

"The pirate's significant," he said, turning back to the issue at hand. "Too many of these guys, too much going on for it not to mean something."

"I agree."

"The fort," he said.

She nodded.

"You don't have to go with me."

"I want to," Amanda said.

"It could be . . . it's probably dangerous."

"I know that." She paused. "Two is better than one."

"Isn't that a song?"

"Shut up."

"We don't know what we'll find. It could be nothing," he said.

"You don't believe that."

"No."

"Then don't say it."

"Aye, aye," said Finn.

"It's just . . ." She sounded frustrated. "We both know this is it. A fort? How perfect is that? A remote fort at that, and on an island? Give me a break! You guys should have figured this out a long time ago."

"We were close. We just didn't know it. We didn't figure it out."

"Stitch," she said, remembering the story.

"Yes." He considered this a moment. "The thing is . . . I like Stitch. Stitch is cute. Mischievous, but cute. I could never quite see him looking so mean and chasing me and Maybeck like that. But now, I'm thinking: spell. I'm thinking the Evil Queen can make us do just about anything she wants. Cute or not. Look at what's happened to Luowski and the others! She feeds off people's ambitions and desires."

"Makes sense to me." Amanda sneaked a peek around the rock. "How are we going to do this? Alligator-infested water. A pirate the size of the front door of Mrs. Nash's house."

"How are you and your arms doing?" he asked, knowing that each push weakened and tired her.

"It's pretty lame when I'm a DHI. Not much push to the push. But I can try."

"There are rocks down there," he said. "If he hit his head on the rocks, it wouldn't bother me one bit. Better than into the water where he'd make a lot of noise."

"So we want to come at him from over there," she said, pointing to the right of the bridge.

"We want you to," Finn said. "Me, maybe not so much."

They quickly worked out the details of their attack. Amanda waited as Finn crept down the hill and came at the pirate from straightaway.

"You there!" the pirate called out. He snatched an ancient pistol from his belt.

Guns? Finn thought, wondering if it was from a gift shop or for real, and having no great desire to find out.

"You take another step," the pirate said, "and you'll eat lead, palsy-walsy."

Only then did the pirate's head swivel as he caught movement out of the corner of his eye. Before he ever saw Amanda, he was airborne. The pirate crashed into an outcropping of rock and did not move. For about ten seconds.

Before Amanda could ask, "Is he . . . dead?" the pirate was twitching and reaching for his head.

"Run!" Finn said, grabbing Amanda's hand and scurrying across the rickety Superstition Bridge.

\* \* \*

Philby, entrenched at his computer, accessed the server remotely and typed in his backdoor password, waiting for the remote connection. A printout of Jess's latest sketch sat alongside his keyboard. He didn't understand *where* it was, but there was no mistaking *who*: Maleficent!

Excitement welled within him. His mother's cooperation stunned him; secretly he still thought that at any moment she might come storming into his room, shouting at him to shut down everything and go back to bed, that she'd suffered a moment of weakness and had come to her senses.

So he worked fast, frustrated by a slow Ethernet connection that was as unpredictable as the weather.

In the background, he registered a sound, an unmistakable sound, from inside the house: the sliding-glass door opening. The one to the Florida room—a large screened-in porch at the back of the house. Why was his mother going out in the middle of night? Maybe she was sleepwalking. Maybe the entire conversation he'd had with her had been with a woman sleep-talking.

He typed faster, urging the connection to speed up.

Elvis meowed from the living room. There was one thing about Elvis: he only made that particular sound when he wanted to be picked up or petted. When he made it for a second time, Philby actually looked out his bedroom door as if he could see through walls. (He could not.) Because there was one thing about his mother: she could not resist Elvis. She spoiled the cat like it was a rich uncle who might bequest his entire estate someday.

It was a family joke: if Elvis meowed twice, Mom wasn't home. Had she really fallen asleep so quickly? She'd seemed pretty worked up—

The screen changed, and Philby pulled his attention back to his computer.

He was in.

* * *

Thankfully, gorillas knew nothing about broken glass. As the first of the three explored the broken hole through the control room's glass door, he cut his hand. Jumping back, he stuck his hand in his gaping mouth and whimpered like a baby. The injured gorilla then showed the other two his blood, and all three stepped away from the door as if it possessed powers.

Behind them, the Evil Queen could not stop adoring herself in the stainless steel mirror. She seemed oblivious to everything going on around her.

"You might be wondering what a dame like me is doing in a place like this," Cruella De Vil said to Charlene. "And to tell you the truth, I hardly know!" The way she laughed made Charlene wonder if that hadn't been what had shattered the glass. "It's because I know the way of the world—our world, the modern world. Think about it: Queeny out there is from a world lit only by fire. She can hardly be considered worldly, like some of us. Eh, girly?"

"You'll never get away with this," Charlene said, holding up the Return fob. "One click of this button . . ."

Hugo spun around in his chair, his hand on a lever. "I wouldn't be so sure. If your friend there takes one more step toward me, it's lights out, everyone. If you push that button as the power fails, there's no telling what will happen to us—to *all* of us. We might be gone forever."

"Is that true?" she asked Maybeck, who looked ready to pounce.

He looked over at her with a terror-ridden, perplexed expression, his usual confidence sapped.

"Now, now, little girl, don't be foolish," Cruella said. "Hand that over to me this instant." She flicked the ash off the burning cigarette at the end of her ebony-and-ivory holder, aiming the ember at Charlene's face. "You wouldn't want to see me when I'm mad."

Maybeck scooped up an office chair, holding it above his head threateningly. "Whoever you are," he said to Hugo, "you're new at this. Let me tell you something about being a DHI: the slightest bit of fear and you're partly human, partly hologram. It's a glitch in the system that's never been worked out. So if you think this chair is going to pass through you, you're mistaken. Now, let go of that switch."

Charlene matched each advancing step Cruella took, backing away from her.

"Drop the chair!" Hugo shouted, his hand still on

the switch. "Do it, or we all go *poof!* And if Goldilocks there pushes that button, we might just . . . evaporate."

Maybeck's eyes darted. Cruella's burning cigarette was closing in on Charlene's face.

"Do it," Maybeck said. He wanted her to push the Return.

If I push the button, I drop the fob and we'll lose it again, Charlene was thinking. She banged into the counter behind her. Her hand felt a drawer handle. She hooked a finger into the handle and pulled the drawer open slightly. If she *knew* where to find the Return, they could come back to get it. She held it in her hand over the open drawer.

Cruella eyed the Queen through the office windows, clearly wanting her powers to throw spells. But the Queen was still struck by her own reflection.

Hugo Montcliff's hand remained on the oversized switch. "You hit me with that chair, pal, and you're going to be the one who throws this switch."

"I suggest we all calm down," said Cruella. "This is what we call a stalemate."

* * *

As they crossed Superstition Bridge, Finn and Amanda heard the voices from within Fort Langhorn. They hurried to the left to avoid being seen.

"I can't believe it!" Finn said.

"It sounds like a convention or something."

"Of Overtakers."

"You think?"

"I promise." Eager to get a look inside, Finn moved toward the fort's open gate. He sneaked a peek, his heart beating painfully in his chest with what he saw. The Horned King from *The Black Cauldron*. Gaston. Prince John from *Robin Hood*. He'd seen all three in a single glance. Milling throughout the center courtyard were pirates and a dozen other characters Finn had seen before but couldn't name.

He slipped back next to Amanda, breathing hard. "This is it," he said, winded by nerves. "Their hideout."

"What now?"

"If the Queen and Cruella are asleep, there's a good chance they're in there," he said.

"We're going *in* there?"

In the distance, across the bridge, the pirate was stirring. He'd be on his feet any minute. He'd sound the alarm. The bridge was the only way off the island.

"We've got serious problems," Finn said. "Follow me."

He led her around the side of the fort so the waking pirate wouldn't spot them. "They're all in there," he told her. "You can't believe how *many.*" Then he said somewhat desperately, "There are only five of us. Seven, counting you and Jess."

"Ariel told Willa there are many, many more. That they're waiting for a leader."

Finn skidded to a stop.

"What?" he gasped. "Why didn't I hear about this?"

She shrugged. "Girl talk," she said. "She knows . . . we all know how hung up you are on living up to Wayne's expectations."

"That's not true."

"Isn't it?" said Amanda.

"Who said I'm the leader?"

"You see?" she said. "That's what I'm talking about."

They continued along the fort wall, sneaking past the door leading to Pappy's Fishing Pier and kept following the wall as it turned again.

"Don't be mad."

"I'm not mad," said Finn.

"You're stewing."

"What's that?"

"That's what Mrs. Nash calls it when you get so mad you won't talk. She doesn't let us stew. Everything gets out in the open."

"I'm not stewing," he said.

"If you say so."

Then he stewed some more, not knowing what to say. They rounded the third corner.

"Are we just going to go around in a full circle, or what?" she asked.

"I remember coming here with my family years ago," he said. "And maybe I'm mixing it up with the tunnels on the other island, but I'm pretty sure there's a secret escape tunnel running from the fort."

"That's what we're looking for?"

"That's what I'm looking for, yes."

"And if we *find* it?"

"I'm going in there."

"No way, Finn."

"Not you, don't worry."

"That's not what I'm talking about! You can't go in there with a zillion Overtakers inside."

He stopped. They pressed their backs to the logs as he said, "Listen . . . Look . . . I don't know exactly how to explain this, but I'm not even sure you're going to wake up tonight. Okay? I'm freaking out here. These people, these *things* are ruining everything, and they're only getting stronger. We . . . the five of us . . . the Keepers—and you and Jess, and Wayne and Wanda— we either stop them or . . . that's just the thing: I don't know what. I don't know if any of us will be around, or if we'll be lying in bed unable to wake up, like you are right now. I'm not playing hero here. I'm afraid. I'm afraid to go to sleep. Afraid to go to school. I can't live like this. I'm going to find those two and stop them. Obviously, they're only the tip of the iceberg," he said, the voices of Overtakers rising over the wall. "But I'm not losing you. I'm not running away."

She leaned across and kissed him, and despite him being a DHI, it felt to him as amazing as it had in front of Mrs. Nash's.

When she pulled her lips off his, he said, "See? There's still magic in the Parks."

"Is that it?" she asked, pointing.

At first he thought she was disappointed in the kiss. Then he saw a rock wall coming out from below ground.

"The escape tunnel!" he said, greatly relieved.

\* \* \*

Philby found his loyalties tested. He didn't want to leave the connection to the server, but Elvis was still out there meowing. Philby had definitely heard his mother open the sliding door to the Florida room. So what was going on? What if it wasn't his mother? What if Hugo had returned?

Blood overcame photons. He sneaked out into the living room to check it out. The room was dark, as was the outside. It was late. Neighbors' houses were shuttered for the night.

In the greenish glow of some of the kitchen appliance displays, he spotted Elvis rubbing up against the open sliding glass door and meowing. The fan in the Florida room spun lazily. A breeze blew outside, clattering the palm fronds.

Philby walked on his toes, slinking forward.

"Hey, pal." A low voice. Not his mother's.

Philby jumped and banged against the sliding door's metal doorjamb.

A kid—a *giant* of a kid—had his hand over Philby's mother's mouth and her arm wrenched up behind her back. Her eyes were bulging, pleading to her son through palpable terror.

"You must be Luowski," Philby said, his voice eerily calm. He'd never truly hated before. He'd never had the urge to hurt someone like he had now. The boy's size meant nothing; what he'd heard about him meant nothing. He was hurting his mother, and that was all there was in the world—the only thing that existed.

"You will let her go right now," Philby said.

"Oh, yeah? Or else?"

"I will rain down a world of hurt on you the likes of which you've never known."

Luowski spit out laughter, but Philby sensed concern lingering down under the boy's calm exterior.

"I don't think so," Luowski said. "I think you will do *exactly* as I say, or the world of hurt will be on your conscious, pal. And it won't be raining down on me, believe me." He goosed Mrs. Philby's arm up more tightly, and Philby watched her strain under the pain.

"It's 'conscience,' nimrod. You're out of your depths . . . beyond your pay scale . . ." Philby said, as he edged closer. "You have stepped so far over the line that I'm not going to let you go back. You can beg, but I won't hear you."

"Tough? You, nerd boy? Think so? You're going to show me your Internet modem, and we're going to shut that puppy down. Then, we're going to give it . . ." he stole a glance at his wristwatch, ". . . fifteen, twenty minutes, and I'll be on my way."

He'd told Philby much more than he'd meant to. Whatever was going down with the Overtakers, it was happening this very minute. *Right now!* In fifteen minutes it would all be over.

"Got to pick on girls, big guy?" Philby said. "Big Mr. Greg Luowski picks on a mother because he's too afraid of a Kingdom Keeper."

"Am not!"

"Have they told you what we can do? What we're capable of? I'm guessing not. I'm guessing the Queen either put you under a spell or made it sound like a really cool thing to take us on, to join up with her. But she left out a few details, I'm willing to bet. Like the fact that I can walk through a door or a wall when I'm a DHI. Like I can walk into your home and find you, or your mother, and there's *nothing you can do to stop me*. You might want to think about that before you continue down the road you're on, Greg. You will never hear the end of this. This will never go away."

Luowski tried hard to look composed.

"Never. Ever. You let her go right now, or you'll have five of us in your house and no evidence that anyone was ever there but you and your parents. Whatever happens will be put on you."

The thing is, Philby was freaking out his own mother. But sometimes there was collateral damage. He had to accept the fallout.

"You and me, Luowski," Philby said. "Leave her out of this. Or are you too chicken?"

"Nice try."

"You've seen what Finn can do. I know you have. Amanda, too, I hear. How about me, Greg? What can I do? Did you think about that before you came *into my house*? Because you should have."

Luowski was sweating now, either from the heat, or from everything Philby was saying.

His mother bent her knee and drove the ball of her heel up and into a spot between the boy's legs that made Luowski's eyes squint shut as he screamed. She elbowed him in the chest and dove to the side as her son charged.

Philby never thought about what he was doing. He was all about adrenaline and instinct—this caveman urge to protect his mother. He lowered his shoulder and hit Luowski in the chest like a football tackle, knocking the boy off his feet and into a rattan chair. The chair spilled over. They blew through the screen door, shredding it, and rolled out onto the patio.

Luowski was more bear than human. His strength returned, and Philby felt it like a machine had been switched on. Finn had described the supernatural strength of being thrown by Luowski, but only now as he felt his shoulders crushed by the boy's grip did he fully get the picture. Luowski was an Overtaker, not just another big kid.

Philby felt Luowski's muscles contract: he was going to throw him into the wall of the house; he was going to crush every bone in his body. He was going to kill him.

"Greg!" Philby's mother's voice.

Luowski was as programmed as any other kid: when an adult called your name, you looked.

A spray hit Luowski's face—bug spray, Philby realized by the smell. The boy-giant released Philby and slapped his hands over his eyes, crying like a wild animal.

"Ahhhhhhh!" He staggered around the lawn, wiped some of it clean, and took off running as Mrs. Philby charged at him, can outstretched, ready to deliver another dose.

Luowski was gone. Philby's mom stood there panting. But a smile curled proudly at her lips.

"We showed him," she said.

"WHAT IS GOING ON!?"

Philby's father.

"What the heck happened to my Florida room?" He was in a pair of tighty-whities and a T-shirt. He looked . . . disappointed.

"Dad, it was—" Philby said.

"—a gator," his mother said, interrupting. "But Dell and I handled it, didn't we, sweetheart?"

Philby looked up at his mother. Maybe she was under a spell as well.

"Yeah, we did."

"Go back to bed," his mother told his father. "We can deal with this in the morning."

His father, looking totally perplexed, knew better than to tangle with his wife when she was holding a can of bug spray.

"You're all right?" he asked the two.

"No," Philby's mother said. "We're better than just all right. We're good."

Definitely some kind of spell.

* * *

Finn blinked, allowing his eyes to adjust. Some light filtered in from the mouth of the tunnel, where Amanda stood guard. He was helped by the faint glow of his DHI. But soon the entrance was well behind him, and the depth of the tunnel began to choke out all light. A glow came from behind him and he spun around, ready to strike out.

"It's me!" Amanda hissed.

"What are you doing here? We had a plan!"

"You had a plan. I had . . . reservations. Isn't one of the rules that Keepers never go alone?"

"There are exceptions."

"Like when the odds are a hundred-to-one against us?"

"I explained: If we're separated, it gives you a chance to come rescue me."

"Yeah, like that's going to happen!"

"It's called strategy."

"It's called stupid. I'm much more help here with you than back looking at the stars and getting all freaked out by the wind in the bushes."

"So, you're afraid," he said.

"No, no," she said sarcastically. "I'm real used to this."

"Hey," he said, indicating the faintness of his blue outline. "I'm scared, too, in case you hadn't noticed. I don't exactly love small spaces . . . like tunnels, for instance. But here we are."

"Here we are," she said.

They crept forward, deeper into the narrow tunnel. Water dripped down the walls. A sharp edge of rock appeared just ahead—the tunnel divided. But no, Finn realized—the tunnel to the right was blocked by a wooden door.

"Now that's interesting," Finn whispered.

"The wood is new," she said. "Really new."

"Yes. Not a bad place to lock yourself away for a little nap." The door was locked. He understood what had to be done. "I'm going in there," he said. "I can go *all clear* long enough to get through the door—I know I can." He tried to psych himself up for it, as it would require a complete brainwash to get his full DHI back.

"That would leave you alone in there. And, by the way, me *alone* out here."

"Yeah," he said.

"Please, don't."

His blue line grew stronger without his closing his

eyes, without concentrating. It's her, he thought. He was feeding off her concern for him.

"At one o'clock," he said, "you need to be back at the hub."

"Please . . ."

"With or without me."

"Don't even go there." She sized up the door. "I can push it open."

"It would take everything left in you, and it might turn out to be a broom closet. No. Save your strength. We may need it."

"Do not humor me," she said.

"I'm being confident. I'm *feeling* confident." His blue line was exceptionally strong. His toes and fingers tingled. He offered her a fleeting smile, and he stepped through the door.

\* \* \*

"I will crush you like a bug," Maybeck said, his arms still rock-solid as he held the chair aloft.

"When I pull this switch there won't be any you. So what then?" said Hugo.

"Enough with the yakety yak," Cruella said, "Just pull the switch."

"Get that *thing* from her, and I will," Hugo said. "We can't risk them happening together. Do something!"

Cruella aimed the burning cigarette closer to Charlene's face.

Charlene glanced at the wall clock, trying to stall for the remaining three minutes. She couldn't help Finn and Amanda Return—that would have to still be up to Philby—but the fob offered her and Maybeck a way out. The rising confidence in Maybeck's eyes suggested he might know what she was thinking.

*Click.* The minute hand moved forward. Two minutes to go.

Finn was always on time for everything, but he wasn't necessarily early.

"Tell them why they're doing this, Terry," Charlene said.

"Oh, yes, by all means. Please!" said Hugo.

Maybeck's eyes found the clock. "Because Maleficent's prison cell is controlled electronically, and this facility provides Disney World's backup power."

Judging by the state of alarm on Cruella's face, he'd hit a home run. Charlene tried to keep her own surprise from showing. This was the first she'd heard his theory.

"So, really," Charlene said, "where do you think the rest of us are right now?"

"PULL THE SWITCH, YOU LITTLE TWIT!" Cruella shouted at Hugo.

Charlene's thumb warmed the plastic button on the

fob, rubbing back and forth, so tempted to send them all back from where they'd come.

* * *

Finn inched forward, a tightness gripping his chest immediately, his DHI's blue outline dimming. His eyes slowly adjusted to his own faint glow.

The cave walls sweated, the air dank, the space narrow and confined. His head swooned. He moved forward tentatively as the tunnel turned slightly, and he gasped.

Cruella De Vil. Asleep on some furs atop an air mattress. He leaned closer; her eyeballs danced beneath her eyelids. It looked . . . *horrific*.

Just beyond Cruella, the Evil Queen slept on her back, hands folded across her belly, her crown in place. Her lips and nose were twitching. She seemed to be grinning slightly.

He had them.

For a moment, the shock of the discovery proved too much; he simply stared. If he could tie them up, gag the Queen so she couldn't throw spells, then wait for sunrise and the return of the Characters to their various attractions, then maybe, just maybe, the Imagineers had two more prisoners. Two more generals, Shan-Yu would have said.

He had his two shoelaces. A sash around the Queen's robe. A plan formed in his head.

The way their eyes moved behind their lids was disturbing. He couldn't stop himself from looking.

He checked a watch that hung from Cruella's neck: 12:59. In one minute he would be Returned—that is, if he and Amanda were close enough to the hub. He had no desire to test the system. But he needed more time. He began unlacing his shoes frantically. They would never get another chance like this.

\* \* \*

Spinning in self-admiration, the Evil Queen's green-outlined DHI, glued to her own reflection, noticed three gorillas behind her. *Gorillas?* In the distant realm of consciousness, a flicker of reality spoiled her celebration of her unparalleled beauty, returning her to the moment at hand. She dropped the stainless steel sheet and it landed loudly.

Charlene caught the changes to the Queen through the control room windows. There was Maybeck, his arms beginning to shake from holding the chair for so long; Cruella, advancing the glowing end of her cigarette at Charlene's perfect complexion; Hugo Montcliff, his hand on a master switch.

"What are you three doing standing around?" she

heard the Queen complain. "I said 'Get them!' "

The gorillas charged the door, more afraid of the Queen than some broken glass.

Charlene was no Jess—but she could see the future. The gorillas were going for Terry. He would not have a chance.

Maybeck heard the door break open and understood that he was the target. He had never hurt another person—not like he was about to hurt this kid. But he brought the chair down onto Hugo holding the switch with a vengeance.

Hugo Montcliff saw the look in Maybeck's eyes and knew the fate that awaited him. He was, in fact, going to be squished like a bug. He pulled the switch.

Charlene pushed the button. The fob fell into the drawer.

The two facility workers taped into the chairs screamed through their gags in unison; the kids and the two costumed freaks *vanished*. Like a magic act. Now you see them, now you don't.

* * *

Finn was just tying the Queen's hands together when she sat bolt-upright. He screamed at the top of his lungs and fell back.

Seeing Finn so close, the Queen screamed as well,

the released terror echoing off the tunnel's sheer stone walls.

Cruella's eyes bugged open. It took a moment for her to reorient herself.

In the uncomfortable moment that followed, the only sound was the steady drip of condensation coming off the rock walls.

For Finn, their coming awake was like living a horror movie. The Queen began untying her hands with her teeth. Cruella rolled over on her furs. Finn saw the Queen's hands coming loose—her ability to throw a spell was only seconds away. He backed off, looking down at his own hands with their faint blue outline. In his current state he wasn't going to walk through the door any time soon.

"Well, what do we have here?" the Evil Queen said, knowing perfectly well what she had here. She had Finn. Cornered.

He banged his back into the door. He willed himself to *all clear*, but knew it was hopeless. He was terrified of the Queen; what chance did he have?

"What's happening to him?" Cruella asked.

Finn looked down at his hands—sputtering and translucent. Like nothing he'd ever seen.

"Where'd he go!?" shouted Cruella.

"Who turned out the lights?" the Queen said.

Finn stood still, wondering why everything had gone pitch-black and why they couldn't see him. It took him several long seconds to grasp the situation: he was in DHI shadow, his DHI no longer providing a glow in the tunnel. *Invisible.* The projectors had apparently been turned off. By who? More importantly: why? His first guess was Philby.

"No, no, no!" Cruella said. "It's the power failure. We did it! We succeeded! By tomorrow morning at seven o'clock we'll be whole aga—"

"SILENCE!" the Queen erupted. "Say nothing more. He's still here, you fool. FIND HIM!"

"I can't see my own nose!" Cruella complained. "And I have a big nose."

"Hold your arms out. We should be able to *feel* him."

Finn knew everything the Queen had said was true. He made himself small, arms at his side, and ducked down into a squat, his ears intent upon hearing the sound of their shuffling feet as they moved toward him.

He was going to be caught. The tunnel was too narrow to slip past them. His best chance was surprise. He charged.

Cruella shrieked. He felt her arms spin like a propeller. He averted his face, knowing the Queen was next.

"Umph!" she said, as he hit her and went down with her onto the air mattress. She grabbed for him, but he rolled and clawed the wall and moved off her. He glued his back to the wet stone, anticipating their next move.

"This way!" the Queen roared.

In their haste, the two moved past him.

"Do you have him?"

"NO! Do you?"

Finn hurried past the two air mattresses, hands outstretched, and found the wooden door. He felt left, right, up, down—*there!* A dead-bolt lock. He turned it.

The door came open.

He heard footfalls racing in front of him.

"Is that you?" he called to the sound.

"What's going on? I can't see a thing!" came Amanda's terrified voice. "There were noises. . . ."

"Get to the bridge!" he said. "I'll explain later!"

"GET HIM!" he heard the Queen's voice echoing from behind him.

*You can't catch what you can't see*, Finn thought.

Reaching the mouth of the escape tunnel, Finn and Amanda rushed out into total darkness.

"It's a blackout!" he said, realizing there wasn't a single light on in the entire Park. Only the moon offered any chance to see or be seen. As many times as he'd been in the Parks at night, he'd never seen it like this.

"If there's no power, how can we exist?" she called out.

They rounded the final corner of the fort. From inside came shouts and cries. The Queen must have raised the alarm. Overtakers began pouring out of the fort behind them.

"Who knows?" he answered. "But here we are. We can talk. We can hear each other. Who cares? We've got to get out of here."

They ran past the wobbly pirate they'd knocked down a few minutes earlier. Finn crashed into him and the guy went down again. A stream of Overtakers crowded the bridge.

"MIIINNNNNNNIEEE!!" Finn shouted.

They both heard a motor start in the distance.

Finn glanced back at the Overtakers.

"Faster!" he called out.

* * *

"What's happening?"

"Mom," Philby said. "I don't have time to explain it all. Not exactly sure, anyway."

She'd gone from tyrannical Keepers hater to poster mom, sitting by her son's side and watching him manipulate a dozen windows on his computer screen simultaneously.

The server had never faltered, but without warning the Projection icon had turned red, indicating a full Park-wide failure of all projectors.

"It's some kind of power failure, I think," he said. "The projectors are out, but the server is still up. It's probably on a battery backup of some kind. But if that's right, it won't last long. Five minutes. Ten, at the outside. I've got to get them back."

"I thought you said they *were* back," she said.

"That was Maybeck and Charlene. Yeah, they Returned okay. It's Finn and Amanda."

"The sick girl . . ."

"Yeah . . . We hope not."

"So, can you help them?"

"I'm late. And I'm kind of busy here."

"I'll shut up," she said, straining to sit back, but then sticking her face alongside his shoulder.

Philby executed a few lines of code and pushed Enter.

The screen filled with data that then began to scroll automatically.

"What's that?" his mother asked.

"It's okay," he said, fed up with her questions, but trying to sound patient. "It's begun. A few minutes is all, and we'll know."

Finn and Amanda—invisible—jumped onto the raft, joining Pluto and Minnie.

"Go!" Finn said to Minnie, who startled, and looked around trying to see him in the moonlight. "Please! Take us back!"

Minnie threw a lever and the raft pulled away from the dock ahead of the Overtakers' arrival. Once to the other side, an invisible Finn kissed Minnie on the cheek before he and Amanda jumped off.

They ran hard, Pluto at their side, keeping up with them effortlessly.

When Pluto barked sharply three times, Finn looked behind them.

The wolf, head to the ground. Moving like a tornado toward them.

"We've got company," he told Amanda.

"How can he possibly—?"

"Who knows? Smell? Maybe he's after Pluto."

The hub and Cinderella Castle came into view and, as they did, all the lights in the Park pulsed once and went dark again. With them, Amanda's DHI sparkled, eerily translucent, and then vanished again with the loss of power.

"Almost there," Finn said. He caught up and

reached for her. Trying to feel her. He bumped her back with his fist, reached down her arm, and took her hand.

He tingled all over.

He knew that feeling. Knew it only too well.

# 12

FINN AWAKENED IN HIS BED, his clothes damp with sweat and the fetid smell of the tunnels. His mother sat in a chair two feet away.

"Mom?"

"Oh, thank God! Are you okay?"

Finn took inventory of his condition. "I'm fine."

"You crossed over."

*Duh!* "Yes." He sat up sharply. "Can I use your phone? I've got to text Philby."

She had her phone in her hand. She passed it to him.

i'm bak. others?

yes. all 4. amanda 2. she's good.

Finn released a huge sigh of pent-up anxiety. He explained things to his Mom. She raised her hand for a high-five and Finn looked at her strangely.

She lowered her hand. "Too much?"

"And then some," he said.

"So, it's over?"

"I wish," he said. "I failed." He agonized for a moment. "I had them. . . ."

"Who?"

"The Queen. Cruella. *I had them!*" His mother's phone rang. "That's Philby for me." He answered the call.

Their conversation was intense. They spoke in a Kingdom Keepers shorthand, Finn relating what had happened on the island, and the discovery of the fort; Philby relayed what Maybeck had told him about the activities at the power plant, including Hugo Montcliff being a DHI. That news was the hardest to take. Finn tried to swallow away his terror. Other kids as DHIs. Where did that leave the Keepers?

Philby told Finn about Charlene winning back the fob and dropping it into a drawer in the control room. Despite some losses, there were gains, he realized.

Finn told him, "Something happened during the power failure when I was in projection shadow. Cruella said something about tomorrow morning. That by seven it wouldn't matter. The Queen stopped her. She didn't want me hearing it."

"Maybeck's theory is that the power failure has to do with the prison break, which makes sense, but we have no way to know if it's true or not," explained Philby.

"Don't we?" Finn said.

"I'm listening."

"This is your stuff, not mine, but didn't you say that counting Hugo that made five DHIs for them?"

"Yup."

They had yet to identify the remaining two, but Finn now had an idea. "Have you checked the server log since the power failure?"

The line crackled.

"Are you there?" Finn asked.

"Thinking. Checking . . . Stand by. . . ."

Finn heard Philby's fingers clacking on the keyboard through the phone.

Philby mumbled, "I thought I was supposed to handle the techie stuff."

"Whatsup?"

"Bandwidth bump. How'd you know that?" Philby said. "Stand by. . . ."

More clicking from his end.

"You're not going to believe this," Philby said.

"Try me."

"The prison?"

Finn nearly came out of his chair. "Yes?"

"I think it's in the Animal Kingdom. There's something I've got to show you. Check your e-mail . . . now."

A moment later, Finn opened the e-mail from Philby, recognizing Jess's artwork immediately.

"She drew that *tonight*," Philby told him over the phone.

Finn studied the diary entry. A gate? A ladder on its side? Bunk beds? Something hanging on the wall. Or was that a window?

And if it was a window, that small, that high on a wall—where would that be? A basement. Only basements had weird, tiny windows like that.

Basements and . . .

. . . prison cells.

Finn felt physically sick to his stomach. He leaned over his trash can thinking he was going to hurl. His mother patted him on the back.

"What's wrong, dear?"

It was like being blindfolded and spun around, trying to hit the piñata, only to have the piñata hit back at you. Smack you in the head.

A prison cell.

Finn said, "I know how they're going to do it."

\* \* \*

Finn's mother waited at the curb, the car running. He knocked on the door, rang the bell, then knocked again.

Wanda Alcott answered, fully dressed. Finn knew

there was no way anyone could dress that fast, much less an older lady—she had to be at least thirty. It meant she'd been awake all night. It was past four AM. Doing what? he wondered. Monitoring the situation, perhaps?

"I need to talk to him," Finn said.

"If it's about the power failure, we're looking into it," she said.

"We were there," he said. "The cogeneration facility."

She looked stunned. She nodded thoughtfully. "The supervisor mentioned children."

"One was an OT. Two were us: Maybeck and Charlene. All DHIs. The Return's there. We need it back. Now. We're not safe until we have it back. It's in a drawer. You have to get someone to get it for us."

"I can do that."

"I know you can; that's why I'm here."

"He's safe. I appreciate your concern—"

"It's not concern. Not for him. The power failure was part of the jailbreak. They're going to bust them out."

"Yes. I'm sure that was the intention. The power failed there for nearly ten minutes. But it's all under control. The . . . Our guests are where they belong."

"No," Finn said, "they're not. Do you have clearance? Can you get me into the prison?"

She stared at him.

"I need to see him. I need clearance."

"That's not going to happen," she said. "No one sees him. You'll have to tell me."

"I'm not telling you. I'm sorry, but I can't. I'll only tell him. Face to face. No more video. No more tricks."

"That's impossible."

"By seven this morning," Finn said, "they'll be gone. And it'll be on you. Think about that."

She did just that.

"What's happened to you?" she said. "When we spoke earlier—"

"Everything you said at Epcot was true. You've been a tremendous help. An amazing help. I need you to help me one more time."

"When did you get so all grown-up?" she asked.

"It's been a different sort of night."

"I guess."

"And I'm tired," he said apologetically.

"Amanda?"

"Is fine. She Returned, with the spell broken." He waited only a matter of seconds. "I'll try on my own, but they won't listen to me."

"You don't even know where it is," she said.

"And if I do, will that convince you?"

Her eyes went wide. She opened her mouth to speak, but nothing came out.

"Good," Finn said.

Less than a minute later, he marched back to the car and indicated for his mother to roll the passenger window down. "I'll be with an adult," he said. "She's Wayne's daughter."

"I know, remember?"

"Oh, yeah. I know it's late. I don't expect you to understand but—"

"If your father finds out, you'll be looking for a new mother."

"I only have one mother."

"That may change," she said, although she glowed from his comment. "Your father will be at the breakfast table promptly at seven-thirty. You'd better be too, buddy boy, or I don't know what." Her eyes grew glassy. "I'm scared," she said.

"Don't be."

"For you. Not for me."

"I know, Mom."

She rolled up the window, looked at him once more through the glass, and drove off.

\* \* \*

Wanda drove Finn into the Animal Kingdom through the backstage vehicle Security entrance, where it took five minutes of phone calls to get Finn approved.

"I still can't believe you knew about this," she said from behind the driver's wheel. The dashboard clock read 5:37 AM. Finn felt wide awake.

"Philby has a different kind of magic," he said. "Ones and zeros."

He'd never been to this particular part of Animal Kingdom, a warehouse structure near the elephant cages.

"It was originally designed as a medical quarantine for western lowland gorillas. When a military coup denied our chance to obtain the animals, the facility went unused for nearly a decade. Then the problem arose. Some modifications were made to transform it into a high-security retention facility," Wanda explained.

"A prison."

"It has continued to be listed as an animal housing facility. You'll forget you ever saw it."

"Saw what?" he asked.

"That's the spirit."

She stood before a video camera and pushed a button. She then had to swipe an ID card, and place her index finger on a biosensor—the same kind they used at the Park entrances.

"My father has been housed here since the Fantasmic! threat. He's viewed as too important—he knows too much, so he's kind of a prisoner himself."

A light turned green and the door unlocked. They entered. The hallway was blocked by a double set of security doors with glass two inches thick. They went through a security check as at an airport, and then down a flight of stairs. Another hallway. She pushed a doorbell, and a moment later the doorjamb buzzed, and she let them inside.

Wayne was sitting on a small couch. He looked older, reminding Finn of a lamp that had been repaired—much the same, but something different. The twinkle in his eyes remained, but his voice was dry and salty, like that of a man who didn't speak much.

"Welcome," he said. He motioned Finn into a chair facing him.

Finn saw through an open door to a bedroom. It was not an office, but an apartment; Wayne lived here. He seemed older and weaker. Finn felt a pang of sadness.

"Why?" Finn asked.

The man's white eyebrows arched.

"Why here?" Finn said.

"The funny thing about the past," Wayne said, "is it's behind us. There's nothing we can do that will change it. The future is much the same—out of reach. When you get to be my age you realize you have only right now. This moment. You are over there. I am here.

For how much longer, neither of us knows. Let's not worry about me. Tell me what you want."

"Who said I want anything?"

"We all want something."

"What do you want?" Finn asked.

"To hear what you want," the old man answered.

Finn sighed. There was no arguing with Wayne. Why had he tried?

"I'm listening," Wayne said.

"Jess drew this place. I think she did. . . . I need to see if it's what she drew." Finn unfolded his computer printout of Jess's diary drawing. "Something is going to happen before morning."

"It has been quite the eventful evening," Wayne said. "I would doubt much more will happen before morning. They tried and they failed."

"The blackout," Finn said.

"Yes. Ingenious. We lost power like everyone else. Normally . . . well, there's a system in place, but my understanding is that's what they sabotaged. Quite brilliant, actually. But thankfully, it failed."

"You know this because . . . ?"

Wayne took hold of a television remote and worked the device. A flat-panel screen came alive, divided into four quadrants. Four jail cells. Two contained Maleficent and Chernabog. Two others were empty.

Finn gasped. Maleficent's cell was identical to Jess's drawing. He tapped the printout.

"You have to take me there," Finn said.

"Have to?"

"Please take me there."

Moments later, a guard led them through another series of electronic doors.

"They'll admit us, Finn. But by rule, we won't be allowed out until the shift change at seven AM. You need to understand that before going in."

"Seven AM?" Finn said. He told Wayne about Cruella's mention of the exact time. "It's less than an hour."

"Even so. We won't be leaving."

"I'm good," Finn said.

They entered and were passed off to a burly guard with shoulders as wide as a doorway, and a nose that looked like it had been flattened by something unnatural. Two gates later, they were passed off to yet another guard, and now Finn recognized the jail cells from the video.

He and Wayne stopped in front of Maleficent's cell. The prisoner slept peacefully.

Finn whispered to Wayne, "Please ask them to turn off the security cameras."

Wayne said back, "Protocol dictates twenty-four-seven coverage."

"They're counting on that."

Wayne viewed him curiously.

"Let me guess," Finn said. "During the power failure, it was pitch-dark down here. I'm guessing a fire alarm *during* the blackout." Wayne looked impressed; Finn knew he had scored. "Because that combination—power failure and fire—would mean the cells opened automatically for the prisoner's safety." Most of this had come from Philby's extensive research following Finn's proposal of a variation to Maybeck's theory.

"There are measures in place," Wayne said, not disagreeing. "That's about all I'm allowed to tell you. Suffice it to say, not even a moth left this building at that time."

"No," Finn said. "But if you don't turn off the cameras, you're going to lose your prisoners."

"That's an oxymoron," Wayne said. "The cameras *show* us the prisoners."

"How much do you know about augmented reality?"

"I'm quite familiar with it. We use it a great deal for interior projections."

"DisneyQuest?" Finn asked.

"Do I know about DisneyQuest? Of course," Wayne answered.

"Is Downtown Disney wired for DHI projection?" Finn asked, already knowing the answer. Philby had been knocked sideways by his earlier discovery.

"It's on the sheets. It's in planning."

"I witnessed two DHIs projected *inside* DisneyQuest. Outside, as well."

Wayne was about to tell him that was impossible.

"AR technology. Security video cam projection."

"I understand the technology, as I've said," Wayne said, continuing to whisper.

"TURN OFF THE SECURITY CAMERAS!!!" Finn shouted into the cell.

Maleficent didn't stir. Didn't twitch.

Wayne looked back and forth between the sleeping fairy and Finn.

He shuffled over to a white wall phone, lifted the receiver, and spoke. The guard wouldn't take his eyes off Finn, punishing him for the intrusion and inconvenience.

Wayne rejoined Finn and pointed to the nearest security camera. It had a red light atop it. There were cameras for each cell, and several more for the hallway.

Finn didn't watch the camera, but the prisoner.

"There now," Wayne said, as the red light went off.

Maleficent remained visible in bed.

"Satisfied?" Wayne asked.

"Let's go," said the guard. He reached out for Finn, who broke away.

"Give it a moment!" Finn said.

"We're done here. Shift change is coming up."

Wayne said, "Please, Finn. Let's not make a scene."

"Philby said there's a thirty-to-forty-second buffer to keep the DHI video smooth."

That hit home; clearly Wayne knew this as well. He glanced at his watch: an antique Mickey Mouse watch.

"Very well," he said.

The guard's impatience enveloped them both. It had been a long night.

With all three men watching, Maleficent popped, and vanished.

"What the—?" The guard hurried to unlock the cell.

"No!" Wayne reached out and stopped the man. He turned to Finn. "I think I owe you an apology."

"Without Jess on our side . . ." Finn said. "If I'd put her under that spell instead of Amanda, we'd have never known."

"Somebody had better tell me what's going on," the guard said angrily.

"No one's left this wing?" Wayne verified.

"No, sir. Not since shift change at ten PM."

"*Before* the blackout," Finn said.

"Yes, sir," the guard said to Finn, suddenly with deference and respect.

"So," Wayne said. He seemed to be waiting for an answer from Finn.

The guard whispered, "Are you telling me that . . .
*thing* is loose somewhere in here?"

"Not exactly," Finn said.

He asked them to repeat the camera procedure with
Chernabog. Five minutes later they determined that he,
too, was nothing but a DHI hologram.

The guard, sweating profusely despite the air conditioning, reached for his radio. Wayne stopped him.

"You don't want to do that," he said. "They'll sound
the alarm, yes?"

"Of course."

"We'll take a rain check," Wayne said. Turning to
Finn: "So they're asleep in here?"

"They have to be. During the combination of
blackout and fire alarm, they escaped from their cells.
They couldn't leave the prison because of your precau-
tions. They had to get somewhere and get to sleep.
Quickly. I imagine they've been awake for a day or
more, to ensure their fatigue. Once asleep, once the
power went back on, their DHIs took their places in
their cells."

"How brilliant of them!" Wayne said.

"They intend to walk out of here during the shift
change," Finn said.

A wall device sounded. Finn recognized it as the
same tone used between classes at school.

"LOCKDOWN!" Wayne shouted at the guard.

"You told me not to radio!" the man said, fumbling for his walkie-talkie.

"I didn't look at the time! Lock it down!"

The guard hollered into his radio, but the eyes of all three were on the wall clock.

Wayne shouted frantically, "The guards must nap somewhere."

The guard shook his head, his ear to the radio. "Shift change's already under way."

"Tell me! Damn it, man! Show me where they nap!"

"I'll get them fired!"

"NOW!"

The guard took off. With sirens alarming, down the hallway, up the stairs they ran. Wayne moved like he was thirty years younger.

Together they reached a plain gray door marked STORAGE. The guard tried his key, but it wouldn't go in.

"The lock's been jimmied. The key's not going to work." He leaned his shoulder into it. "It can only be opened from the inside. We're cooked."

Finn checked the clock: 7:05. The shift change had already begun. Too late? Finn wondered. "It's me," Finn said. "I can do this."

"I'm afraid so," Wayne said.

The guard looked totally confused.

"The guard has a Taser. All you need to do is get the door open," Wayne said.

"We hope," Finn said.

Wayne nodded.

"What exactly are you two talking about?" the guard asked.

Finn closed his eyes, took a deep breath, and pictured the dark train tunnel.

He walked through the door.

He heard the guard say something Finn would never repeat.

\* \* \*

Finn's brief *all clear* passed nearly instantly. He was through the door, but too tired to hold his *all clear*. He flipped on the light switch. The storage room was a small, L-shaped cinder block. Mattresses were stacked along the far wall. Metal shelving held toilet paper, paper towels, and soap. He saw brooms and buckets, blankets and plastic bowls.

The guards had fashioned the space into an improvised bunk room to take unauthorized naps. Finn stripped back the blankets. He jumped back as he discovered a bare-chested guard. The man's hands and feet were taped, his mouth gagged.

Finn was able to open the door from the inside. The guard outside hurried in.

Finn said, "Two guards. Two uniforms. The shift change!" He ran down the corridor, Wayne surprisingly close on his heels.

The lockdown was in full effect. They were blocked from leaving at the first station they encountered. Wayne shouted back and forth with a guard on the other side, making demands that were not accepted.

"Wayne!" Finn shouted, pointing through the thick glass to a flat-panel display rotating between security views.

He pointed to the frame showing the facility's final door—the door to the outside. To freedom.

"Check out that guard's neck. The collar."

"Green skin . . ." Wayne muttered. He sounded sad, defeated. Maleficent in a guard's uniform.

"Chernabog was too big," Finn said. "She must have transfigured him into a man. He's the one at her side."

On the video, the door shut, and the two figures were gone.

* * *

Attempts were made to stop the two. Radio calls shut down the Park's Security exits by road. Dog teams searched the Park for scents prior to opening, but

427

perhaps because of the abundance of wild-animal odors, failed at their task. The Park opening was delayed seventy minutes, visitors standing at the gates waiting in the heat. They were told a computer malfunction was to blame.

At last the Park was opened, and tens of thousands of guests streamed inside.

Maleficent and Chernabog were not seen again.

Despite repeated efforts to trap the Overtakers on Tom Sawyer Island, the fort went unused by them. If it had once been a hideout, as Finn and Amanda continued to claim, it was no longer.

# 13

Seven DHIs—the Keepers, along with Amanda and Jess—sat along the catwalk surrounding the water tower in Disney's Hollywood Studios.

Their DHIs shimmered slightly against the night sky, but even from several feet away they looked perfectly real. The technology improved with every software upgrade.

"What now?" Charlene asked.

The mood was not good. Despite the Keepers' control of the fob and their preventing a takeover of the power plant, the Evil Queen had engineered Maleficent and Chernabog's escape. Right under their noses.

"We find them," Finn said. "And we find wherever they've moved their hideout to."

"We can help," Ariel said. "But we need a leader."

All eyes shot down the metal railing at Finn. "We want to help," Finn said to her. "But I can't see the characters following one of us."

Ariel laughed. "One of you? Oh, no!" She covered her laugh. "I'm sorry! I don't mean it to sound like that. But we have a long and *storied* history." She giggled, self-amused. "*Our* leader. There's only one leader."

Finn thought back to Shan-Yu's comments about emperors and leadership.

"Mickey," he said.

Ariel's face sagged. "Yes."

"Where is he?" Willa asked.

"Minnie is so sad. No one knows for sure. He might be in hiding. He might be . . . We just have no way of knowing. They've taken down his house, you know? Minnie's, too. 'Updating,' they call it. Don't believe it. It's all because of 'the Night.' "

None of the Keepers had ever heard of a particular night or event. As a group, they looked at her curiously.

"We heard noises from his house on that night," Ariel continued, oblivious to their confusion. "A struggle of some kind. He's not been seen since. The family will listen to him. *Our* family. What you call the characters. He can bring us together. We thought . . . You see, we understood . . . We believed *you* were sent here to find him for us."

"Us?" Philby said. "But we never knew he was missing!"

"We've guarded the secret. Not even the white-hair knows." She meant Wayne.

"But why?"

"He's too important. He *is* the magic. The Green One knows. She understands his power."

"Maleficent," Charlene muttered.

Amanda squeezed Finn's hand unseen. He squeezed hers back. For a very long time, no one spoke. The crickets and night animals made a buzz that filled the air. A breeze blew. Somewhere down there was Frollo. The Green Army. *There was much to learn*, Finn thought.

"What frosts me," Philby said, "is that three weeks later and still there's been no kind of discipline or investigation into Luowski and Hugo."

"They stopped wearing the contacts," Amanda said. "There's no proof of any of it."

"They're building an army," Maybeck warned. "Just as we thought. We'd be wise to do the same."

"Is this their general, I wonder?" Jess reached into her pocket and passed down the sketch of the uniformed officer. It reached Ariel and stopped. She studied it, looked up, and studied it again.

"What is it?" Finn asked.

"This is no general," she said. "It's Captain Peter."

"WHO?" Philby, Finn, and Maybeck said in near unison.

"Captain Peter Roseman. The *Disney Magic*. The cruise ship. I've worked with Captain Peter before, several times."

"The cruise ship," Philby said.

"They want to steal the *Magic*," Willa said. "Not the magic—small *m*. The *Magic*—capital *M*."

Finn stood up so quickly, his DHI knees went through the chain banister. "That's the next Keepers installment! The cruise line! We have that opening scheduled for what—?"

"Two weeks," Maybeck said. "A Saturday. Grand opening is Port Canaveral."

The other Keepers clambered to their feet. Only Ariel was slow in getting up.

"We've got to say good-bye for now," Finn said to the mermaid.

"I hope you'll come back and visit?"

"Actually, we may need you."

"And your other friends," Charlene said.

"We'll see if Wayne can arrange some kind of character spectacular on the cruise," Finn said.

Ariel nodded, not knowing exactly what they were talking about. "Sounds lovely."

Finn thought of Minnie and Pluto. He pulled the fob out of his pocket and held it before them. "Everyone ready?"

Nods all around.

"How strange that a thing so small possesses so much power," Finn said.

"But it does," Philby said. "That thing is the key to it all."

Finn nodded. He held his hand over Ariel's and said, "Will you hide this for us?"

"Of course," she said. "Willa knows how to find me."

Finn looked around at the faces of the Kingdom Keepers, thinking: We're not done here.

And then he pushed the button.

# ACKNOWLEDGMENTS

The research for the Kingdom Keepers books continues to branch out and expand with each new book in the series. My world is expanding at the same rate as that of the Keepers. It's a cliché that you can't do a project without certain people, but it remains a fact. I'm indebted to hours and hours (days and weeks in some cases) from any and all of the following. Each of these people brings with them the knowledge of colleagues and the help of assistants, either too many to name, or those who wish to remain anonymous. But it takes a Kingdom to make these novels. So, in no particular order thank you to those at Disney: Laura Simpson, Chris Ostrander, Megan Fuchs, Alex Wright, Scott Otis, Richard Fleming, Sam Medina, Jerry Coleman, Les Frey, Cindy Johnson, Alisha Huettig, and Jessica Ward.

And it takes others to turn the research and my stories into actual books and book tours and research travel and a million e-mails and Google searches, and on and on. So, thanks to Amy Berkower and Dan Conaway at Writers House; Matthew Snyder at CAA; Wendy Lefkon, my Disney Books editor and dear friend; Jennifer Levine and Deborah Bass, publicity; Lisa Laird, speaking agent; my office manager of fourteen years, Nancy Litzinger Zastrow (happy recent marriage!), and Phoebejane McVey VI, in

St. Louis. To David and Laurel Walters, who have actual day jobs, but who make the time in insanely busy lives to still copyedit repeated drafts. And to Dave Barry, who may not want anything to do with these books for all I know, but affects all of my work nonetheless—he really is the smartest man in the room.

Special thanks to Genevieve Gagne-Hawes for her thorough story and character editing during the multiple revisions of the book. Gen, you are a real Keeper.

For those I've forgotten, I haven't actually forgotten you or the help you've provided, only your names . . . No lawsuits please.

—*Ridley Pearson*
*2011*